The Blacksmith's Wife

ANNE DOUGHTY

Allison & Busby Limited
12 Fitzroy Mews
London W1T 6DW
allisonandbusby.com

First published in Great Britain by Allison & Busby in 2016.
This paperback edition published by Allison & Busby in 2016.

A CIP catalogue record for this book is available from the British Library.

10 9 8 7 6 5 4 3 2 1

ISBN 978-0-7490-2091-0

Typeset in 10.5/15.5 pt Sabon by
Allison & Busby Ltd.

The paper used for this Allison & Busby publication
has been produced from trees that have been legally sourced
from well-managed and credibly certified forests.

Printed and bound by
CPI Group (UK) Ltd, Croydon, CR0 4YY

For Peter
Friend, editor, husband
29 November 1933 – 26 April 2013
As promised

CHAPTER ONE

Ardrea, County Armagh
April, 1845

Sarah Hamilton opened her eyes suddenly, the traces of a pleasant dream fleeing like a mouse disappearing down a hole before she could grasp anything about it. She smiled to herself, got quietly out of bed and glanced down at the sleeping figure of her husband whom only a vigorous shake would waken.

She knew by the dim light filtering through the curtains on the small south-facing window that it was early. Still too dim to read the time on the clock on John's side of their bed, but bright enough for her to tramp barefoot across the wooden floor. She peeped out at the small plantation of trees partly masking the small, humpy green hills that stretched away in all directions from their long, stone-built roadside dwelling; northwards to the low-lying fields and meadows bordering Lough Neagh; south through winding lanes and sloping orchards to the cathedral city of Armagh, their nearest market town.

She never knew why she troubled to move so quietly when John was so hard to wake. He had the gift of sound sleep. Whatever the troubles and frustrations of the day, however taxing and difficult the work in his forge which occupied the furthest end of the two-storey thatched house, he managed, almost childlike, to fall asleep the moment he got into bed, unless, of course, he turned towards her and took her in his arms, the gentleness of his lovemaking a sharp contrast with the strength and power of his body.

Sarah had always loved the early morning. As a child, brought up by her elderly grandmother on the outskirts of Lisnagarvey – a flourishing market town some eight miles from the growing port of Belfast – she had lost both her parents in the summer epidemic of typhoid; only months after her family had moved to Ulster from Yorkshire to take up a new opportunity in a flourishing textile business run by a former neighbour.

Her grandmother and one of her brothers had survived, but her sisters and other brothers had not, so Sarah remained in the care of the old woman. Sarah Lamie, who had lived with Sarah's family for many years, had always been an early riser and young Sarah was already accustomed to being wakened at an early hour.

'Sleepy head, still in bed,' the old woman would say, laughing. 'God's given us a new day,' she would go on, smiling with a joy Sarah had never seen displayed in others of her age.

The cottage, found for them by their former neighbours

who had taken her brother Charles into their care, was tiny and sparsely furnished, but they wanted for nothing. Her great-grandparents had been among the first Quakers to come to Lisnagarvey from Yorkshire in the 1700s and it was part of their belief that no one should be neglected, neither for their talents, which might not be obvious to anyone, nor for their physical needs. When the potato store went low, someone would appear to refill it and there was always meal, or flour, in the heavy crock behind the kitchen door.

They had no money to speak of; the only income the willing gifts from the handful of parents whose children came each day and made up the small group her grandmother taught to read and write, to keep accounts and to mend the plain clothing that both men and women wore.

Sarah smiled to herself as she remembered the neat undecorated dresses: grey or black, or palest blue with large white collars, always neat and spotlessly clean. She had always longed for colour, for dresses with pretty floral designs, pinks and blues, with frills and decorations, or embroidery, but even after her grandmother died and she lived alone, taking over the old woman's task of teaching the young, she respected the old woman's memory by continuing to dress in the Quaker manner. Only in her embroidery and tapestry work, which helped her to be financially independent, did her passion for colour find an outlet.

The light was stronger now and the first pale gleams of sunlight were catching the rag rug she had laboured over in the dark nights of the recent winter. Full of colour, the fragments came from garments torn beyond repair and thrown away by the wealthy, collected up by the women in the workshop in Lurgan run by her brother – scraps of fabric to be shared out and used by those with the skill, patience and imagination to create from such meagre resources.

John had watched her evening after evening totally fascinated by the speed at which she sewed; the tiny needle caught the light of the lamp and the water-filled globe that stood close beside it, enhancing its gleam so she could see more easily for the intricate work.

'Ah don't know how ye have the patience for that,' he said often enough, shaking his head. 'Them wee stitches – shure I can hardly see them even when I know where to luk.'

'And what about the patience for making a dozen horseshoes and every pair a match?' she'd said, laughing. 'Is it not the same thing?'

He'd nodded and agreed that it was a fair point, but he was not entirely convinced and remained amazed at what he saw as her great skill.

As the light strengthened and pale gleams began to touch the barely leafed trees in the nearest hedgerow, she saw that it had been raining in the night. From the tips of new leaves and on the long thorns of the slowly leafing hawthorns drops of water hung, shimmering in the tiny breeze which had sprung up.

She heard her grandmother's voice as clearly as if the old woman were standing in the room behind her: 'See, child, what need have we of jewels? Hasn't God given us the jewels on the trees?'

It was just an early spring morning like this one that she had first met John. The memory of it still made her smile. It was market day in Lisnagarvey and in the afternoon she had finished her teaching early so she could go and buy threads and fabric from the traders who had laid out their goods in the square surrounding the Town Hall.

The whole place was thronged with people: noisy with men who bargained and then slapped hands, and hawkers who shouted out the virtues of their wares. The pavements were very crowded, but somewhat cleaner than the square itself where calves, sheep and some horses had changed hands in the course of the morning. She never knew quite how it happened, but suddenly she was struck a glancing blow on the side of her head. Not painful, but startling. It was so sudden and surprising enough for her to lose her balance, trip and fall on the edge of the pavement.

The next thing she knew was that a bolt of cloth had dropped down on the pavement beside her and a young man with blue-grey eyes was kneeling beside her, a look of total distress on his tanned face.

'Ach, dear a dear, are ye hurted?' he asked anxiously, looking round him as if he might find some resolution at hand to this totally distressing event. 'The mare moved just as I was unloading the bolt,' he explained, as if that might help him. 'Are ye all right? Will I call a doctor to come and look at ye?'

He put his hand to her dishevelled hair, moved it back from her face and searched her cheek minutely for any sign of damage.

She had laughed then at the innocence of the man who,

in his concern, had touched her as easily and gently as if he were her mother.

'No, I'm not hurt at all,' she replied, surprised at the slight shake in her voice. 'It was more the suddeness of it. Do you often swing bolts around the place?' she asked, smiling weakly.

'Ach no,' he said sheepishly. 'Sure there's a knack in it, I'm sure, but I haven't the right way of it,' he added, as he helped her to her feet.

'What about your weaving? Has it come to any harm?' she asked more steadily, as he retrieved her empty basket from between the feet of some bystanders, who had now paused to watch him from the corners of their eyes.

Paying not the slightest attention to the curious glances of people who passed by, he looked her up and down yet again as he handed the basket back. He'd not spared so much as a glance for the heavy roll of cloth still lying at their feet where it had fallen.

'Never worry about that,' he said, picking up the heavy bale as if it were a small parcel. He propped it on its end against the side of his pony and trap. 'Would you come and drink a cup of something at the tavern? It might help ye.'

'But what about selling your week's work?'

'Ah no, I'm not here to sell it. I'm just delivering it to a draper for m' brother. He's the weaver. Shure I can get a wee lad to watch it fer me while we go an' have somethin'. They say sugar in tea is good for a shock. Did ye iver tell of that?'

'Yes, I have indeed, but not everyone has sugar.'

'Aye, yer right, but now say ye'll walk over to the tavern

wi' me so I can make sure yer all right. It wou'd set m' mind at rest,' he added persuasively as he took her arm.

She had gone with him to the tavern and sat in the dark, smoky interior already thick with heat from a roaring log fire, the press of bodies and the smell of cooking food. It was there the draper found them. A good-natured man, he'd seen an unfamiliar pony and trap and an equally familiar-looking bale of cloth. He'd listened to the story the small boy had told him, gave him a threepenny bit, carried the bale to his own cart and come to the tavern to pay his debts.

As soon as he'd pocketed the money for his brother, the young man asked if he could drive her back home to save her the walk.

'I'm afraid I still have all my messages to do,' she said quietly. She would never forget the look of disappointment on his face when he had no choice but to let her go.

It was a week later when she once again walked the length of the market square and she realised she'd been watching for him. Now it was her turn to be disappointed for he was nowhere to be seen.

The sun was clear of the trees now and beams of light cast long shadows towards the house. They glinted on the diminishing hayrick that had provided for the mare during the winter months, turning the tousled strands they touched into threads of gold. She smiled to herself when she remembered how it had all been resolved.

After three weeks of hoping she might meet him again by chance, she had told herself firmly to stop being foolish.

There were other markets for cloth, and besides he'd been delivering the cloth for his brother, so he wasn't even a weaver himself. She had no idea how he earned his living. Absorbed in her own thoughts as she made her way along the crowded pavement, she was startled by his 'Good day, ma'am.' There he stood beside the pony and trap, waiting in exactly the same spot where he'd had his accident with the bolt of cloth.

As for John, he knew he'd no reason at all for going back to Lisnagarvey, but he still puzzled back and forth in his mind as to what he could do to see her again. He'd only taken the cloth for his brother so there'd be money to put food on the table while he was suffering with his chest. There'd be no bale of cloth to go to market till George was fit to work again. But if he was well enough to be back at his loom, then he'd be well enough to take the cloth himself.

John had to admit it was far too far to travel just for a market. Either Armagh or Richhill market could provide anything he needed for the forge, or for the house. But the thought of going to Lisnagarvey would not leave his mind. By the time he set out, some three weeks later, he knew he was going there simply to look for a tall girl in a pale blue dress with a smile in her eyes that seemed to be there all the time.

'Are ye lookin' for jewels on the tree?'

The voice was soft and full of sleep. She turned and saw him sitting on the side of the bed rubbing his eyes.

'Yes, I was, but then I fell to thinking about a man who knocked me clean off my feet,' she said honestly, as she came and sat beside him.

14

She could never quite get used to the fact that anything she ever told him, no matter about how long ago it was or how seemingly unimportant it might be, he would remember, sometimes quoting a phrase or a saying back to her, or asking her if he had indeed got the right way of it. Places he'd never been, people he never knew, it was all the same to him; they were parts of her world and she had shared them with him. So he remembered.

'Are your feet not froz'n on the cauld floor?' he asked, putting his arm round her. 'Or did you mind to stan' on the rug like I told ye?'

'Yes, they are, and yes, I did,' she said quickly. 'But they'll soon warm up when I'm getting the breakfast. I was just thinking I'd better wake you up for you said you've to go into Armagh today. Is it Hillock's you're for?'

'Aye, we need angle iron again, and a lot of small stuff forby,' he began. 'But shure we cou'd warm your feet far better in the bed,' he added, drawing her closer.

'John, dear, I'd love to come back to bed, but do you remember you said you needed a word with Scottie? He'll be expecting his bowl of porridge.'

'Aye,' he agreed, 'he doesn't get much at home in the mornings. The poor old Granny isn't fit for it,' he said, looking sad.

'But there'll be no Scottie tonight, will there?' she said, stroking his cheek.

'Indeed there won't,' he replied promptly, pulling her to her feet and into his arms. 'Don't tire yourself out now doin' too much,' he added, after kissing her vigorously.

'And what about you coming back tired with carrying

all that heavy stuff and going straight back to your own work in the forge?'

'Never you think o' that,' he came back at her with a smile, as she slipped lightly from his arms and left the washstand to him.

She pulled on her working clothes over her shift, a hard-wearing dark skirt and one of her oldest blouses, pushed her feet into her shoes, ran a comb through her long, dark hair and stepped out onto the echoing wooden stairs that dropped steeply into the big kitchen below.

John had damped down the fire at bedtime. Now, she leant over the smoored fire and opened the hot centre, where a curl of blue smoke rose from the hot embers. Carefully, to avoid getting her fingers burnt, she placed small pieces of bone dry turf and sticks amid the glowing embers she'd uncovered. Straightening up from a task that always made her back ache, she brought bowls, plates and mugs from the dresser and began placing them on the scrubbed wooden table.

She turned away from the table the moment she heard the sticks crackle. Pleased with her efforts on the fire, which it had taken her a while to get used to after the tiny fireplace in her old home, she added pieces of coal with the tongs. Very soon there'd be a cheering blaze and she could hang the kettle over the leaping flames. It sat on the hearth, filled and left ready at bedtime.

The porridge she'd prepared herself the previous evening was cooked and ready for the early start. It just needed to be stirred thoroughly, reheated and served up with a jug of fresh milk from the larder on the north-facing wall just outside the back door.

She stepped out into the loveliest of April mornings: the sky blue, the air mild, the night's rain on the tramped earth all around the house drying in the light breeze. She paused and stood looking for the most recent signs of the coming spring. As she turned back into the house she glimpsed a familiar figure climb through a gap in the hawthorn hedge and take a shortcut across the field to where she was standing.

'You're in good time, Scottie,' she said, smiling as the boy, the younger of the two apprentices, came up to her, out of breath from hurrying. Although he was still shy and awkward with most people, he did manage to look at her and nod a greeting.

'Boss said there's horses due. He wants a word,' he explained abruptly, his eyes darting to and fro, resting only briefly on her face.

Fourteen years old and lightly built, Scottie now had only a slight trace of the Galloway accent he'd had when he began his seven years' apprenticeship with John Hamilton of Ardrea. His uncle, a farmer from near Dumfries, brought him to the adjoining townland of Greenan to live with his grandmother for this purpose.

'Can ah see to the stirabout fer ye?' he asked abruptly.

For all his awkwardness, he had always offered to help her. If he caught sight of her going to the well while he was in the forge, he'd ask John, or the journeyman, Sam Keenan, if he could go out and give her a hand with the heavy buckets. He was never refused, for both men knew he worshipped her, giving her the love he'd have given to his own mother if she hadn't died giving birth to his younger brother.

'Thank you, Scottie. I think I hear the kettle singing, so I can make the tea now and you can have the crook for the pot,' she replied, as they went back into the kitchen where the sun was now just high enough to glint through the south-facing window.

She was spooning the stirabout into three bowls when John clumped down the stairs looking very clean, a fragment of shaving soap below one ear. He was wearing his 'going to market' suit, older and much worn, unlike the new suit he'd bought for the small gathering in Grange Church almost two years earlier.

Sarah eyed him carefully, noting the clean shirt and the well-polished boots. He was not a vain man, but as a young man his mother had always insisted that he dress for the task in hand. It was one thing, she had said, wearing much-mended and stained clothes in the forge, but that was no excuse for not being well-turned-out when there was no dirty work to be done.

Sarah felt sure she was a good woman, from all John had said about her, but one who had never had good health. Several of her children had died in infancy and she herself died soon after her much older husband, just as John, her youngest surviving son, had completed his apprenticeship with Robert Ross of Killuney. A hard time it had been for John taking over his father's house and forge, trying to make enough money single-handedly to pay for his food as well as the rent to the local landlord, Molyneux of Castle Dillon, never mind learning to cook and bake bread with no woman in the house to do it for him.

Sarah had listened regularly to the stories he told against himself: about how he kept burning the spuds, tripping over the bread left to prove on the harnen stand on the hearth, or leaving the milk on the larder floor and finding their neighbour's cat had got through the tiny window designed to let the air in and left its hair in the jug.

He was never angry or frustrated; he always laughed at his mistakes and never failed to admire her well-practised skills. That was when she'd first used the phrase: '*And what about all the matching horseshoes?*' – words that had become a joke between them.

The chairs scraped on the stone floor as the two men stood up.

'Thank you, Mrs Hamilton,' said Scottie with a little nod, before he put his cap back on and disappeared out the back door, the way he'd come in.

John lingered a little longer, knowing it would take Scottie and Ben, the older apprentice, a few minutes to put the mare into the trap, check out the buckles and straps on her harness and make sure she had the nosebag she'd be needing before their return.

'Is there anythin' you need for the house? Tea or sugar or suchlike?' he asked, slipping his arm round her.

'No, we're fine for provisions till we go in together on Saturday. You've enough to do today and plenty to carry. Will you be late?'

'Ach no. Shure they know me and are well useta what I need. But it'll be after dinnertime. Ye may give the boys their share and keep mine under a plate fer when I get in.'

'I'll keep *ours* for when you get in,' she said, correcting him.

'Aye well,' he nodded, pleased. 'Don't go empty in the meantime. Have a bite to keep ye goin'. Sure goin' empty might not be a good thing,' he added, with a sly smile.

'There's no knowing, as the saying is,' she replied, laughing, knowing what he was thinking.

She held him for a moment after he kissed her before they got to the front door. The pony and trap stood waiting in beside the great stone pillars that marked the house as a place of business and not just a home. She watched him as he walked out, stepped up lightly into the driver's seat and took the reins from Scottie.

As the mare responded to his words, he raised a hand in salute and they moved off onto the roadway, turning right into the green sunlit countryside that spread out all around them, clear in the fresh morning air and visible for miles around from this high point on Drumilly Hill.

CHAPTER TWO

As the sun rose higher it bathed the hilly landscape in sunlight and cast short shadows beneath the hawthorn hedgerows. Sarah Hamilton went round the house, opened all the downstairs windows, ran upstairs to the bedroom, struggled with the window there – it had a habit of sticking – and then propped open the front and back doors with the heavy metal doorstops John had made as practice pieces when he was still an apprentice.

She was hoping to bring some freshness into the kitchen where she had baked bread for most of the morning and was now boiling potatoes for the midday meal. Standing for a moment at the front door, leaning her tired back against the doorpost, her eyes shaded from the bright light, she decided it was not just mild, it was actually warm, the first day of real warmth after the winter. Not that the winter had been a hard one, she reflected, but for days on end it had been so wet and dreary she would have welcomed snowfall for the bright reflected light and the patches of blue sky that had been absent for so long.

She paused only briefly before going back to her work, well aware that until she had done all the dusty and dirty jobs and no longer needed to lean over the griddle or the fire, she couldn't go back upstairs with a bowl of hot water. Perspiring and uncomfortable, dusty from both flour and fine ash, she longed to wash and change from her working clothes. Indeed, as the morning proceeded, she realised it would be warm enough to wear the lighter of her two better skirts with one of her pretty handmade blouses that hadn't seen daylight since the shortening September days had brought the first chilly mornings.

The last of her jobs was bringing water from the well just behind the forge. It was in no way a 'dirty' job, given the cobbles were not muddy and were already bone dry after the light showers in the night, but it was a job better done before she went upstairs to add her bowl of hot water to what remained in the jug on the washstand.

However careful you were balancing the two heavy buckets, it was easy enough to trip on a stray bit of metal and spill water all over your skirt and shoes. It was even more likely to spill when her back was as painful as it had become this morning.

As she stepped out of the door and moved along the whitewashed, south-facing front of the house, she heard Sam Keenan's hammer beating on the anvil. Even if John hadn't been in Armagh, she would have known it was Sam, the tall, angular journeyman. John had taken him on as his first employee when Sam had finished serving his time with one of the Rosses a couple of miles away at Mullanisilla.

His hammering was heavy and steady; the long, strong strokes were interspersed with lighter ones to disperse the tension built up in the body from the impact of the heavy blows. John's hammering was much less dense and the small dancing pattern between the heavy blows, which all blacksmiths used to offset the vibrations of the weighty blows, was much lighter than Sam's. She always felt there was almost a hint of gaiety in John's rhythm and texture.

As for Scottie and Ben, it was easy to tell when they were at work. With both of them, despite the difference of two years in their apprenticeships, there was a hesitancy in the rhythm. That was something that would go, John had explained to her. By the time they had served their full seven years' apprenticeship their muscles would be developed. By then they would each be able to lift the heavy anvil unaided. Only then would you hear the pattern that marked out the man, in the same way as his writing would, the way he signed his name, for example. That was, of course, if it was something he could do in the first place.

She had just removed the wooden cover from the well and was about to prime the pump from the jug of water kept under a bucket in the grass beside it, when Scottie dashed out of the forge and stopped abruptly beside her.

'Let me do that, missus,' he said quickly. 'Ye shou'dnae carry them heavy buckets no more than ye shou'd pump up water,' he said, without looking at her.

She smiled to herself, remembering sadly how protective

he had been when briefly, last year, she had carried their first child.

John had been so delighted that as soon as they knew themselves he'd told the good news to all three workers in the forge. Sam, Ben and Scottie had all nodded. Sam and Scottie wished him joy. Sam, married with two children and one on the way, kept his thoughts to himself. When he saw Scottie dash off to carry her buckets, he just smiled knowingly. He had more idea of how a woman would cope when there was no one there to help her.

Ben, of course, despite his extra years of experience in the forge, was so overcome with shyness that he said nothing. To be honest he was silent most of the time. Unlike Scottie, who would have lifted even a sheet of paper if he thought it would help her, Ben seemed indifferent to other people, speaking only when he was spoken to and even then in a halting and stilted way.

Scottie was certainly the lively one of the three. He had a deftness of manner both with objects, like the pump or the bellows, and also with the handling of animals. Whenever there was a young horse, or one known to be nervous, due to be shod, John made sure Scottie was there to hold him, that Sam had not sent him to deliver a repaired or sharpened tool to some farmer who lived nearby, nor was he on some other errand like collecting a bag of turf for making the fire on the stone circle outside the forge when there was the broken hooping on a cartwheel to mend.

Ben had already begun shoeing horses and doing it quite well under John's sharp eye, but John thought Scottie was still too young and too light of build to begin shoeing himself. He told her that he felt sure Scottie's soothing manner with animals would make him a great success with the many horses and ponies that came to the forge.

Sure he was still only fourteen and had a bit yet to grow. It would be all the same to Scottie whether his clients were as different in temperament as the tall, nervous hunters kept by the local gentry and the heavy, plodding horses owned by the ploughmen who moved from farm to farm, working for more than one farmer. Scottie would settle them all.

'Ther'yar,' he said, opening the wooden lower doors of a tall, glass-fronted cupboard in the kitchen. He swung the buckets and set them down inside without spilling a drop on the recently scrubbed floor. 'Ye need to mind yersel',' he added hastily, as he disappeared at speed back to the shears he'd been sharpening when they'd heard her footsteps on the cobbles.

Sarah sat down in the nearest chair, suddenly very weary, a shooting pain in her stomach momentarily taking her breath away.

'Perhaps,' she said to herself in a whisper as she put a hand to her sore back. 'Perhaps John will have his wish.'

Early last week he'd dropped a shy hint that unless he was mistaken she'd not bled for a wee while now. She'd admitted that she'd been thinking that too, but she then told him the reason she hadn't said anything was because she didn't want to raise his spirits and then for him to be disappointed again.

They'd lost their first child after three or four months and John had been distraught, anxious during the day when she was poorly and in pain, and beside himself at night when she couldn't sleep. Finally, the next day, he'd overruled all her protests and sent Sam to fetch the doctor from Armagh. He was so agitated when the man himself arrived that to begin with the doctor told him firmly he'd never yet lost a father to a miscarriage.

'Look on it as a try-out,' he'd added, more gently when he'd examined Sarah, told her what would happen next and gave her strict instructions as to what she was to do. 'The body needs to be sure all is in order before it goes on,' he insisted, addressing them both. 'Don't hurry to make up for this loss. Give yourselves time. Sure you've plenty of time for a fine, long family, if that's what ye want. This is no setback at all in the longer view.'

But it was Sarah's neighbour, Mary-Anne Halligan, at the foot of the hill, who had come to visit and spoken even more directly than the Armagh doctor. She was well-known as a midwife even though she'd never had any formal training except what her own mother and grandmother had taught her when she was old enough to help with their work.

'I've hardly iver met a wumman who went the full way wi' the first'un,' she began, settling herself comfortably by the fire with a mug of tea and a fresh scone. 'But the doctors wou'd niver tell ye that. Ach, I suppose they don' want t'upset ye or get ye worryin', but shure ask any wumman ye know an' she'll likely tell you it were the second, or the third, aye, or even the fourth, God help us, that brought a fine, healthy baby. Don't pay one bit of attenshun to the Job's comforters. Ye might well be a ma the nixt time, but give yerself a wee while first to let yer inside settle down. Just tell yer good man when it's a bit chancy.'

Sarah had no idea what she meant and had to ask.

Mary-Anne looked at her in amazement: 'Did yer ma niver tell you 'bout these things afore ye got married?'

She'd explained then how she'd lost both parents to the fever one summer long ago and how she'd been brought up by her grandmother who was actually her own mother's nurse. The old woman had lived with the family for many years and had never married or had a child herself.

Mary-Anne had nodded, said 'Ach, aye,' and settled down to tell her how women that were neither rich, nor even well-off, managed to space their children at two-year intervals.

'If ye don't believe me, take a luk at the parish register,' she went on, when Sarah had listened wide-eyed. 'Clear as spring water, and written there for those that can read, a chile ivery two years for as many as ye want, if ye just keep to the safe times o' the month. Am not sayin' but there's ither ways o' doing it, an' some wimen are glad just to say "no", but shure if yer fond of other, like you and yer man, isn't it a nicer way o' doing it?'

Sarah thought over again what Mary-Anne had said as she went upstairs and peeled off her clothes. She stood naked, looking down at her body. Perhaps she was larger, but if she was, it hardly showed. She couldn't be sure but she thought her nipples were larger and certainly they tingled very often like they had done the year previously. Despite all her doubts, the notebook she kept in the chest of drawers, with her underwear and the folded cloths she used every month, made one thing quite clear. The last time she'd bled was the end of January. It was now the third week in April.

She laughed suddenly. 'Sure time will tell all,' she said aloud.

It was a favourite expression of John's. The logic of it was perfectly clear, but she always insisted that time itself wasn't the problem. What was hard to deal with was the *not knowing*. So many things, she insisted, you could cope with, no matter how difficult they were, if you knew exactly what they were in the first place.

He had a way of looking at her, his face immobile, his eyes wide as he took in every word. Well, he was, of course, taking it all in. It was one of the first things she had noticed about him. He listened to what people were saying. If his responses were simple, or homely, it meant he was still thinking about it. Sooner or later, when he'd given his mind to it, he'd come back to the subject again and ask her what she thought of his conclusions.

John had been to school, could read and write, as most blacksmiths could, but as far as she could see it had been a very limited schooling. To her surprise, he knew very little of Irish history, though he had once recited for her the kings and queens of England. He possessed only a few books, but read the local newspapers avidly each week. When encouraged he could tell stories about local characters and events going back well into the previous century.

As she buttoned her blouse and straightened her skirt, which did indeed feel a little tighter on the waist, she remembered him describing in great detail the Battle of the Yellow Ford in 1598 and explaining why the lane connecting the road over Church Hill with the rectory to the east of it was called Bloody Lane.

She felt better as she glanced in the mirror and lifted the heavy jug from the washstand. She made her way down the steep stairs and threw the soapy water away outside the back door, but she left the jug sitting by the door instead of refilling it at the well. She didn't want to distract Scottie again from his jobs. Sam and Ben might well cope with the extra work, but John was not due back till after dinner time.

She fried up chopped onions and mashed them into the potato with a generous lump of butter, ready to serve onto the three warm plates. Then remembering what John had said, she buttered a piece of fresh bread and poured a glass of milk for herself. She had just brought in a jug of buttermilk and another dish of butter for the table when she heard the scrape of boots outside the front door.

Sam took off his cap and led the way, sniffing appreciatively while Ben and Scottie sat down in their usual places.

'Are ye off yer food, missus dear?' asked Sam, dropping his cap on the floor by his chair and making sure the two apprentices had done likewise.

'No, Sam, I'm not,' she replied, realising she was indeed very hungry. 'Boss's orders. He said if I was going to have my meal with him when he came back I was to be sure and eat a bite to keep me going.'

'Aye, he was right there,' he nodded, glancing up at her as she brought the piled-up plates to the table.

She caught the glance and wondered. Sam was the family man and maybe saw what she could not see. Mary-Anne from the foot of the hill came up to see her now and again.

She'd spoken more than once of the clues a woman might get if she did but notice them. She said men picked them up as well, but they noticed different things.

'I mind once a man tellin' me that he always knew when a wumman was "that way" as he called it, because she had a good colour. "Lit up", wos what he said. "A brightness in the eyes and a spring in the step" . . . afore they got too big that wou'd be,' she added, just to make things plain. 'An' indade, I think now he was right. I've often seen the signs that a wumman would be sending for me, long before she thought of it hersel'.'

They were all hungry and the food was tasty; all three men nodded when she looked at the cleaned plates and asked if they'd like to scrape the pot. She got up, brought the blackened pot to the table and shared out the remains between them, glad that, as always, she made sure there was plenty. Simple food it might be and very seldom was there meat or fish, but as her grandmother used to say when they sat down to food in their tiny cottage, 'Isn't hunger the best relish you could have, and how better to get it than to do your work well.'

There was no doubt the work in the forge made for clean plates.

It was an hour or two later, the dishes washed, two meals safe under enamel plates on the hearth, when Sarah took out her sewing and sat down gratefully by the fire. The morning tasks had been no different from other mornings but she admitted she felt more tired today than usual. Perhaps, she thought to herself, after John came home and they'd had their meal together, she'd walk down to see Mary-Anne while he changed his clothes and went back to the forge. But as she made up her mind that's what she'd do, she heard a clatter on the cobbles outside.

Smiling with delight, she dropped the sleeve she was working on with the blouse to which it was to be fitted. He was actually a bit later than she'd expected, but it would still be early enough when they'd eaten together for her to go to see Mary-Anne before she started making her evening meal for her husband, Billy and their two sons.

At first she couldn't make any sense of what she saw. Daisy, the mare, was covered with sweat and was foaming from her mouth; her eyes were wild with fear and a long scrape on her side dripping blood onto the cobbles. The trap was empty, the reins trailing. There was no sign whatever of the materials John had gone to buy.

And there was no sign of John.

She stood there, her heart in her mouth. Something terrible had happened, she was sure, but there was nothing to tell her what it might have been. Or so she thought. It was Ben, Ben of all people, who spoke out when all three of them appeared from the dark doorway.

He stared at the trap as if transfixed, but then, almost unnoticed, he moved round to the other side of the well-polished and much cherished vehicle, John's pride and joy, the first thing he had ever bought for himself, having saved up for years while working as a smith.

Ben stared at score marks on the side of the trap and then ran his hands over the rim.

'What is it, man, what can ye see roun' there?' demanded

Sam, when he glanced over at him and saw, to his total amazement, that tears were streaming down Ben's cheeks.

'They ran inta somethin' about the height of anither trap only stronger like, a dray or a cart maybe. The mare musta took fright. She ran that fast the trap cowped over aginst somethin' hard. Musta been a stone wall or suchlike an' the boss got thrown out. We may away and luk fer him on the road,' he said, turning his back and walking out between the great stone pillars which were the trademark of a working forge or a strong farm.

Sarah looked at Sam and knew from the expression on his face that what Ben had said made sense to him. Scottie hadn't even heard; his head was buried in Daisy's neck, his arms around her as he stroked her and comforted her. She was steady now, her eyes no longer bulging, her nostrils no longer dilated. As Sarah stared at the pair of them, she saw Daisy snuffle at Scottie's familiar, warm work clothes. Comforted by his touch, his enfolding arms and his known voice, she tossed her head, stopped fidgeting and stood quite still.

'Now don't worry, missus,' said Sam quickly, seeing the look of utter distress on her face. 'Shure the boss is a fine, strong man. If he's taken a bit of a fall, sure he'll get over it. I'll away after Ben and get some of the Halligans from below to give me a han'. We'll fin' him all right an' bring him home straight away, niver ye fear.'

The lovely sunlit afternoon passed so slowly that at times Sarah was convinced the clock had stopped. She tried to occupy herself in the house knowing that Scottie was beside himself and wouldn't know what to say to her. He'd taken Daisy from between the shafts of the damaged trap, rubbed her down and put her out to grass, making sure she had water and hay. The bleeding from her left flank had stopped so he left it alone, knowing that if he tried to clean the long gash, it might only start bleeding again.

'A'll away and watch fer them on the hill and tell ye when they're comin',' he said, appearing unexpectedly, putting his head hastily round the kitchen door and running off without waiting for any answer.

She lifted her head from her sewing lying untouched in her lap and watched through the window as he climbed up the nine-barred gate and then scrambled precariously onto the pointed top of the right-hand gatepost, the one with the best view down Drumilly Hill. There, he settled himself, the light breeze blowing his unkempt red hair across the pale freckles on his cheeks.

It was a long time before he saw any movement at all on the road: a tinker woman plodding up the hill, a child on her back, a heavy case of her wares in one hand, a small boy holding the other.

Scottie watched her move slowly towards him, her back bent with the weight of her stock, both children silent with tiredness.

'Missus in?' she asked abruptly, as she drew level with the ever-open gate.

'Not the day,' he replied promptly. The missus knew the tinker woman and whether she bought anything or not, she'd always give her bread and tea and milk for the child and the baby.

Her face remained unchanged. Had Scottie paused to ask himself if she believed him, it would have given him no clue to anything she ever thought.

Time passed, the breeze strengthened, the shadows lengthened. His backside had grown numb with cold through the cast-off trousers someone had given to his granny, when finally he caught a movement on the road. It was minutes later before he could make out what it was. Neither cart, nor trap, nor ploughman with horses, but four men carrying a heavy burden between them, one at each corner of a door, on which lay a figure, a white bandage on its head, the booted legs hanging over the end of the makeshift carrier.

He watched as they drew closer, not knowing what to think, unable to see the face of the figure lying sprawled face upwards. It was Sam Keenan at the leading edge that looked up and caught sight of him. In one single gesture he told Scottie the last thing he ever wanted to hear. He simply shook his head.

CHAPTER THREE

Scottie didn't know what to do. He sat on his precarious perch and watched as they carried the body of his much-loved boss through the gates and into the cobbled space in front of the house. All he could see of Sarah Hamilton was the speed with which she moved when she heard the sound of boots. She dropped to her knees, her back to him, leaning over the body of her husband.

The four men, having lowered their burden gently to the ground stood awkwardly, looking down at her as she touched John's face, so clean and white, its year-round, open-air tan completely disappeared. She couldn't quite grasp why he was so white or why his clothes were soaked through, but she saw immediately that he was dead.

For the last hour or more she had sat unmoving by the fire trying to accept that there had been an accident, that

John might be injured, he might even be disabled. That would be a terrible thing to have to face. She had given no thought at all to his death for that was to give up hope and she had been taught long, long ago by her grandmother that one must never give up hope. Hope is God-given and we must cherish it and rely on His sheltering arms to find a way forward from the most heartbreaking of disasters.

'Have you any idea what happened?' she asked calmly, looking up, aware of the grief and unease of all four men; Sam Keenan, John's everyday companion and friend, Ben Hutchison, his senior apprentice, Billy Halligan, his nearest neighbour and his elder son, Jamsey, now in his teens. John had known Jamsey since he and his brother were children coming up the hill after school to watch him working in the forge.

He had been fond of them both, slipped them the odd penny for sweets, listened to the news of their doings. Now Jamsey stood, like the others, as still as they could, muscles aching from the efforts of the last hour and the exhausting pull up the hill with their sad burden. Ben and Jamsey glanced from Sam Keenan's grime-streaked face to Jamsey's father wondering what either of the older men would say, what words of comfort they would offer a woman only two years a wife, a loving, hard-working wife whom they all knew John had worshipped.

It was Sam Keenan who spoke for them both.

'We foun' the load of iron and suchlike in the verge down in Ballybrannan. He wos on his way back from town. Somethin' must've come towards him from th'other way, just on that bit where it narrows. The mare must'ave took a bad fright; the cart cowped up and John was throw'd out.'

He paused, watching her face, but she just waited for him to go on.

'He might 'ave taken a fall an' be none the worse of it, but by bad luck there wos a wee bit of a stream wi' a stone bridge over it. He hit the stone and fell over inta the water.'

'So he drowned?'

'No, I don' think so. We foun' him in the water wi' a gash on his head but it wasn't bleedin'. It might be his neck's broken.'

Sarah nodded and leant forward to loosen the white bandage. She wondered how and where the four men had found a white bandage: a proper bandage, not a piece of old, but clean linen or even someone's handkerchief.

It fell away, revealing a long, deep gash across his forehead and temple. It was a purplish colour, but there was no blood whatsoever. It looked as if the bandage had no useful purpose, except perhaps to spare her the sight of that heartbreaking gash, which had cost him his life, one way or another.

She paused only a moment and then said, 'You could all do with a cup of tea and a bite of cake. Could we take John into the sitting room?'

They all bent down together, grateful for activity and as they did Mary-Anne Halligan hurried through the gates, gasping for breath and wearing her best dress.

Without a word, and to Sarah's great surprise, she threw her arms round her. 'Ach, God love ye, I'd a been here sooner, but I was cleanin' out the dairy an' I was in my dishabels.'

Sarah smiled. Her beloved John was dead and here she was thinking that it was a long, long time since she had heard that word. Her grandmother had once explained to her that 'dishabels' was a corruption of the French word *déshabillé*, which, of course, meant old clothes, those not suitable for receiving company.

She glanced down at her own clothes, grateful she was wearing one of John's favourite blouses with her second-best skirt. She was not in her dishabels. She was grateful for that and as she responded to Mary-Anne's embrace, she asked, 'Was it you put on the bandage?'

'Aye, surely. But shure there's no bandage to put on yer heart.'

'No, there's not, but I've other people to think about now,' she said honestly, as the enormity of what had to be done began to print out in her mind.

'Shure Billy an I will give ye a han'. Come on in and we'll make a cup a tea an' see what ye want us all to do.'

Mary-Anne and her family were as good as their word and, within a few hours, John's brother, George, from nearby Grennan, arrived with his wife bringing tea, sugar, bread and cake for the visitors who would come when they heard the news. George paused only to greet Sarah and then drove into Armagh to summon the undertaker, leaving his wife, Alice, to keep her company along with Mary-Anne.

Visitors began to arrive within the hour and Alice and Mary-Anne made pot after pot of tea.

Sarah was amazed in the hours that followed at the outpouring of grief over her loss and the warmth and love directed towards her, something she would never have expected for a relative newcomer to a long-settled community where everyone knew each other and had known them all their lives.

She received their greetings, answered their questions and watched the practicalities disappear in front of her. By the end of that long day, John lay in his coffin looking trim in his best suit, only a much smaller, rectangular plaster now marring the face that had been so familiar to all who came to the forge. The funeral was arranged, as custom was, for two days after the day of death, long enough for everyone to pay their respects both at his home and in the churchyard.

Through it all, Sarah remained steady and smiling, welcoming all those who came, putting at ease men who had never met her before, women who felt obliged to cry, kind neighbours so anxious to help in any possible way.

She was so steady that neighbours nodded together and agreed that 'sure it hadn't hit her yet'. What Sarah herself thought was that she was not alone in her grief and that for now it was her task to comfort others; whether it was Scottie weeping in her arms when he finally came down from his perch on the gate pillar, or her own brother, Charles Gregson, who rode, white-faced, from Lurgan as soon as he got word via the stationmaster, who sent one of his porters to bring him the news in his factory on the outskirts of the town.

She hadn't seen her brother since she and John had their very quiet ceremony almost two years ago in this same month of April. Now, in the churchyard surrounding that small grey church, built by an earlier Molyneux, the local landlord, John would lie in the family grave with the other Hamiltons who had lived and died in this parish in the last seventy-five years.

The hours of that long day passed and of the two that followed leaving only a passing impression of faces, known and unknown and regularly repeating phrases, 'I'm sorry fer yer trouble, God love you.' 'Can I do anythin t' help ye? Say the word, for John was a good fren' to us all.' 'Ye couldn't meet a straighter man. He wos that good-hearted he'd give ye his last sixp'nce.'

They sang his praises so that their words echoed and made a kind of litany in her head as she lay totally exhausted in her empty bed the night after the funeral. Wide-eyed for the most part, she occasionally drifted into sleep, saw John walk through the door, come and put his arm round her and draw her close. Then she woke in the silence and thought of all that she had to do, the letters to be written, the arrangements to be made.

She got up very early the next morning, a Friday, and found to her amazement that Mary-Anne had spent the night on the settle bed. She had the fire going and the porridge already bubbling.

'Oh, Mary-Anne, you are too good to me. You've done so much to help and that settle bed is hard as nails.'

'Not as hard as what ye've ti' face.' Mary-Anne replied promptly. 'Shure it's little any o' us can do. An' ye might have took bad in the night wi' the shock of it all, standin' by the grave an' shaking hans wi' half the world an' a word for all o' them, in yer condishun.'

For a moment, Sarah thought she meant her widowhood, then she looked at her face. No, that was clearly not what she meant.

'Did ye not know?' Mary-Anne asked, shaking her head.

'I wondered,' she replied honestly. 'And we *were* hoping, but I couldn't be sure.'

'An' when did ye last bleed?'

'End of January.'

Mary-Anne shook her head again. 'An' you an educated wumman!' she said, a wry smile on her face, as she counted the weeks aloud on her fingers. 'A wee one due after the harvest and no forge and no money in yer purse. How are ye goin' t'manage? Will yer brother be able to help ye out? Now come over to the table and eat yer porridge while there's still oats in the crock.'

Sarah ate her porridge as obediently as a child. When she had finished, she thanked Mary-Anne for all she had done and insisted she go home to her menfolk. She asked her to come up anytime she felt like it, for she'd always be glad to see her, but she wasn't to worry about her.

'If I'm not well, I'll send Scottie down for you, I promise. Just knowing you're there will help me. Really it will.'

'Ye'll not have Scottie for long, wil'ye?'

'What do you mean?'

'Shure there's no one now to run the forge, they'll have to find other work somewhere or other, an' Sam Keenan has a wife and two childer an' one on the way. He'll be out lukin' on Monday.'

Sarah felt a sharp stab of pain in her stomach but said nothing. She took a deep breath and was grateful when it subsided. But the full weight of Mary-Anne's words did not subside. The picture of a silent forge came home to her. Loss upon loss. That was what faced her, her and her unborn child and these three men who'd become part of her life with John. He was gone, but they still lived and all three had family of one kind or another dependant on them.

'Then I'll have to run it,' she began. 'There's three men depending on it as well as me, and a child, all being well,' she went on, as calmly as she could manage, given that she had just this moment remembered it was Friday.

Friday was payday and she wasn't sure what she might find in her purse. If anything.

She sat at the kitchen table with her empty bowl pushed away from her so she could lean her arms on its bare, well-scrubbed surface. She was thirsty and thought of making a pot of tea, but felt so tired the effort seemed too much for her.

The forge was silent. It was almost as if the silence were louder than the familiar sounds had been. She had no idea what the day might bring. Unfamiliar with the local customs, she had not expected the procession of people known and unknown that flowed in and out for the two days and nights before the funeral and the equally unexpected sudden silence after the burial itself, when, apart from Mary-Anne, it seemed only the closest of relatives could visit.

She grasped the meaning of locking up the forge, the large padlock clearly visible from the gates, now closed for the first time since the solid thatched house had been her home. But what about Sam Keenan and his wages?

Normally, each Friday when she had done the morning jobs, she took out the cash box into which John had put the takings during the week. She'd made up Sam's wage, the sum she and John had agreed was needed for the expenses of the house and the small sums both Ben and Scottie received, amounts laid down in the apprentice documents along with the agreements about food and clothing and the provision of appropriate bedding if required.

Scottie went home to his granny at night, using the shortcut across the fields, but Ben, who only went home on a Saturday night, slept in the loft over the forge, washed at the well each morning and came for his bowl, or his piece, as soon as John appeared in the forge to light the fire.

Her head was beginning to ache as she puzzled away at the total disruption to the well-organised system that now lay in ruins with John's death.

Speaking strongly to herself, she got up and fetched the battered cash box from the cupboard below the dresser, sat down again gratefully and opened it. She sighed: there was just enough for the three men, but nothing left for running the house.

She took a deep breath, well used to the erratic nature of their income, where one week the price of a pair of gates would more than pay the wages, and the next, with a reliable customer unable to pay till the end of the month, or till after the harvest, she would have to dip into the reserve.

The first reserve was an old brown handbag that had belonged to John's grandmother. There, behind the bank book, the rent book, their birth certificates, and their marriage certificate, were a few tattered and grimy notes. There was almost enough but not quite.

She opened the bank book and glanced through the entries: the long series of small entries which preceded the buying of the trap, big deposits after a good harvest when farmers brought hard-pressed machinery to be repaired or renewed, and regular withdrawals in winter with little work in the forge and extra fuel needed in the house.

A bank book, she reflected, was a different kind of diary.

It too charted important events, reflecting good times and bad. When she came to the withdrawal of the money for John's wedding suit, the one in which he'd been buried, she felt quite overcome, a kind of sick nausea grasping her chest.

'Are ye all right, missus dear?'

She looked up, feeling dizzy, the figure in front of her slightly blurred.

'I giv' the door a knock, but whin I diden hear ye at your work I thought ah better luk in. Yer powerful pale. Ken I get ye anythin'?'

'Thanks, Sam. Would you make us a pot of tea? I think I'm just tired. I haven't slept much.'

'Ach sure it'sa desperit hard time for ye,' he said strongly. 'Aye an' fer all of us. Whit'll we do at all wi'out him?'

'We can only do our best, Sam,' she said sadly, as he hung the kettle on its chain and poked up the fire. 'And I'll need you to keep me straight. There's things I might not know about the forge and no John to put me right. The accounts I'm well used to, but some of the big bills for supplies I'd need to have warning of.'

'D'ye mean yer goin ta run it yersel?'

'What else can I do?'

'Sure, maybe we thought ye'd go ta live with some ither of yer family or teach we'ens like ye told us ye did once,' he said, looking at her in amazement, a hint of relief already creeping into his voice.

'Sam, I *have* no family, except my brother, and he has his work cut out for him trying to run a factory. It's a hard time for him with orders letting him down. He's never married but he looks after the old couple who took him in when we lost our parents. He has nothing to spare.'

She paused, the effort of speaking almost too much for her, the nausea flowing over her again, this time with cramping pains in her stomach.

The kettle was rattling its lid and as Sam moved around making the tea she laid her head on the bare table. She wondered if she was going to cry. She felt so peculiar. She couldn't describe it. Even if the good-hearted Sam had asked her how she was feeling, she wouldn't have known how to answer him.

He put a jug of milk on the table, fetched mugs from the dresser and poured tea for them both, then, suddenly remembering, he dug his hand into his trouser pocket and brought out a crumpled note.

'Here y'ar. I near fergot,' he said apologetically. 'A couple o' men who owed us money come upta my house lass night to pay up. Shure everyone knows a wake is desperit hard on food and drink, even if ye don't buy whiskey, that's forby the big bills,' he said, knowing very well John's brother had gone for the undertaker from Armagh.

She smiled slightly as she smoothed out the battered note.

'Well, we're all right for this week, Sam,' she said quietly. 'If you'd reach behind you into the left-hand drawer of the dresser you'll find the wee envelopes I use. I'll make them up for you and the boys.'

She drank thirstily from her mug, felt a little better and watched him pull out the drawer where she kept the account books, the ancient cash box, paper, pens, a bottle of ink and a box of nibs.

'They these?' he asked, smiling, as he handed them to her.

She nodded, feeling strange again as she opened the cash box and began to put together tattered notes and coins.

'Ye don't luk well, missus,' said Sam, who was now studying her closely. 'Wou'd ye maybe need to see the doctor?'

She'd certainly not ever felt like this before. She knew the colour had drained from her face and the stomach cramps had begun again more vigorously. As she sat trying to put together the familiar amounts and take in what Sam had just said, she felt a dampness between her legs as if her monthly bleeding had started suddenly when she was unprepared.

'I think, Sam, I might have a word with Mary-Anne. I'll go down in a wee while when I've finished my tea.'

'Ye'll do no such thing,' he said, with a vigour that surprised her. 'You'll sit where ye are and I'll away down and get her an' bring her up t'you.'

He paused only long enough to throw back his tea, pocket the three envelopes and bid her firmly to stay where she was. She heard his boots on the cobbles and the whine of the gate hinges which needed oiling and then, gratefully, she laid her head down on the table, her one thought that she now had a week to work out what to do before she ran out of both money and food.

CHAPTER FOUR

Mary-Anne arrived in a flurry, her skirt flying, clutching a bulging shopping bag. Sam was out of breath as he hurried to keep up with her. She took one glance at Sarah, who had raised her head when she heard the gate whine, and insisted on her lying down right away. She watched carefully as Sarah moved slowly and awkwardly from one steep wooden tread to the next, Sam Keenan close behind her, blocking the narrow stairway in case she should miss her step.

By the time Sarah got up into the bedroom, she was exhausted; a cold sweat was breaking on her face and her legs threatened to give way under her. She dropped down on John's side of the bed, the one nearest to the door and heard, rather than saw, Sam and Mary-Anne come in behind her.

Before she'd even had time to collect herself enough to thank Sam for his help, Mary-Anne had hustled him out of the room.

'Away home, good man,' she said quickly. 'Come back down, or send wee Scottie, or one of the childer in 'bout an hour,' she went on. She dropped her voice to a whisper, *'In case I need sen' for the doctor.'*

Sarah heard the words quite clearly but found she hadn't the energy to protest. She simply lay back as she was told, aware of Mary-Anne pulling off her boots and undoing the buttons on the side of her skirt.

'Now, lift up yer backside up if ye can, like a good wumman,' she said softly, as Sam's boots echoed on the stairs and they heard him pull the front door closed behind him. 'Are yer monthly cloths in the chest?' she went on.

Sarah wiped her forehead after the effort of raising her lower half so that Mary-Anne could remove her skirt and her damp knickers. She did say, 'Yes,' but the sound that came out was only a whisper.

It was all her friend needed. She bent down, pulled out the lowest drawer first and immediately found what she wanted. She'd never met a woman yet who didn't keep well-washed, but stained cloths, somewhere handy in the bedroom.

She spread a couple of the largest squares underneath Sarah's lower half, then draped the skirt across her body.

'Now, just you close your eyes an' have a rest, an' I'll lie on the bed beside you. Shure it's not offen I get an excuse to lie down,' she said cheerfully, as she took off her own boots and lay down gently on top of the bedclothes, without creating so much as a squeak from the bedsprings.

Sarah wanted to thank her, but couldn't find the energy to speak.

To her surprise, she found tears running freely down her cheeks. Why tears, why now? she wondered. Were they for John? And why now, when they'd stayed away through all the long hours since he'd been brought home? Suddenly, quite unexpectedly, she thought of Helen, her dear childhood friend, the only person other than John with whom she had ever shared a bed.

Helen was inches smaller than she was herself. She was blonde with curly hair, while she herself was dark, her hair long and straight. Helen seemed always to bubble with life and energy while Sarah was quieter, more thoughtful, sometimes almost solemn. 'Chalk and cheese,' her grandmother had called them, laughing, when she saw them coming back from a walk together, their arms round each other's waists.

The much-loved, only surviving child of another Quaker family, Helen was one of the handful of children her grandmother taught. They had always sat beside each other, run errands together, shared whatever books or paper they received as gifts. They had been inseparable all through their childhood, their birthdays only three weeks apart. Then Helen had fallen in love at only seventeen, a man some six years older than herself, but the son of close neighbours whom she had also known from childhood.

Seeing what joy they had together and sharing the hopes they had for their future with them, Sarah had been so happy herself. But her joy in their relationship was short-lived. Helen's parents opposed her marriage to a man who was not a Quaker.

Helen had gone ahead and married him with Sarah as one of her witnesses at the registry office in Armagh. By then, Helen's intentions having been made clear, she was pronounced as being 'out of unity' by their Monthly Meeting. With her grandmother no longer well and unable to attend Meetings on Sundays, Sarah herself stopped attending.

Sarah's eyes closed. Helen had been so hurt, not only by the pronouncement of their local Monthly Meeting, but by the coolness and even rejection of her family and many of her friends. She'd said that Sarah was the only person who had not changed in any way towards her as a result of her marriage.

But change had come upon them all. Happy as Helen and Daniel were in their love for each other, Daniel ran into difficulties with the cotton-spinning business he'd inherited from his grandfather. Customers, many of them Quakers, who were committed to fair trading, simply withdrew their support. His business began to fail. In desperation, they decided the only thing to do was emigrate. Like thousands of Presbyterians, Catholics and Quakers before them escaping discrimination and unfair levies and taxes, they decided to go to America, where Daniel had cousins in New England who would help him to get started again.

Helen had wept when she told Sarah what they'd decided and Sarah had wept with her when she accepted it was probably the only way. Yes, they would write and indeed they still wrote long, open letters to each other, but on that memorable occasion the tears had poured down her cheeks, tickling her ears and she couldn't find her hanky. Just like now.

The hours passed as she moved in and out of sleep. She heard Scottie's voice and felt the gentle movement of Mary-Anne on the bed beside her as she went down to speak to him. The light of the well-lengthened April evening had turned to a golden glow when Sarah found herself suddenly jerked from an uneasy, dream-filled doze by a sharp pain that made her body twitch so violently that Mary-Anne, who now lay beside her again, woke instantly.

Sarah gasped as Mary-Anne got to her feet in seconds, came round to her side of the bed, got down on her knees and put both hands on her stomach.

'There now. Take deep breaths,' she said softly, in a tone Sarah had not associated with Mary-Anne until today. 'Shure the worst is near over, the pain itself won't harm ye – the only danger is fear and ye've no call for that.'

She felt the pressure of Mary-Anne's hands and sensed a warmth flowing from them. It reminded her again of childhood and her grandmother laying hands upon her when she was in any sort of pain, or was anxious or troubled.

'Pain is all the same in one way,' the old woman had

often said. 'Whether it is your heart or your head, if you are troubled in body, or in spirit, then you need to ask for healing. Now, sit down here on the floor where I can rest my hands upon you. Be still and listen to what comes to you. What picture comes into your mind? A person, or a place, or an object. They have a message for you. Just listen and keep still. Let the pain be the pain, it cannot harm you in itself.'

Sarah closed her eyes again and focused on Mary-Anne's hands and the warmth that flowed from them. To her surprise what she heard was John's hammer on the anvil. The long, slow strokes and the dancing rhythm in between. She would never forget that dancing rhythm. That was John, that was his trademark and he had left it with her. Like Helen had left her with laughter and her grandmother with love and comfort, John had left her a gift of love and lightness, epitomised by that dancing rhythm. These gifts would, in time, bring comfort. They could not replace his sheltering arms, but they would be with her for however long she might live.

'Ach, that's better, yer smiling,' said Mary-Anne, as she moved away the skirt she had spread over her, replaced it with a cloth and put her hands back on her stomach.

There was pain, but it seemed to be happening to someone else; her body trembled, twitched and was still. Mary-Anne did what she had come to do. It was over. She had lost John's child, but she had been strengthened in love. She fell asleep with Mary-Anne holding her hand, lying on the bed beside her.

* * *

It was dark when she woke, the pain gone, her mind clear again. In the fading moonlight through the undrawn curtains she could see Mary-Anne fast asleep beside her, still fully dressed, on top of the bedclothes. She moved very carefully so as not to disturb her, her own body stiff from long hours of lying on her back. She took it very slowly, managed to stand up and walk shakily to the south-facing window. She leant against the outshot made by the chimney stack coming up from the kitchen below.

As always, the projecting whitewashed flue was slightly warm from the heat rising from the fire on the hearth below, no doubt now banked down by Mary-Anne or Scottie. The fire on the hearth never went out, unless by accident on a night when a high wind blew up, roaring round the exposed house. Then, the wind could whip up even the well-damped-down embers so that in the morning there was only a pile of ash and a dusty hearth.

The fire had not gone out in the almost two years when she and John had tended it together, cooked their food on it, enjoyed its warmth and comfort evening after evening, as they sat and talked while she sewed or John read to her from the local paper.

Today must be Saturday. She counted on her fingers to be sure. Tuesday was John's visit to Armagh, Wednesday a day of visitors and arrangements, Thursday was the service and burial in Grange churchyard. So yesterday was Friday. Sometime then she had lost her unborn child. At her feet she saw a pile of cloths. The one on top, larger than the others was clean, the stains ancient, but below she knew there were fresh bloodstains on the rest of the pile where Mary-Anne had staunched the flow and then washed her.

Loss and yet more loss, she thought calmly, aware that the moonlight was fading and already there was a hint of light in the eastern sky. Another day was dawning, and the fire had not been allowed to go out even during the biggest event in her life. She knew what her grandmother would say: *Sure we cannot know what we are called upon to do, but the good Lord will help us whatever our grief or sadness. We must just trust him.*

Her grandmother had suffered the loss of the young man to whom she'd been engaged. She had never married, but she had not let what had happened embitter her. She had an easy smile, a cheering word for everyone she encountered, a glow which radiated all around her. Sarah could see her wrinkled face, her stooped figure, her hobbling walk. They made no difference to her indomitable spirit. She had died in her nineties, sound of mind though confined to her chair by the fire, her body so light that Sarah had not the slightest difficulty lifting her for bed or commode.

She too had died in April, on a morning of sunshine and showers when Sarah herself had looked out at their small garden and told her that there'd been rain in the night, that there were 'jewels on the trees'.

Reluctant to disturb Mary-Anne who had so freely admitted that she seldom got time to rest, Sarah did not go back to bed, but as the light grew stronger Mary-Anne stirred.

'Are you all right?' she asked in her normal sharp voice.

'And why would I not be with such a good nurse?' Sarah replied briskly.

'Aye, well,' she began more gently, 'shure it's hard if ye have no family to give ye a hand when yer not right. T'was the least I could do. Shou'dn't someone be helpin' you and you sayin' you were keepin' the forge goin' because of Sam Keenan and his we'eans and Ben and poor wee Scottie. That wee lad has no one here belongin' to him but his oul granny. An' she wou'd never say a kine word if there was some cuttin' remark she cou'd make,' she added sharply. 'Some oul people bees awful bitter, an' sure what good does it do? We all have our time, rich or poor, and that's the end of it.'

She had got up, sat on the side of the bed and now came to join her at the window. To Sarah's surprise, she held out her arms to her. 'Ye'll not be like that,' she went on, 'ye'll be like me twin sister, me double.'

Sarah saw the tears suddenly pour down Mary-Anne's face. She moved into the open arms and embraced her warmly.

'What age was she?' Sarah asked, stroking her hair.

'Ach, only seventeen,' she replied, finding a handkerchief in her skirt pocket. 'It was TB. I had it too, but threw it off. Some people do,' she added, seeing Sarah's puzzled look. 'But now I have you, haven't I?' she said, a shake in her voice.

'Oh yes, now you have me. We'll have to do what we can for those who need us.'

'Aye,' Mary-Anne said strongly. 'An' the pair of us need our porridge as soon as we stir up the fire.'

The day passed slowly, a real April day of sun and showers. As the time passed, both good news and anxiety streaked the hours with a turbulence that matched the weather; interludes of brightness swept away by renewed anxiety and disappointments to follow.

After she had finally persuaded Mary-Anne to go back to her family, that she was perfectly all right, just a bit shaky on her feet, the postman was her first caller. He came, saw the front door propped open as usual, tramped down the short corridor to the kitchen door and found her sitting at the table, surrounded by papers, account books and an open cash box.

'A powerful crowd at the funeral,' he began awkwardly, not meeting her eyes.

'Yes, I was amazed the church was so full,' she replied, trying to make him easier, 'but then John and his family have been here a long time and he knew everyone, didn't he?'

'Aye, he did that and a good word for everyone. Sure you'll miss him sorely. Whit'll ye do?' he finally asked, plucking up courage and looking at her for the first time.

'Well, I'll try to keep things going as best I can, but I don't know how I'll manage. I'll have to see what can be done . . .'

He saw her look at the papers and the cash box and shook his head.

'I'm afeerd I'm not the bringer of help. I wisht I was,' he said forcefully, as he took a large white envelope from his battered mailbag and handed it to her. 'I think I maybe know what thon is, an' sure cou'd they not 'ave waited a wee while?' he added sharply.

'Well, it has to be done; it's someone's job to send it out,' she said opening it, aware that he was watching, his face creased with concern.

'Is it what I think it is?' he asked, his tone so soft she felt herself close to tears.

The single sheet of paper with its engraved heading was difficult to unfold, but the black figure for John's burial was even stiffer than she might have imagined. She handed it to him and smiled.

'I'll have to sell my jewels, won't I?'

'D'ye have any?' he asked, a trace of relief breaking into his voice.

She shook her head, smiling. 'My grandmother used to tell me I didn't need jewels, I had jewels hanging on the hawthorns every time we got sun after rain. And then she'd say "But we do have some tea in the caddy." Will you have a cup with me while I have it?'

He thanked her but had to say no. He'd a long round to do, it being Saturday, but he wished her good luck and said he'd hope he had something better in his mailbag for her next week.

She heard his boots on the floor of the corridor and saw his short, sturdy figure cross the cobbles to the gate, which now stood open. A few minutes later, she heard hammering from the forge. Everyday life had begun again for all their friends and neighbours, but nothing would ever be the same for her. She put the bill in the empty cash box and closed it firmly. She now had six days, not seven, to find her way. The bill was one more mountain to climb.

CHAPTER FIVE

Sarah couldn't imagine why she had gone back to the old brown handbag belonging to John's grandmother. She remembered clearly that she'd found a single battered note there on Friday morning when she'd tried to make up Sam's wages and the small sums due to Ben and Scottie. As she sat down at the kitchen table with the worn and battered object, she told herself she was being silly, wasting time when the morning tasks were still only half completed and there was dinner to make for Scottie and Ben at midday and bread to bake for their evening meal.

In the end, she just laughed at herself as she picked up the handbag and struggled with the broken catch, then tipped out the familiar contents on the table. Bright beams of sunlight fell on packets of faded parchment and lit up the swirling curlicues and flowing text of manuscript writers who made a living from copying documents of all kinds.

'Rent book, bank book, copy of lease,' she recited, as if by speaking the words she could persuade herself more effectively that there was no money there.

She was, of course, quite right. Neither banknote, nor coin, half-crown, florin nor shilling, slipped from between the folded and only recently disturbed packets that held the birth certificates of both John and his elder brother, George, and the death certificates of his two sisters and those of his mother and his father. She had once looked at John's birth certificate and saw a name she now recognised as that of Mary-Anne's mother, the midwife, who as midwives often did had registered the birth herself to make sure it was actually done.

She set aside the most recent document, their own marriage certificate, without unfolding it and took up the packet of death certificates she'd never looked at. Now she drew them out of a torn and yellowed envelope, surprised at how thick the four single page documents appeared to be. That was when she found a tiny book, not unlike the bank book, though much slimmer. It was what made the envelope fatter than she'd expected. It's pale, faded, printed cover declared it was the official record of the Friendly Society Burial Fund.

Curious about something she had never heard of, she opened it, saw the names of John's parents of the townland of Ardrea and Parish of Salter's Grange. The print was so small she was glad of the strong light as she began to read the requirements of the society and the terms under which they would provide a burial fund for their members.

Intrigued, she worked her way through the agreements and exclusions and noted the premiums which she'd now been informed could be paid weekly, monthly or yearly. The same hand had recorded the tiny amounts of money on line after line, page after page, from the 1780s to the 1830s when John's parents had died within a few months of each other. Two pages, each with a single diagonal stroke and the words 'Paid up' recorded sums of money that seemed surprisingly large considering the smallness of the premiums.

The few remaining pages in the slim booklet were blank but for a slip of paper which said in a quite different hand: *Documents for sons of deceased held by Ulster Bank, Armagh. Premiums paid half-yearly by arrangement.*

She had no idea what arrangement that might be, but she knew where she might be able to find out. She opened the bank book she'd looked at the previous day – the one she'd used herself many times in the last two years. There, leafing back to the beginning of John's own account with the bank in Armagh was the record 'F. S.' every six months. A small amount, so small and so infrequent she wasn't sure she noticed it herself. If she had, she certainly didn't remember asking him who, or what, F. S. was when she was first trying to get a picture of their income and expenses.

The most recent entry for F. S. was January 1845, so the next was due in July, except that John was gone. Like both his parents, a strong, dark line would be drawn diagonally across the unfinished page. Without question there would be an amount far greater than the bill now shut up in the cash box in the top left-hand drawer of the dresser.

For some unknown reason she could not begin to understand, she found herself in tears and discovered once again she had no handkerchief in her skirt pocket.

It was Sunday afternoon before she came back to the kitchen table with the hasty calculations she'd made the previous day. Now, on an equally sunlit April day, the sun high in a blue sky, the countryside springing to life, the newly leafed trees bending in a fierce wind, she sat down with all her account books and the cash box containing the largest bill she had ever seen.

The wind was so strong it made the doors rattle and earlier she'd had to rescue the water buckets as they rolled across the cobbles. She knew the noise would stop her from concentrating so she left them anchored with a big stone knowing she'd need them later.

She'd have to go to the Ulster Bank tomorrow morning. Until she did, she could neither do her delayed weekly visit to the grocer's shop in English Street for tea and sugar, yeast and table salt, nor to the Guardian office in English Street to collect their weekly newspaper, which would still be waiting for their Saturday visit together.

Until she got to the bank she would not know exactly the amount to be paid out, but at a time when interest rates were steady she had already worked out a likely number based on the final figures for the two payments made in respect of John's parents.

She took the grocer's calendar from the kitchen wall and studied the pattern of weeks till the end of the harvest in September. Today was Sunday 27th April, the month nearly gone. Then she opened her own still new-looking account books, their marbled covers fresh and bright, and studied the weekly totals for the same period, May to September for 1843 and 1844.

In both their years together, they had been able to put away enough money in those summer months to help them through the colder months of the year when the forge was often quiet and extra turf and coal was needed in the house. Last week, she had not been anxious about the small amount in the brown handbag because she'd known the balance in the bank was enough to see them through May and into the much busier time that continued until after the harvest. All being well.

But all had not been well. John was gone. Only one time-served smith now worked the forge and there were two apprentices to be fed and paid small weekly sums, unless, of course, John's death should have broken that contract. Probably she ought to find out, but it had not occurred to her, any more than it would to John, to use a legal right to avoid doing what she thought was fair, keeping the boys on to finish what had been promised.

The truth was she could not predict what the forge's income might be with only Sam and the two boys. Sam was a good worker and skilful enough, but she knew there were jobs John always did himself. The only figures she could be sure of were: the outgoings; the weekly envelopes for Sam, Ben and Scottie; the cost of feeding Ben, Scottie, herself and Daisy, the mare, in winter; and the regular recurring cost of metal and nails, lubricant and tools, like the load shed down in Ballybrannan.

That would be another bill arriving soon, usually with a month's grace, but at least almost every item John had loaded on the trap was now where it ought to be in its place in the forge. Once the people in Ballybrannan had found out from Sam and Mary-Anne's husband, Billy, and son, Jamsey, what had happened, it had all been brought back, in bits and pieces, whenever a trap, or a carrier cart, or even the bread man, was found to be coming up to the top of Drumilly Hill, a fair way to carry long, heavy pieces of angle iron, or the sacks of horseshoe nails retrieved from the stream below the road.

She remembered the slightly startled look on Sam's face when she'd spoken lightly of selling her jewels, but it certainly hadn't taken her long to check if there were any items at all whose value might help out. No, there was nothing of value except, perhaps, poor Daisy herself who was already pining for her master. Then there was the trap, once John's pride and joy, now badly damaged and quite unusable.

The visit to Armagh was not an easy one. Sarah had been prepared for people in shops and in the Ulster Bank, to offer condolences and she'd promised herself she wouldn't shed tears. What she had not expected was the difficulty she encountered on her very first visit which, of course, with not a penny in her purse, had to be to the bank.

There behind the counter was a young man she did not know; from his bearing clearly not a new employee, but someone older, smart and well presented. His smile was mechanical; he addressed her as 'Madam', looked dubiously at the Friendly Society book and shook his head, explaining patiently as to someone not very familiar with the dealings of a bank, that they could not release funds from the Friendly Society without a death certificate and obviously she could not draw money from a joint account if the joint account holder was deceased.

It did not surprise her at all that the burial fund would require the presentation of a death certificate, nor that it might even take some time for the amount to be calculated and paid out, but what did surprise her was the fact he appeared not to know that a death certificate had to be paid for. It would be one of the first expenses to be met from the burial fund. At that point, she asked for the manager by name, was told he was on holiday and would return next week when he, no doubt, would be happy to deal with her claim.

She had turned on her heel, walked out without a word, tears of anger and frustration falling unheeded on the pale blue fabric of her second-best dress. She tramped down Russell Street without seeing either its handsome houses or the wrought-iron railings of the Presbyterian Church, crossed the road at its foot and sat on a stone seat under a tree on the Mall where she wept silently and asked for help.

Her grandmother had always taught her that in our greatest need help will come, but we must ask for it and then wait patiently. Whatever her own difficulties with the rigid rules of the Quakers in the Lisnagarvey Meeting, she had always felt that what her grandmother believed had sustained her throughout a long and often hard life.

The old woman believed that 'all would be well and all manner of thing would be well', a quote, she said, from a good lady in Norwich called Julian. As a little girl, Sarah had been puzzled by a lady with a man's name, but she'd come to understand that *things being well* was a matter of acceptance. Until you accept what has happened you can't do anything about it.

Had John not died she would not have been in the bank on such business; had the kind and friendly manager not been taking leave, no doubt before the end of the financial year, she would not have had to deal with a young man, clearly an aspiring manager, certainly not a local. The manager, who had known John for years and herself for two, would have treated her with sympathy the moment she produced the burial fund book, an errand always difficult, even if the person involved had not suffered the loss of a beloved young husband.

But accepting that still left the question of being without a penny. She could not now pay the undertaker as she had planned, nor purchase the required death certificate. She couldn't even buy tea and sugar, both of which were about to run out. Then she remembered the newspapers, last week's and today's, both of which would be waiting on a shelf behind the small counter of the Guardian office where she regularly bought nibs and ink as well as the new account books.

Well, she could at least apologise to her grocer for not being able to pay last week's bill nor buy any of her usual supplies this week. 'Paying last week's bill,' was one of the puzzling things John had to explain to her when she first came to Armagh and they went together into town for her first weekly shop.

It seemed that you always went to the same grocer, in John's case, Cousers, where his parents had shopped. You could say you 'dealt' with a particular grocer because you were always a week behind with your payment. He explained that the 'indebtedness' was a kind of contract. If someone told you that they were 'paying their bill', it meant there'd been some falling out and they were taking their custom elsewhere.

She smiled for the first time that morning and thought of the friendly assistants in Cousers. They all knew her now, whether John was able to bring her in the trap as he so liked to do, or she had to walk into town by herself when he was too busy to leave the forge. At least she could assure them she was not taking her custom elsewhere. That would be something to set against the distress she had felt in the bank.

She walked in to the dim interior and was touched by the familiar smells of spices and fresh sawdust on the floor, grateful for a continuing thing in a world where suddenly everything seemed to be different, bleaker, sadder and unfamiliar.

The shop was quiet, no other customers in sight, but the moment she appeared the tall, angular figure of the senior assistant caught sight of her, excused himself from where he stood instructing two of the young lads on the weighing of dry goods and hurried round to her side of the counter with one of the tall counter-height chairs they provided for their customers.

'Mrs Hamilton, dear, sit down,' he said warmly. 'Did ye walk it or was one of yer neighbours comin' in an' lifted ye?'

'No, Harry, I walked it. It's a lovely morning and I was glad to see the sun and the trees,' she replied, suddenly finding tears threatening to spill down her cheeks.

'Ach now, don't mind the tears, missus dear, shure wasn't many a one shed in here when we got the news from yer neighbour, Mrs Halligan. Yer good man, an' a good man he was, shure, he had a kine word for everyone. What'll ye do wi'out him? Will ye go back to yer own people? We'll be heart sorry to lose ye,' he said, bending towards her, his body placed firmly between her and a customer who had just stepped through the door.

'I have no people, Harry,' she said honestly, wiping her eyes and blowing her nose. 'I've a brother in Lurgan, but we were orphans. Our grandmother took me in, but he lived with friends of my mother and father. They died of fever when I was small. This is my home now,' she said, managing a smile.

'An' whit about the forge an' all? How will ye manage?' he asked, a look of concern on his lined face, his bushy white eyebrows raised in puzzlement. 'John was no great han' at accounts, I know that; a great smith I heerd tell, but he useta laugh about it himsel', said he diden know how I could tot up a bill in my head an' it always right. Did you take them over?'

'I did indeed,' she replied easily. 'I was brought up with accounts,' she explained, 'it was simply part of what my grandmother taught her "wee scholars", as she called them.

Many of their parents would have been in business, like my brother.'

'An' woud he maybe be able to help ye out,' he asked tentatively, his face full of concern.

'No, Harry, he couldn't,' she shook her head sadly. 'He has a textile business in Lurgan, still going, but times are hard in textiles, as you know, with competition from overseas. He supports the old couple who took him in when our parents died. He has his hands full, as they say,' she added, giving him a weak smile.

'If there is anythin' at all I can do t' help ye, will ye tell me? Shure hard times comes til' us all an' aren't we bound to help each other?'

She nodded, grateful for his kindness, but afraid tears might let her down again if she spoke. Then she remembered she'd come to tell him that she couldn't pay last week's bill.

'Harry, I did come for a few things but I'll have to leave them for today. I didn't want you to think I'd gone elsewhere, but I wasn't able to get money from the bank,' she said honestly.

'An' did ye have money there?' he asked, looking startled.

'Oh yes, thank goodness. And there is a burial fund as well. I didn't even know about that. Your man in the bank wanted a death certificate which, of course, I now can't pay for.'

'Ach aye, there's paperwork an' suchlike, but did they not give ye whit ye asked fer from yer account?'

She almost smiled at the look of blank incomprehension that caused his bushy white eyebrows to shoot upwards in amazement.

'Shure the Hamiltons have always banked with the Ulster,' he went on, clearly angry. 'What was wrong with them at all?'

He sounded so shocked that she smiled in spite of herself and said a few cautious words about the replacement manager.

'Ach well, shure we can get roun' that,' he said, relieved, as he dropped his voice further. 'Me sister works for yer man the undertaker. I'll send roun' one of the wee girls with a note to collect it for ye while we see t'yer shopping, an' then ye can go back t' the bank and ask for Ethel Magowan. She's me sister-in-law but ye won't know her. She's the chief clerk and works in the back. She'll sort out yer man, have no fear,' he added firmly as a broad grin spread across his face.

CHAPTER SIX

Harry Magowan smiled as Sarah paid him for last week's shopping and thanked him again for the way he had resolved her problems. He brought her shopping bags round from behind the counter where he'd kept them while she went to the bank. Now, he walked to the door with her, handed them back and smiled even more broadly as he said he'd look forward to seeing her next week.

As she stepped out into English Street, the pavements now more crowded, Sarah felt tiredness suddenly overtake her, the prospect of the long walk home somewhat intimidating. But she was so grateful for all that had happened in the last busy hour that she set out briskly.

Harry's sister-in-law, Ethel Magowan, a square, robust woman with iron-grey hair and small round spectacles, had been every bit as good as Harry had suggested. She'd taken

Sarah into the manager's office, he having conveniently gone out for lunch, and sat her down at his desk. There, Ethel glanced at the death certificate Harry had provided, and produced a form for the redemption of the burial fund. While Sarah filled it in, the older woman concentrated fiercely as she calculated the exact figure for the matured policy. It was the largest sum of money Sarah had ever seen and only a pound less than her own calculation. Ethel Magowan then proceed to open a new account in Sarah's own name. Then, and only then, did she manage a small smile as she reassured Sarah that 'our manager would always be ready to assist her with help or advice'.

Now, with a larger than usual amount of money in her purse, most of which would go into the brown handbag for unexpected bills of which there might be more, she thought longingly of sitting down, but she couldn't face the noise and bustle of any of the places where she might have ordered a pot of tea or a bite to eat. She gathered herself once again, stepped out briskly, then, as she was about to walk past the Guardian office further along English Street, she remembered the newspaper.

For once the place was empty but for a young assistant she had never met before. Suddenly, grateful there would be no need to mention John, she simply gave her name and collected two newspapers: one from last week and today's edition which still smelt of printers' ink.

Sliding them down behind the tea and sugar at the back of one of her shopping bags, she was suddenly taken by the thought that John would never read to her again. He would never comment on the doings of the gentry: their marriages, their coach passages through Armagh on the way to their country estates, the honours bestowed upon them on their visits to London. Nor would he read out the deaths recorded, the fires in the mills, the weekly admissions to the workhouse, or the comments on the state of the weather and the likely effect upon crops.

She handed over pennies from the small change Mrs Magowan had thoughtfully suggested when she'd counted out the notes of her withdrawal. She decided she would cancel the papers. But not today. That job would have to wait. Today, she just had to get away, to pick up her bags and head for home before she was ambushed again by her tears.

To her surprise there was hardly a vehicle to be seen on the Loughgall Road. Once she passed the blocked-off entrance where the gates of the new railway station would stand, she saw nothing moving except children and dogs.

One or two women standing at the doors of the small stone terrace of Gillis Row nodded to her, as they rested from their morning's work and held their faces up to the sunlight, but beyond the noise and clatter of Drumcairn Mill and the entrance to the Richardson's house at Drumsollen, where two men were erecting new gates, all was quiet, sunlit and empty.

She sat down to rest once or twice where the hedge bank was a convenient height, but once sitting down she found herself restless, a deep sense of being alone invading her. How different from bowling along in the trap, John pleased to have an outing and her company and to be away from the forge for a while. It always seemed that even Daisy was in good spirits and was herself happy to be on the road with him.

She got to her feet quickly. No, that was not the way. She'd had so much kindness and support from Harry and his sister-in-law: Harry open and approachable, his sister-in-law apparently tight-lipped and severe, but in the event just as committed to helping her. *Give thanks in all things, look forward not back.*

She smiled, then had to wipe away tears again, as her grandmother's words came into her mind. She got to her feet, picked up her bags and set off again, reminding herself that Riley's Rocks was not far away. John reckoned that was the midpoint of their journey. He always insisted that Daisy knew that too, for she always speeded up at that point on the way home, knowing there would be food and some small treat when she got back, before she was unharnessed and then turned out into her own field.

The sun was now high in a clear blue sky, Sarah felt hot and sticky, and longed for the cool of the house, the fire kept in but smoored down by Sam or Ben so that she could boil up the kettle as soon as she arrived back. She thought longingly of a large mug of tea. Not the day for the best china, nor even the large, everyday delph cups and saucers, only the half pint mugs John had once bought in the market in Armagh would serve her need.

It was as she turned off the Loughgall Road into the Ballybrannon Road that she heard a vehicle come up behind her and then stop a little way ahead.

'Can I give ye a lift, missus? Are ye goin' far?'

'Thank you, that would be very kind. I'm going to

Drumilly Hill, to the forge,' she replied, raising her voice.

A short ginger-haired man jumped down from the cart and with a word to the horse walked back to meet her.

'Ach dear,' he said. 'Wou'd ye be Mrs Hamilton, Mrs *John* Hamilton?' he said slowly, his voice so soft and the look on his face so plain she knew what was coming next.

She nodded, not trusting herself to speak as he held out his hand and grasped hers firmly.

'Mrs Hamilton, ye don't know me, but Sam Keenan is a very old friend o' mine an' I was heart-sorry to hear about yer good man,' he said, reaching out for her bags. 'I'm Paddy McCann and many's a time yer John helped m' brother an' me out over at the Cart Manufactory when we'd rims to fit. He and Sam wou'd come over of an evenin' and giv' us a han' if it was a difficult job, aye or sometimes even when we jus' had more work than we cou'd cope with,' he added, as he lifted her shopping carefully into the high-sided cart. He shook his head sadly and went on, 'Yer John was a great han' with metal. I'm a good carpenter, but that wasen much help when it came to fittin' rims,' he added laughing shortly. He paused. 'Now give me yer han' an' I'll help ye up the wheel. It's far higher than yer trap wou'd be and no step fer ye, but he's a good, steady horse and won't move on ye.'

'Thank you,' she said, catching up her skirt and gripping the side of the cart with her other hand as she climbed steadily up the wheel. She settled herself on the bag of straw with which he'd padded the driving seat. 'I have to admit I'm very tired,' she confessed, knowing she'd have to make an effort to smile and say a few words to put him at ease.

But before she'd given it any thought at all, he shook the reins and the horse responded promptly.

He turned to face her, and looked at her in amazement. 'Did ye walk the whole way as well?' he asked.

'Yes, I did,' she said, nodding. 'I *was* half expecting to get a lift when I got to the main road, but it all seems to be very quiet on a Monday. I think more people must go in on the market days, or Saturday, like ourselves, but I had things to see to . . .'

She broke off suddenly as she recognised the small stone bridge where Daisy had taken fright. He glanced at her quickly and pressed his lips together, his face screwed up in distress when he remembered what Sam Keenan had told him.

'Ach dear, ye'll think of him ivery time you pass that wee stone wall, but sure he was one good man. He'll be in a better place right enough, but it's you hasta go on by yerself. I heer ye want to keep the forge goin'. That's why I was comin' over t'see you forby gettin' this fellow a set of new shoes,' he said vigorously, as they left the bridge behind them. 'That trap of yours was a lovely thing, even I says it as shu'den', seein' I made the most of it, but sure it's not a bit of use t' you the way it is. I'll give ye a very fair price to make it like new. Then ye can keep it, or sell it, but it'll not break yer heart again ivery time ye see it like ye will wi' that bit of stone wall.'

Sarah could hardly believe how quickly they arrived home; Paddy's horse, several hands higher than Daisy and of a stronger build made light work of the hill. As they passed

Mary-Anne's house, Sarah was aware of the ring of hammer on anvil – the first time in days. She knew it was Sam. It was nearly always Sam when she and John came back from Armagh together.

Then, when they heard Daisy's step on the cobbles, Scottie would run out to take the reins while John helped Sarah down. Ben would follow more slowly to carry the shopping bags into the house and take to its place anything John might have collected for the forge.

Now, on this sunlit Monday, no one appeared till the clatter of Paddy's horse on the cobbles brought Scottie to the door of the forge to look out and see who it might be. Usually, if it was a customer known to them, he could tell from the sound of the hooves, but this strong black horse he could not recall.

'It's missus,' he called over his shoulder, moments before Paddy drew up by the front door. The hammering stopped instantly and Sam and Ben came out to meet them. Scottie grabbed her bags and ran off into the house while Ben took the reins and stood awkwardly by the horse's head watching Sarah as Sam and Paddy helped her down.

Tea, Sarah said to herself, as Paddy and Sam greeted each other, the old friends that they were. That was what she most wanted, but now it would have to be tea and a piece of cake. Paddy was not only a customer, albeit one she didn't know, but he was also a visitor, come on an errand of kindness. If there was one thing Sarah had observed in her two years at the forge it was that a welcome was always given, gentry or neighbour, even if it was only a glass of spring water offered when it was warm and the road was dusty. 'Sure it's only like a smile,' John had always said, 'isn't there always a way of showing a bit of kindness?'

Her heart sank as she thought of the effort of making Paddy welcome, but she need not have been anxious. As she came into the kitchen, having issued an invitation to all of them, she saw a woman straighten up from putting the kettle on its hook over a blazing fire. Mary-Anne turned the moment she heard her step, came and put her arms around her without a word.

Sarah let Mary-Anne hold her, but it was all she could do not to burst into tears like an overtired child. Another step in the short corridor leading from the front door to the kitchen told her she mustn't relax. But it was only Scottie, in whose eyes she could do no wrong.

'Can I come too?' he asked tentatively.

'Of course you can,' she said, watching the anxious look disappear. 'You've been busy too, I'm sure, and you must meet Paddy McCann. Would you go an' tell Sam to give us a few minutes till the kettle boils? We'll need the big teapot today.'

Mary-Anne had brought milk as she always did on a Monday, and had already found cake in the tin.

'Sarah, I cou'd find no tea or sugar. Why did ye not send down to me? I cou'd have give ye some to keep you goin'. I knew when Scottie came down lookin' for buttermilk this morning ye must have run out. Did ye get a cup o'tea at all today?' she asked sharply. 'Scottie said ye'd left them champ to reheat for their dinner and I was jus' wonderin' what ye might have had left fer yerself.'

Mary-Anne was anxious to know why Sarah had been

so long in town, fearing there'd been some difficulty, but she insisted that Sarah sit by the fire and rest herself while she cleared the table and carried away the stacked up dishes. Only when she'd made sure Sarah had planned a proper bite to eat to make up for the dinner she hadn't had, did she ask if she could come up and see her in the morning and hear her news then.

Sarah was grateful for her thoughtfulness and said she was always welcome but made her promise not to come up till it suited her. After she left, Sarah sat unmoving as the fire burnt low again. She felt so tired she wondered if she could manage one more word to anyone. She knew perfectly well that when Paddy's horse was shod he'd want a word about the trap. It was too far from the busy manufactory on the road between Grange Church and Cabragh for him to just call back another time.

The beam of light falling on the well-swept floor from the south-facing window had changed its angle. Sarah opened her eyes and looked at the patch of sunlight which had moved across the room and now lit up the space in front of the dresser. She could not quite believe it: she had fallen asleep in her chair in broad daylight. It was one thing John dozing off after a long, hard day while she was still preparing their supper, but she'd never fallen asleep before during the day.

She stared at the tiny dust motes which rose and fell spinning and catching the light, moving in the slight draught from the open doors. The front door always stood open, except in the worst of weather, and the kitchen door was always propped open through the long working hours of the day, as she was in and out with buckets of water, or collecting potatoes from the store, or turf for the fire.

Sometimes she needed the cool draught to help dry the floor when she had scrubbed it, or to disperse the smoke when the wind was blustery and blew down the chimney. Looking around her, it seemed as if she had always lived here, tending her own house, making a place of comfort for the husband who worked so hard to make a good living and to support both them and the family they hoped to have.

It occurred to her that she could celebrate what she'd had or bemoan what she had lost. She smiled to herself. Whatever doubts she might have about some of the strictures and regulations of the Quakers, and the nature of the queries they put to themselves so regularly, she was sure her grandmother's vision of what their lives should be would never leave her. Her grandmother would have loved John too, loved his honesty and his kindness. He was someone who could be trusted implicitly.

'Ach, ye've had a bit of a rest. I diden knock in case ye were asleep an' then I'd a come back anither time.'

'Well you nearly caught me, Paddy,' she said smiling easily. 'I thought I'd never fall asleep in a chair, but I did.'

'Aye, an' why not? Ye've hard enough to work an' ye've a lot on yer mind. I wrote you a price in case ye'd gone to lie down,' he added, producing a page torn from the jotter they kept in the forge for totting up bills and making lists of things that needed replacing.

'That *is* a very fair price, Paddy,' she said, glancing down at it as he handed it to her. 'Are you sure it's enough?' she went on quickly, thinking of the bills from the forge for labour or machinery that needed repairing. 'I don't know anything much about carpentry, but I know the trap is in a very bad way. Would you even be able to take it back with you?'

'Aye, if you say the word. Sam's made a rig that will hold it together if we take it slow, and Ben and Scottie say they'll walk alongside to take the pressure off on the bad bits o' road. I think we can manage. D'ye think yer Daisy wou'd be up to it?'

'Don't ask me, Paddy,' she said, laughing. 'Ask Scottie. He's got the measure of Daisy.'

'Aye,' he said, his face crinkling into a grin. 'Some people has gifts they may niver even find out about, but he was lucky. He came to a forge an' him no size at all t'be a smith, but yer good man saw somethin' in him an' took him on. That was *his* gift; he cou'd see the good in people, like m'frien', Sam Keenan, an' him a Catholic he diden even know. I'd say ye have the same gift as yer John had. Ye'll always know who ye can trust. Ye'll only need to take one luk at them.'

CHAPTER SEVEN

As April ended and the hours of daylight lengthened further, the evenings faded slowly after sun-filled days which brought the first real warmth of springtime. Sarah decided that these lovely evenings were her worst time of the day.

Morning and afternoon she was kept busy, whether it was bread to bake, potatoes to boil for the midday meal for Ben and Scottie, washing and cleaning, or caring for the fire so it neither burnt up and wasted fuel, nor fell so low she could not be ready to cook, or boil a kettle for tea should someone call. Like a ladder up the day, she sometimes thought, she had no need at all to wonder what to do, she simply had to take the next step, and then the next.

There was, she admitted, a reassurance in the continuing things; the echo of hammer on anvil, of hooves on cobbles, the postman stopping to pass the time of day, a hasty visit from Mary-Anne bearing her order of eggs and milk, or Jamesy, Mary-Anne's son, coming up the hill with the heavy can of buttermilk, a favourite, so John said, with all those who worked in forges. '*A king compared with water,*' he'd commented, as he explained that it cleared the throat of smoke and ash dust better than water ever could.

She told herself it was not surprising she should miss John most in the few hours of the day when they were at leisure, but she couldn't fail to remember the mild, gentle evenings in the last two summers when they'd walked the lanes towards Loughgall, or Kilmore, or Salter's Grange. Often they'd greet old friends of John's working in tiny front gardens where by June there would be bright flowers: dahlias and roses and tall spikes of lupin. Sometimes they'd catch the unmistakeable scent of tobacco and find round the next corner an old man leaning on a gate puffing clouds of blue smoke into the warm air. John, it seemed, knew everyone and all those they met had welcomed her with an enthusiasm she had never expected.

Now, in the first full week of May, the kitchen calendar unmarked by any event, she sat by the fire, a small continuing thing when so much else was gone. Of her lonely bed she tried not to think, for there, despite being weary from the day's work, she often remained sleepless, her tears flowing unbidden, her mind refusing to be at peace.

Sometimes in the last days of April, but seldom predictably, Mary-Anne had appeared in the evening. Having recently taken her mother-in-law into their home, the old woman now being able to do little for herself, it had inevitably made extra work for Mary-Anne. She never knew when Billy, or one of her sons, would see her weariness and say, 'D'ye want to take a wee run up an' see Sarah an' we'll see to Granny?'

Billy himself was a kind man and thoughtful enough, but often he was so tired out by evening and so burdened by his own responsibilities he didn't notice how worn Mary-Anne had become. Their farm, with its well-built house and good grazing, was small, enough to provide for all five of them, but only if all went well. Mary-Anne was quite open about the fact. It wasn't just a matter of working hard, she'd explained, and goodness knows Billy and the boys did that, but bad weather, or the sudden injury or death of an animal was always a threat; a major disaster meaning a bill that could not now be paid.

Mary-Anne, like Sarah, was the one who tried to keep track of their income. She played her own part as well in adding to it: keeping chickens, selling her eggs and making butter. Sometimes she did have a gift from a woman she'd helped through labour or miscarriage, as she'd certainly had from Sarah, but as often as not the women she helped were less well-off than she was. She was too kind ever to ask for anything from them.

Her evening visits were a pleasure to them both; the bond of love they'd made during Sarah's loss of both husband and child strengthened at each meeting by the honesty growing between them, each confessing to their burdens and anxieties, cheering and encouraging each other, offering help with a problem shared, exchanging small gifts of cake, or vegetables, or a piece of cloth to mend a garment.

It was Mary-Anne who offered to see that Sarah's

newspaper was collected each week when Billy or one of the boys went to town. She assured Sarah she was welcome to go into Armagh with them, but if she had no need to go, they could still collect her paper with their own and bring it up in the evening, or with the next delivery of milk, eggs or buttermilk.

Sitting one evening, her back aching, with no new piece of needlework started and ready to hand, she thought of Mary-Anne's offer. Still folded and sitting unread in the deep-set window, the neglected newspapers mocked her. Already there was another one awaiting her. The affairs of the world went on and there would always be news, if only from the far-flung parts of the island, places whose names she'd learnt from the old atlas her grandmother used when teaching her pupils about 'our island' and the exact place within it where they lived.

She read both papers hastily, skimming over events in Newry and Monaghan, Nenagh and Leitrim: the births, deaths and marriages and the movement of regiments to and from Armagh Barracks. It was on the very last page of the more recent one she found a comment on the weather that alerted her to something she had completely forgotten. She read the item again more slowly: *Since Thursday evening we have had some refreshing showers, which have tended greatly to improve the early-set potatoes. The healthy appearance of the crops in the neighbourhood promises an abundant harvest.*

Well, that would be good news for Billy, who had been planting now for weeks. John himself had put in two rigs of potatoes in the 'garden' – the cultivated area of Daisy's field next to the back of the house. That would have been three or four weeks ago. Now she thought of it, unlike Billy who grew for the market as well as for themselves, John planted three crops, the final one much later in the year. That one, late-harvested, was the one where the potatoes were clamped. That store saw them through the winter.

Without the newspaper she would not have thought of that. Now she would have to ask Ben or Scottie to show her how to dig in the seed potatoes. Preparing them to be set she knew about, for she had sat with John while they cut the potatoes together after he'd explained each piece for planting had to have one, and only one, good sprouting eye.

Perhaps she did need her newspaper after all.

So deep in thought was she about the planting of potatoes and when the next lot should go in that she didn't hear the tentative knock at the kitchen door, though the door itself was still open.

'Are you all right, missus?'

She looked up in surprise. It was Ben standing there wearing battered, but clean clothes, his hair sticking to his head. It looked as if he had just washed it. He was looking down at her anxiously.

'Ben, come in. I didn't hear your step I was so busy thinking,' she said quickly, totally amazed by his unexpected appearance.

Unlike Scottie, who ate his evening meal and then hurried home across the fields to sleep at his granny's house, Ben used the bed provided up in the loft, as required by the terms of his apprenticeship. What he did between closing up the forge and going to his night's rest she had no idea.

'I had something to ask you. If it's convenient,' he said studiously, as if the lines had been well-rehearsed.

She looked up at him and smiled. He seemed to have grown recently, or perhaps she had just become more aware of him: a solid presence, observing, listening, taking everything in but remaining silent except for the usual muffled 'Thank you', for meals or mugs of tea. The only time she'd ever seen him show any feelings was when he'd looked at the damage to the trap when Daisy arrived home without her master, her eyes bulging, her flank smeared with blood and her sides heaving with exertion.

'Come and sit down, Ben. Would you drink a mug of tea? I was just going to make one,' she added, knowing that if she said otherwise he would be too uneasy to accept.

'That would be great,' he said, as if some burden had been lifted. 'Can I put down the kettle for you?' he said quickly, as she got to her feet.

'Thank you, Ben, I'll see if there's still a bite of cake in the tin.'

She took her time carrying mugs and plates to the table and carefully carved the remaining wedge of cake, sharing it between them. She tried to think what she knew about Ben and found it was painfully little. His parents were dead, like hers, and he obviously had some relative who had sponsored his apprenticeship. It was something she and John had never had reason to speak about. Ben, like Scottie, had an elderly grandmother, but he only went to stay with her on a Saturday night, coming back to his bed in the loft above the forge late on Sunday evening for an early start on Monday morning. She didn't even know where his grandmother lived, though clearly, unlike Scottie's granny in Greenan, it was not nearby.

Ben was, as John always said, 'A dab hand with the bellows'. While she cut the cake, he had knelt down on the hearth and in no time at all she was able to wet the tea and set it to draw. She went out then into the little chilly outshot at the back of the kitchen. There, by the back door, well-scrubbed wooden shelves carried milk, eggs and butter. She filled a small jug and found on her return to her great surprise that Ben was vigorously stirring the teapot.

'Sometimes in the forge the tea gets so strong you could stand on it,' he said easily, as he poured it into the two mugs she'd left ready on the table. He waited for her to sit down and then gave her mug into her hand and passed her one of the two plates bearing the last of the fruit cake.

'Lovely cake, Mrs Hamilton,' he said nodding appreciatively, while Sarah looked in amazement at the transformation of this young man.

He not only looked different, he actually spoke unprompted, and in a voice and manner that suggested he was not a country boy. She could not, for the moment, detect any accent that might identify some other part of the country he might have come from, but he certainly spoke like a young man who'd had some education.

She found herself curious and wondered how she might find out more about him without upsetting him, but before she had time to decide what to do he put down his mug on the hearth and looked at her directly.

'I've something to ask you and I'm not sure how to put

it,' he began. 'It may be impossible and I don't want to play on your generosity, but I want to be released from my apprenticeship.'

It was the longest utterance she'd ever heard him make and she sat silent, touched by his words and amazed by his articulate manner of speaking.

'Why don't you just put it as it comes to you?' she asked gently.

'You mean "as the spirit moves me"?' he asked with a slight smile.

She laughed as she admitted that indeed that was almost certainly what she meant, but not everyone would appreciate her using those particular words.

He looked at her once again and said: 'After my parents died, I went to a Quaker school in Dublin. I was given a place because I had no one to take me in. My parents were Quakers, but my uncle was not. To be honest, he was very hostile to all forms of belief. He had lost his wife in childbirth and from what little I'd heard of him he was full of bitterness.'

'But it was he who arranged your apprenticeship, wasn't it?'

'Yes, he did. I can't understand why he did, because I'd never met him. Apparently he'd been approached by people from my parents' Meeting who'd visited me at school. He agreed to pay for my apprenticeship if they would arrange it, but he made it very clear he did not wish to see me.'

'And did you choose to be a smith?'

'No, I wanted to go on at school . . .'

He broke off, his face twisted in distress. Whatever had

happened to bring him to the forge, in answer, presumably, to a small advertisement in the paper, was still too painful to talk about. She was still wondering what she could say next when, to her great relief, he spoke again.

'I used to go out and walk in the evenings and shortly after I came here I met an old man who'd been a schoolteacher. He lives on the far side of Loughgall and he has books, a whole roomful,' he said, his eyes shining. 'It's a very small room, but every wall is covered with books. He has been so kind to me. He lends me anything I want and I read at night. But I told no one, not even Mister Hamilton. He must have wondered at the amount of oil the lantern in the loft used, but he never said a word about it.'

It was just then that Sarah remembered what Paddy McCann had said to her the afternoon before he took the trap away to be mended. He'd said then John had a gift: he saw things in people they didn't see themselves. Whatever John had made of Ben, when some Quakers from the Ballyhagan Meeting had brought him to the forge, he must have seen something more than a strong pair of shoulders, just as he'd sensed Scottie would be at home in the forge, though at the time he had never seen him handle a horse.

'There's much to be learnt from books,' said Sarah wistfully, thinking back to the days when she too had access to the books of other Quakers and to a small library in Lisnagarvey. Now her books were limited by her having the time to go to the library in Armagh, unencumbered by shopping bags.

'What did you enjoy most?' she asked quickly, realising she'd grown silent. She'd been thinking about Paddy

McCann and his parting comment that Monday afternoon that he thought she had the same gift as John, to see something others might not see.

'Travel and machinery and Irish history,' he replied promptly. 'But it's the machinery that might get me a job if I go. The boss always let me repair machines, but I'd like to build machines and it would stand to me to have mended what's broken. Sometimes, I can see ways that would have made them better in the first place.'

'But you've never told anyone, have you?'

'Only old Mr McMahon. That's why he suggested I go to Canada. He said he could lend me the money for my ticket, but it would depend on being released from the apprentice agreement.'

'Canada!' she exclaimed, taken aback by all she'd heard. 'You'd go alone to Canada?'

'No, I'd not go alone. Apparently, there are parties going regularly from around here, sometimes organised by the minister of a church. There's a couple of families going from around Loughgall and I'd be welcome to go with them. So Mr McMahon says.'

'And when would you go?'

'Later this month. It depends on the ice on the Saint Lawrence river. They want to go to Ontario. The first ships will sail as soon as they hear the ice is breaking up.'

'Do you really want to go so far away? Would you not be homesick for Ireland?' she asked, completely overcome by this revelation.

For the first time in her life, Sarah wondered how she herself could ever contemplate leaving Ireland. For her it seemed unthinkable. She knew little of Ireland first-hand apart from where she'd lived, but the sudden thought of never walking the country lanes or seeing its hawthorns laden with blossom in May was more than she could bear.

'Oh yes, I want to go. If I'm homesick I'll think about it then, but I have to make a life for myself. I'm nearly seventeen and I've no family, just Mary McCleery whom I call granny, though she's not. She was once my nurse and she says I must go, that she's not long for this world, and she'd be happy if she knew I'd gone with good people trying to make a better life.'

'Then of course you must go,' said Sarah promptly, her mind putting together all this new information about his history and his need to make a future of his own choosing. That she could well understand. Long before her grandmother became somewhat infirm, she had run their tiny household, making her own decisions, her own choices. However limited that life had been she'd had a freedom that Ben had never had.

'But there is a problem,' he said slowly.

'And what is that, Ben?' she asked, genuinely puzzled at to what it could be.

'My uncle can't, or won't, repay the loss to you that my going will incur,' he said, glancing away from her for the first time.

For a moment Sarah was puzzled, wondering how his uncle could be required to pay her money, but then she remembered. John had received a settlement for the six years of apprenticeship. He was required to provide board and lodging, a small sum of pocket money, work clothes and no doubt other things she didn't know about. In return, he benefitted by the labour provided, something that increased with each year of training and experience. That was what should now be recompensed.

Afterwards, Sarah wondered if she had been hasty, but however much she argued with herself she could come to no other conclusion. She had, perhaps, spoken as the spirit moved her.

'You'll certainly be a loss, Ben,' she began slowly. 'I shall miss you. But there is *nothing* you have to repay to me,' she went on firmly. 'I'll see what I can do to help you get ready for going,' she added lightly. 'Perhaps if I do some sewing for you, you could do some planting for me before the ice melts.'

CHAPTER EIGHT

However amazed Sarah may have been by the transformation in Ben, it was nothing to the surprise Scottie and Sam had the following morning when, for the first time, Ben gave them 'Good Morning' and made a joke. According to Sam, who came to Sarah with the excuse of bringing her some takings from the forge, Scottie had simply looked at him open-mouthed and speechless.

Ben's news, which he then proceeded to share with them, was indeed a shock, leaving Sam not unreasonably anxious about the future of the forge. Ben's good news was inevitably going to be a mixed blessing for all of them. While Sarah was delighted to see his newly found liveliness and smiled when she heard Sam's story about Scottie's reaction, she had to face the fact that in the not very distant future, probably the end of May, only one of the three key workers remained: Sam himself.

Scottie, however willing, was lightly built for a helper, but more importantly, he had not yet undertaken many of the tasks most needed at this time of year, particularly the shoeing of horses.

Yet once more, Sarah got out her account books and the jotter where she did her calculations. She went back and looked at the reckoning she'd made some weeks earlier when she'd accurately anticipated the amount of the burial fund to the nearest pound. True, there would now be one less small sum to pay to Ben, and one less mouth to feed, but she had calculated for a drop of one third in the forge's summer income. Now, perhaps, she should recalculate for a half.

The question had become how long could she carry on with the forge if the income in summer was not enough to provide for the winter, once the residue of the burial fund was gone?

There was another problem too in losing a well-instructed and practiced young man like Ben. Often enough in the early summer, the whole cobbled area in front of the house and forge was occupied by machines waiting to be repaired. Now that she knew Ben had made a serious contribution to that side of the work, it meant that while last May there were three people turning out repairs, now, as soon as Ben went, there would be only one.

Sam Keenan was well-known locally as a good smith, but soon everyone in the area would know he had neither boss nor experienced apprentice working alongside him. With machines now urgently needed on the land, customers might well go elsewhere rather than risk delays at this critical season.

There is no point in speculating, Sarah told herself. She did three different sums, discounting last year's monthly income by a third, then by a half, then by three quarters. She sighed as she studied the three figures, especially the third one. Without what was left of the burial fund payment, it all looked very dim.

At least, she told herself vigorously, it wasn't as bad as the day before she found the burial fund book in the old leather handbag. That day she knew she had no money in her purse, only enough food to last a week, and nothing predictable coming in.

Amid all the doubts, the only certainties were that when Ben left for Canada, Sam and Scottie had still to be paid on a Friday; her purse would need money to feed and clothe herself and Scottie, pay the rent and the regular bills for forge materials. She had not forgotten there was also a large sum outstanding. However fair it was, and she was convinced of that, the sum due to Paddy McCann when he returned the trap was one which seemed to grow larger as she visualised the money in the bank growing smaller each week.

She was clear that she must give more thought to increasing her income in whatever way she could so the forge itself could keep going. Sam's wife and family depended on his wage, Scottie's granny on the few shillings he took home every Friday night. The life she had entered joyfully some two years ago had fallen to pieces. She had lost both husband and child; now she had to face the possibility of losing her home as well and with it the place in a small community she'd been given by all those who'd known John. In her worst moments, it came to her that there was nothing left to lose but life itself.

'No,' she said to herself firmly, as she closed the account books, put everything away in the dresser and fetched her baking board. 'Don't ever think that way. It serves no useful purpose,' she added. Something would come to help her, she told herself, as she set to work on the day's bread. But she must be on the lookout for it.

May was the loveliest of months: the hawthorn a white cloud in the hedgerows, the newly planted crops springing up green and vibrant. The hammers in the forge rang out early and late. Scottie and Ben planted not only the potatoes, but turnips and carrots, cabbages and onions, some raised from seed by Mary-Anne, some grown from plants leftover from the bundles Billy Halligan had bought in the market in Armagh. He had brought more land into tillage this year, but after weeks of hard labour opening new areas, clearing stones and weeds and manuring he found he'd planted all he could, he could spare no more space from the grazing his animals needed.

There was little leisure for anyone that month. Mary-Anne's mother was failing more quickly so Mary-Anne, with her family hard at work on the land till late, could seldom leave the house to come and visit Sarah. It was on one more solitary evening that Sarah was startled by a footstep in the corridor, both doors still open on a lovely golden evening. Ben stood in the doorway, a book in his hand and asked if she would like to be read to while she did her sewing.

He appeared to know that John had always read the paper aloud to her and as he settled himself he explained that while in winter his friend Mr McMahon had few visitors and he would go to him most evenings, in summer he did have other friends who would visit him. Ben himself still went regularly, but not so often, as he didn't want to intrude upon the talk of old friends.

Sarah had made no secret of the fact that she was working on a jacket and trousers for him. Admittedly, the outfit was second-hand from the market at the bottom of Scotch Street, but Ben could see it was being expertly reshaped to fit him. As he watched, fascinated by a skill he had never before encountered, it reminded her of John when he'd said 'he'd never seen such wee stitches'.

They were, Ben said, the first clothes, apart from the work clothes provided by John, that he'd had since the Quakers had furnished him in Dublin for his journey to County Armagh.

After that first evening, he came often and Sarah knew she would miss his presence sadly when he went, but for the moment she treasured his company, persuading him to read from her own few books of Quaker writings and poetry and from John's treasured copy of Goldsmith's poems, as well as from the books on history and travel, apparently on a long loan from his friend's library.

In the second week of May the news came that the ice was melting in Canada and a ship was leaving from Sheephaven in Donegal on the last day of the month, Saturday 31st. The families in the party from Loughgall had already made a provisional booking with a captain known personally to their minister. Now, with the date agreed, all the prospective emigrants received a list of what they needed to take with them on the voyage.

When Ben brought her his list, Sarah was grateful that the voyage appeared to be so well organised: the agents specified clothes to deal with bad weather and suggested that passengers bring quantities of dried and preserved food to supplement the ship's rations. The rations provided were listed. They were indeed adequate, but certainly not generous.

Clearly, Ben was not the only young person preparing to emigrate with the better weather. The newspaper reported that a party of young women were being sponsored by the Armagh Workhouse and were leaving from Belfast on May 17th, the master of the workhouse himself escorting them by van and rail to Belfast, spending two nights there in order to see them off.

Now that Mary-Anne could no longer visit in the evening she had persuaded Sarah to go down to visit her. They saw each other quite often by day, but the hasty conversations when Mary-Anne brought up milk, or eggs, or buttermilk, meant they'd little time to get to know about each other's life and history.

Mary-Anne was intrigued by what she saw as a totally different life; she was overwhelmed by the thought of Sarah having lost her parents as a child and was curious about her Quaker upbringing. She wanted to know about Sarah's task of teaching little ones, what it was the Quakers believed and what the town of Lisnagarvey was like compared to Armagh. Born only a mile away some forty years earlier in the house where she now lived, Mary-Anne had never been further from home than Armagh itself.

Sarah could see that Mary-Anne was in some ways as lonely as she was herself. Billy worked so hard but was inclined to worry, go silent and retreat into himself. The grandmother was almost blind; she spent most of her time in bed and didn't like strangers. Her sons, Jamsey and young Billy were out and about whenever they'd any time off, seeking the company of other young men and, according to Mary-Anne, some good-looking girls as well.

So the two women sat by Mary-Anne's fire, shared any fragment of news that came their way, laughed when they could and got on with any task that would not prevent them talking to each other.

Unlike Sarah and John, who, newly married, had seldom been visited in their two years together, Mary-Anne and Billy did have evening visitors who turned up regularly. It was one of them, a distant relative of Billy who earned her living making bonnets, that entertained them both one summer evening with an account of the young women going from the workhouse to Quebec.

'Ach, sure the poor things,' she said, drawing up her chair to be nearer the fire. 'They had nothin', neither in them nor on them, as the sayin' is, but some of the gentry must have giv' money to the workhouse to get them fitted out so they'd get a decent place in Canada. Apparently they had a sep'rate emigrant's account for seein' them right. Ivery girl was to get a shawl and a bonnet. That, of course, is how I knows all about it,' she added, nodding confidentially. 'Ye see I had to go up and fit the bonnets an' whin I was there they show'd me all their stuff. Ye see, the women inmates had made the clothes with the linen and gingham and calico bought for them. An' forby the clothes they'd made fer them they'd been bought three pairs of stockin's each, a flannel petticoat and ribbon as well. I hear Adams and John Wilson in Armagh got a good order for stuff.'

'An' what about yerself, Lily, what about the order ye got?' demanded Mary-Anne, a twinkle in her eye.

Lily threw back her head and laughed, a strange, crowing laugh that having once heard it you could pick it out in a crowd whenever you heard it again.

'Shure them ten bonnets 'ill keep me in spuds an' flour for many a long day. An' lovely they were too whin I'd them all trimmed up, the ribbons on thim match o' the ribbons they'd been give for their hair. Shure they'd looked like ladies. Aye, an' I suppose that was the whole idea. If they're well set up they'll get a better place an' shure everyone knows there's a desperit shortage of we'men in all these new places.'

'Had ye thought of goin' yerself, Lily?' asked Mary-Anne, now with a broad grin on her face, while Sarah hid a smile by bending over her sewing.

'Oh aye, indade I did,' she nodded, screwing up her wrinkled face. 'Manys a time sittin' there hookin' ribbon, I thought of them steppin' out, but shure I'm well past the days whin any man wou'd look my way twice. Good luck to them, I sez and thanks be to whativer man or weman set them up, for no name was ever give, and shure where wou'd the workhouse get money for the like of bonnets an' ribbon?'

'Have you no idea who it might be, Lily?' asked Sarah, who had been silent for some time, thinking about the men who came to her grandmother's cottage with a sack of flour, or potatoes, or meal, and who, each time, asked politely if there was anything she had need of.

Sarah could not remember her grandmother ever having mentioned the rent or any other expense to these kind visitors. What she did remember was that her grandmother gave thanks day and daily for the gifts they'd received, explaining to Sarah that, as a Quaker, you were bound to look after everyone in your family, be honest in all your dealings and be generous to those in need if you were fortunate enough to have more than you needed yourself.

'Weel, to tell you the truth, I think it mus' be yer man Molyneux,' she said firmly, nodding her head vigorously. 'I mind my mither tellin' me that one of the Molyneux built Grange Church an' there's a stone on it that sez 1771. That's a brave while ago. But she tole me then an' I've a good memory fer things, that one Sunday he was bein' driven to church in his big posh coach when he luks out and sees a lock o' poor Catholics standin' in the rain, by one o' those Mass rocks ye see about the place. So, he goes on to church and the next thing is he's made enquiries about why they've no place of worship. An' so he builds them a chapel as well.'

'I niver knew that, Lily. I heered the Molyneux were all a bit strange like an' took notions about things. But d'ye think this one might be the same?' Mary-Anne asked.

Lily nodded vigorously and drank deep from her mug of tea.

'The one that's there now, I don't know what his name is, or whether he's a Lord or just a Sir,' she began, shaking her head, 'but he's buildin' a house, well the likes of us wou'd call it a palace,' she added looking them both in the eye. 'Over at Castle Dillon. Three storeys high and steps up and down to gardens, an' statues all over the place, an' an outlook across that bit of a lake where they keep the wildfowl. Beautiful, me brother sezs, fer he goes there regular with turf from his bit o' bog. An' whenever he goes there's a man in a uniform tells him there's a bite to eat in the kitchen whin he's made his delivery.'

She paused for breath and looked from one to the other. 'Now I'm tellin' you this an' its ta go no further fer he might get inta trouble, but one day a year or so ago he's bein' given tea and a piece by a wee kitchen maid an' he says to her, "Is it true there's acorns all roun' the ceilin' in one of the rooms?" An' she tells him it is, an' he asks her a whole lot more questions because there's bin great talk about the place. An' the long an' the short of it is, she tells him there's none of the family coming till the house is finished off an' all the workpeople gone. An' she takes him upstairs an' tells him to just look like he's workin' on the place himself. An' he can't believe his eyes. He sez the ceilings were so high ye'd crick yer neck lookin' up at them, an' everywhere there's pillars and rooms that big ye cou'd put a market in them an' have space left roun' the edges. He came home full of it and sed he doubted if Queen Victoria herself had anythin' better.'

'And you think he gave the money to the workhouse to let the girls emigrate?' asked Sarah, fascinated by her tale.

'Aye, fer he's good-hearted too,' she said, nodding vigorously. 'One o' the smiths that works in their stables had a bad fall last winter an' was laid up fer months, an' Molyneux had his wages sent ivery week an' a basket of food now an' then till the man hisself was back on his feet.' She drained her mug of tea: 'Shure he diden hafta do that; God bless him and send him good luck in all his dealin's.'

Summer came with a rush: the trees were full-leafed, the translucent pale leaves strengthened to a rich green, hedges were alive with the sound of birds feeding fledglings, cow parsley waved white flowers above the tall, rich grasses at the sides of the roads. The days were now so long that when Sarah woke in the night and lay there unable to get back to sleep again, there was already light to see by. Often she got up when the dew was still heavy on the grass and the land silent in the pale early light.

She found it easier to fill the empty hours with a piece of sewing than to lie in bed, wide-eyed, long before the first cock crowed and hours before Scottie arrived at the back door to come and eat his bowl of porridge.

May was a good month in the forge, with customers staying loyal even though Sam was quite honest with them as to how long their work might take. Scottie had now shoed his first horse and Sam had said encouraging words that pleased both her and Scottie himself.

The month ended and Ben said his goodbyes, having asked Sarah if she would write to him as soon as he had an address to send her. She knew she would miss him and she did, even more than she had expected. To her surprise she found that Scottie missed him too. He came asking her for news long before a letter could have travelled back on a returning vessel. In the end, she got out her old atlas and showed him just how long Ben's journey was. Suddenly Scottie seemed to have grown. She noticed he walked now with a longer stride and no longer scurried round the place, his shoulders hunched, his eyes deflected from any watcher.

She herself noticed the different ring of his hammer on the anvil when he was fitting a set of shoes: more confident and more assured. It seemed he had stepped into Ben's shoes as far as the forge was concerned and she was pleased for him.

But takings were down in June. The randomly parked reapers and rakers were all gone and only one pair of gates was propped up awaiting the curved decoration that would crown their topmost bars. The dip in income was more like a half than a third and there were still the same bills for coal and turf, as well as heavy duty iron and angle iron.

July started badly in terms of weather: humid days that made everyone feel uncomfortable and tired, the horses waiting to be shod stamping and skittering with distress, plagued by small flies they couldn't shift with their lashing tails. Scottie did his best with them, but suffered a kick on his right leg which left him limping for some weeks. Heavy rain followed; the humid weather clearing only much later in the month to give brilliant blue skies against which clouds mushroomed upwards into great white castles.

The income in the forge, however, went in the other direction, falling week on week and Sarah spent yet more early morning hours sewing rag rugs with cuttings from fabric her brother Charles sent her, an idea shaping in her mind that she might earn some money from her efforts with a needle and thread.

She was delighted by what Charles had sent and was touched that he'd remembered she'd told him she could use anything he had available. What took away her pleasure in the gift was his covering letter which told her that his business was doing badly, now affected by what he described as 'a general depression in the textile industry'.

He had been let down by some customers who had found cheaper fabric elsewhere. Left with fabric on his hands and no buyers, he'd already had to let some of his women workers go. Worse still, for Charles was still an active member of his local Quaker Meeting, he'd been visited by some of the men who oversaw the Meetings' affairs. They reminded him, as if he should need such a reminder, that if his business failed, leaving debts, then he would be declared to be 'out of unity' with the Meeting.

It was the memory of just such pronouncements regarding her dear friend's marriage that made her feel she herself was out of unity, not because she no longer attended Lisnagarvey, nor had been formally spoken to, but simply because she could not accept some of the precepts that one was required to live by. She had no argument with most of Quaker teaching, but when it came to ostracising a man or a woman for their choice of a marriage partner, or their misfortune, through no fault of their own in a business venture, then she simply could not in all conscience sustain her membership.

Charles's misfortune and the falling income of the forge were only two of many matters that distressed her. She had written to her friend Helen, now in South Carolina, telling her of John's death. No doubt it was a week or two after his death, but months had now passed and with summer traffic across the Atlantic at its height, she had been watching out for a letter for weeks. It was so unlike Helen not to reply immediately when she was in distress that she began to be anxious about her friend herself.

It was at the beginning of August when her brother-in-law, George, arrived over from Greenan. He always came to have his horse shod even though there was a smithy in Greenan itself. He used to joke when he came about supporting the family business, but on this occasion there were no jokes. He came straight in to see Sarah, asked briefly how she was and then said apologetically that, yes, he needed the mare shod, but he had no money to pay for the job.

By the time Sam and Scottie had started work on the mare, Sarah had brewed tea, sat George down by the fire and asked him what had happened.

He looked so distressed that for a moment she thought he might cry, though John had once told her that their father had always said that only women cried and they were men. Indeed, John, soft-hearted himself and easily moved, had never cried in her presence.

'So what *has* happened, George?' she asked gently.

'Ach well, it's easy told. I went to Lisnagarvey market, and indeed you know the very spot I went to. An' I met yer man Wilson who's the factor for a couple of finishers and dyers. I've been dealin' with him for years now an' he knows me well. He just tol' me straight that there's no demand any more, that where he'd once sold cloth t'be dyed and finished, they were now gettin' it in from elsewhere already dyed an' finished an' at a lower price.' He nodded at her and drank his tea. 'Not as good quality, he tol' me and not whit I'd produce, but that diden appear t' matter t' these new people. They want cloth at a price an' they'd foun' it elsewhere an' that's the end of the story. Shure he was lukin' around hisself fer whit he could turn his hand to.'

'So what are you going to do, George?'

'Well, apart from plantin' potatoes in the wee bit a land I have, I'm lukin for harvest work wi' any o' the big farmers. I may have t'go to Scotland like many a one before me. I'd emigrate as quick as a wink if I had the money, but shure there's no use talkin' when I've not what wou'd pay to shoe the mare.'

'What about Alice? What does she think?' she asked quietly, wondering what it would be like to have to cope with three children as well as the sudden loss of their income.

'Ach, she's doin' her best, workin' away at the sewin'. There's still call for napkins for the big houses here and over the water. There's a man collects thim an' leaves her more ta get on with. Pays poor, but it keeps us in flour and oats. She says she dreads the winter wi' no light to see by and likely no paraffin for the lamp. She'd be for off if we had the money.'

Sarah remembered talking about the cost to the families

whom Ben had joined when they'd emigrated at the end of May. She paused for a moment only, and then said calmly: 'George, I know what John would have done if you'd come to him. I think perhaps I could help you get away.'

CHAPTER NINE

The day of George Hamilton's visit was another of the humid days that everyone disliked, one where Sarah looked forward to the cool of the evening, only to find it was no better. She went to bed late that evening, but even then, her eyes closing with fatigue after hours of sewing, she could not sleep.

She felt she'd been hasty in making her offer of help to George. Here she was, trying to see how they could get through the winter with a much reduced income from the forge and she had just committed herself to financing him and his family with a sum of passage money she simply couldn't afford.

Even at the best of times, even if John had still been alive, it was a large sum and needed to be considered carefully. That and the repair of the trap – now, according to Sam

111

Keenan, almost ready to be delivered – would take the bank account to a level considerably lower than it had been two years earlier after John had bought some bed linen for their room and a new suit for their wedding.

She tossed and turned; the bedclothes were suddenly too heavy and too warm, so she got up and went downstairs for a glass of water. She stood drinking it on the stone doorstep at the back of the house and looked up at the sky. Not a star in sight, not even the moon was visible through the thick cloud that had cut out the sunlight all day.

In the darkness a dog barked far away, the sound muffled as everything seemed to be at night. Oh for rain, or wind, or sun, she thought to herself, standing barefoot, the empty glass in her hand. Anything to sweep away this pall of cloud enveloping the land. Enveloping also it seemed her thoughts, which now appeared as clouded and oppressive as the weather.

> *To take Arms against a Sea of troubles,*
> *And by opposing end them*

She smiled to herself, surprised and amused at the sudden thought which had come to her. Where had *that* come from? She remembered immediately that it was Shakespeare. Hamlet. Of course. She smiled more broadly as she peered out into the grey, misty darkness, memories coming back to her. In her childhood, her grandmother had quoted the Bible and Shakespeare so freely and so frequently that she sometimes got mixed up as to which one the old lady was referring. At one time, long ago, she had even imagined that Shakespeare had a hand in writing the Bible. Her grandmother had sat her down and explained patiently.

'No, Sarah dear. Shakespeare was a clever man and he said wise things through his characters, but he was not in the right place at the right time to know about the wonderful things that happened in the Bible, especially in the New Testament when God's son came down to help us all understand things better.'

Her grandmother was so full of life. Even when she was bedridden in her last year, there was a light in her eyes as if she had a source of strength within her that never failed. She had died in her sleep, so peacefully that Sarah, who had moved her own mattress into the small room to be near her, only woke with the sound of rain on the roof to find the old lady lying completely still, looking as if she had just had a pleasant dream.

She took a deep breath, though there was no freshness in the moist air, and made up her mind. She had spoken to George from the heart; she had done what she knew was right. Fairly, it might not seem 'sensible' to someone else, but that was not the point. There was no one else involved. Her job was to travel hopefully and use all her gifts to try to do what she thought best. Helping George and Alice and their children to get away was just as important as trying to keep the forge going for Sam and Ben and Scottie.

Tomorrow, she would go to the Ulster Bank and withdraw the money for the repair of the trap and the family ticket to Canada which George would now need to confirm his provisional booking. Beyond that she could not see. But sooner or later this mist must lift and she must be ready to play whatever part she was called upon to play in events she could not guess at, any more than anyone else.

She shut the door, tramped quietly back upstairs, lay down on the crumpled bed and promptly fell asleep.

Sometime in the night it did rain and, although it was still grey and overcast, Sarah noticed it was cooler when Scottie arrived for his breakfast. As the morning went on, the cloud cleared and by the time she was being driven in to Armagh by Billy Halligan with Jamsey and a small shopping list for Mary-Anne, the sun had begun to gleam through thinning cloud and the first blue sky was appearing.

Armagh was busy, it being a Thursday and a market day, but Sarah's jobs were easily enough done. The manager himself greeted her in the Ulster Bank and made a little joke about her 'going shopping' when he sent one of the young men to count out five-pound notes for her.

Sarah smiled but was quite straightforward in explaining why she was making such a large withdrawal.

'I may well have to sell the trap, Mr Cummings, but without the repairs that have been done it wouldn't be worth anything at all. It was in a very bad way when it was brought back to the forge. I've no idea what it's worth now, but I shall be asking my brother-in-law and my neighbours what they think.'

He nodded easily. 'If I recall correctly your good husband came in to arrange the purchase of the trap some four or even five years ago. I remember he was quite delighted with how well it looked. Has it gone back to the maker?'

'Yes,' she said, nodding firmly, 'A nice man called McCann at the cart manufactory on the Cabragh Road. He actually came to see me after John died and made me an offer for repairing it. He said he knew John,' she explained slowly, the mention of John having been difficult. 'Apparently John and Sam Keenan had helped him and his partner out with hooping cartwheels,' she added more easily.

'That's something we still seem to do in these parts,' he said, nodding and looking rather sad. 'There are those who find us "backward", but I think perhaps they misjudge what we think important. I would celebrate what we call "neighbourliness". It's not something you can value in money. It's more important than that, wouldn't you agree?'

It was several days later when Paddy McCann and George Hamilton arrived on the same afternoon and drank the tea and cake she offered together at the kitchen table. George was unambiguous in his comments. He said the trap looked like new.

'Sure lookin' at that trap of John's sittin' out there beside mine there's no comparison. If I were buyin' and not sellin', I know which one I'd want – if I could afford it, that is,' he said with a wry laugh. 'It's a credit to you, Paddy, it looks really well.'

Sarah suddenly found she couldn't look at the trap without being forced to remember exactly what had happened, but she gathered herself and said firmly that she agreed completely. Polished, varnished and repainted as needed, it shone in the sunlight and she certainly couldn't tell which side had been damaged by whatever vehicle had pushed them off the road on the stone bridge over the little stream where in summer the children went to catch 'sprickleybags'.

As soon as they'd drunk their tea, George took himself off to the forge for 'a word with Sam Keenan', while Sarah got out the old handbag and counted out the money to meet Paddy's hastily scribbled bill.

'Are you sure you haven't undercharged me, Paddy?' she asked cautiously, as she put the folded fivers in an envelope.

To her great surprise, Paddy laughed.

'D'ye know, missus dear, I don't think I've iver been asked that afore. More likely it's someone lookin' a good luck penny or tryin' to beat me down.'

'Well I'll not do that, Paddy,' she said firmly, 'I won't accept a luck penny after all you've done. I'm very grateful to you and I'll put in a word if ever I can for your work. In fact, I'm just wondering if perhaps you could help George sell *his* trap. If you spent some time on the woodwork, it might fetch a better price. They're planning to go to Canada next month and he needs all the money he can make.'

'That's a fair point,' he said, nodding vigorously, 'I'll go an' have a wee word with him afore I go. Now be sure ye let me know if I can iver help ye out again. It wou'd always be a pleasure,' he said, looking her straight in the eye, as he put the envelope into his jacket pocket without even glancing at the notes within.

George was embarrassed at taking the money she'd already set aside for him. He insisted he'd repay it just as soon as he could, but she reassured him that she had enough to be going on with. He could send her dollars if he landed on his feet, as some did, but as far as she was concerned the money was a gift from his brother, John. She also reminded him about the fact the he, like John, had a burial fund. She hoped neither Alice nor his children would need it for many a long year, but she wondered if it was possible to pay it up and take whatever small sum it might release.

'I'm afraid I've only just thought of that or I'd have asked Mr Cummings about it this morning,' she said apologetically, as she walked out of the house with him towards the trap where his horse was munching devotedly from the nosebag Scottie had provided.

'Wumman dear, an' you with enough to cope with, thinkin' about me an' mine and that wee book. Sure haven't you saved all our skins already? I'll be back over t' see you as soon as we get our date.'

If Sarah took comfort from George's appreciation and Paddy's loving work on the trap, her pleasure did not last long. Before she had cleared away the empty mugs and thrown out the few crumbs left for the birds, young Billy arrived breathless from the foot of the hill.

'Ma says to tell you me granny's jus' died. She jus' fell outa the chair an' hit her head on the floor. She says: "woud ye go down to her this evenin' an' give her a bit of a han'"?'

'Oh Billy, I am sorry. That's a shock for you all, even though she was very poorly,' she said, looking at his screwed up face and his uneasy movements. 'Would you tell her I'll be down right away, but I must just see Scottie about his supper? He's well able to make his own if he knows I have to be out, but I must just tell him,' she explained, knowing young Billy never had to think about such things.

'Aye surely. She'll be glad to see ye,' he said, relief in his voice, as he took off at speed to run back home.

Sarah damped down the fire and brought out a clean mug and plate for Scottie. She laid them in his usual place and left the teapot ready on the hearth. He hadn't often had to make his own supper, but he knew where everything was. Whenever he was in the house he watched her every move and often he asked if he could help, so he was familiar with the small, cold pantry beside the back door where he'd find bread and butter. She remembered the strawberry jam Mary-Anne had made, put a helping in a small glass dish, took it to the table and put a bowl over it in case of flies.

She was just about to leave, most of the morning's baking and three quarters of the cake from the tin now in her basket, when Scottie himself rushed in without even pausing at the front door.

'Missus dear, luk, jus' luk. All the good potatoes Ben and I put in afore he went. They were lookin' grate this mornin' when I dug you a bucketful for the dinner, an' now luk at them . . .'

Near to tears, he held out his hand: a limp, blackened and slimy piece of once-green top growth clinging to his fingers.

'There now, Scottie, don't upset yourself,' she said, putting her arms round him for the first time since John died. She felt him cling to her as if he'd never let go. 'We'll manage one way or another,' she went on, trying to reassure him. 'Now don't be upset. Have you told Sam yet?'

'No, I luked in the forge but there was a man waitin' I diden know, so I come on in t' you.'

'You did the right thing, Scottie,' she said, stepping back gently and then patting his shoulder. 'Now go and wash your hands at the sink and see if Sam is on his own now. Come back and tell me. Then we'll see what we need to do,' she said as steadily as she could.

She hadn't the remotest idea what was to be done but she was grateful that Scottie seemed easier. At least she knew she could leave him now to make his evening meal while she went down to Mary-Anne to help with the rituals of mourning.

Sarah arrived at the Halligan's farm at the same time as the woman who was known locally for her competence in 'laying out'. Until the undertaker arrived the old lady would lie on her bed, which had been brought downstairs some weeks ago with a clean bedspread covering her body. When Sarah and Mary-Anne finally managed to have a word she found that the old lady had no shroud, so one had been ordered along with her coffin which should arrive shortly.

What Mary-Anne had said via young Billy's message did not explain to Sarah the number of men in working clothes who were finishing mugs of tea at the kitchen table. Though Sarah knew some of them by sight, she felt sure from their dress and manner that the men were not mourners. She asked Mary-Anne what was happening.

Mary-Anne shook her head, indicated the back door and they slipped out together.

'Ach sure Granny goin' is bad enough,' she said quietly, 'but there's a far worse loss the day, though I maybe shou'den say that. Billy is goin' mad over the tatties. He came in a while before she fell outa the chair an' says all the tops is black an' our only hope is to dig them and see what we can save before the rot goes down the stem and inta the tatties themselves. Sure I can't take it in at all. He worked so hard . . . all three of them did, an' he was waitin' for a contract from the workhouse for so many tons a week. An' now we'll maybe not even have enough for ourselves.'

Jamsey had gone to visit the nearest neighbours. They'd checked on their own potato patches, but knowing the size of Billy's planting they'd come or sent a son to help lift the whole crop though they knew the potatoes would be small.

Behind them they heard the chairs scrape on the stone floor as the men got up and went out to join Billy and his sons who were already at work in one of the fields directly in front of the house on the other side of the road. Back in the empty house together, Mary-Anne tended the fire while Sarah cleared the table and gathered up the dirty mugs and plates to be washed.

'An' that's not all of it either,' said Mary-Anne, straightening up from sweeping the hearth. 'There was a white envelope came this morning and you know what that is, don't ye? Did ye not get one?' she went on quickly, seeing the puzzled look on Sarah's face. 'Shure April and September is the valuation and the half-yearly ground rent. If it didn't come today, then ye can be shure it'll be with you tomorrow.'

* * *

Despite the fact that Billy's mother did not live locally and had few relatives or friends left living at all, visitors came and went all evening. Many stayed only briefly and declined refreshment, which was fortunate as Mary-Anne soon had no cake left and only Sarah's to fall back on.

Sarah listened to the now familiar phrases and wondered what she really thought about them. 'I'm sorry for your trouble,' was kind enough and probably a good summing-up of the well-disposed nature of the speaker to the one who presently had both the loss and the practicalities of a death to deal with.

'Shure she's in a better place,' was more problematic. How did anyone know where the dead now resided? She certainly couldn't see John playing a harp. She wondered where he really was: a speck of dust in the universe; a presence in the places he loved; a cobweb in the forge; a voice inside her head saying helpful things, telling her to 'be of good cheer', to 'wait upon the Lord' when she couldn't make up her mind and wished he was here with her by the fire, ready to struggle with a problem she hadn't met before.

Surrounded by neighbours known and unknown, Billy and Jamsey and young Billy, the two black-coated figures who had arrived with the coffin and the robust woman who had put Granny into her shroud, Sarah felt even more alone than she ever did arriving back to an empty house after visiting Mary-Anne or going into Armagh. She wondered if losing John would ever be easier to bear or whether she would learn to think of something else, or teach herself not to feel the ache of loneliness when she was surrounded by people, but without John at her side.

In the meantime, she simply had to play her part: make tea, or collect up cups to wash, or exchange friendly words with other visitors. It was some comfort that she now had a real friend, one who had helped her at her own bad time, now in need herself.

For Mary-Anne, she would most certainly set aside her own sad thoughts and do whatever would help and support her for the two evenings before the funeral. For the moment she gave thanks that this one was, thankfully, already drawing to a close. She would face up to tomorrow when tomorrow came.

CHAPTER TEN

Granny's funeral came and went, but the anxiety about the potato blight continued day after day, until finally, by the middle of September, it was clear that not every crop had been affected in the same way. Before that, there had been much hasty digging to try to save what remained of the potatoes grown for the winter, but those who held back or, like Billy, had too large a planting to simply dig it all up, discovered that the rot had not spread as expected by those who remembered the bad year of 1838.

Now, in 1845, many potato fields and potato gardens had indeed been affected, but only in part. A few fortunate farms were actually completely unaffected, but in others farmers had still harvested three-quarters or two-thirds of the crop they expected. A few optimistic individuals had waited to see what would happen next. When there was no sign of the blight spreading further through their fields or gardens they had then dug up only the affected plants, allowing the rest to come to maturity. The extended growth period meant in terms of weight that they had almost as good a crop as the previous year.

Sarah gave thanks when she found that Billy had lost less than a fifth of his planting. As he and his sons had made such a big effort to bring more pasture under cultivation, there was no possibility they could dig the whole crop, even with the help of their neighbours that dreadful evening when all anyone could think about were those first signs of limp leaves and slimy stalks. Billy had indeed, like many others, inspected the planting anxiously each day, but by the middle of September, when there was no further outbreak, the Halligans simply dug out all the damaged potatoes and began to harvest the more mature and better-sized ones from their earliest plantings. They got a good price for them in the weekly market in Armagh.

Much of Billy's crop was bought by the Armagh Workhouse when they discovered they could buy better quality potatoes from him than from some of the farmers with whom they had contracts. Later, they decided not to renew their individual potato contracts with specific farmers, but to buy in the market for the best value they could find. Billy now benefitted from reliable buyers and a large crop ready to be dug.

Sarah was amazed at the change in Billy. She remembered the shock Sam and Scottie had suffered when Ben made his first joke, now she had to laugh at herself when Billy welcomed her like a long-lost friend on an evening visit to

Mary-Anne. He sat down opposite her, smiled broadly and asked her for all the news from the forge.

His hard work had paid off and the effects were obvious. Mary-Anne stopped looking so anxious: she began to relax a little after all the extra work caring for Granny and appeared regularly at Sarah's fireside as the temperature of the September evenings dropped down yet more quickly.

Sarah brought the lamps down from their shelf, cleaned them and gave them new wicks. It was a job John had always done and it was one of many simple tasks, now hers, that brought home to her most forcefully her feelings for the evenings ahead. She freely admitted she was dreading the long nights.

The white envelope which Mary-Anne had mentioned anxiously on the day that Granny died duly arrived. Sarah had indeed forgotten when the bill was due, but she hadn't forgotten the bill itself. After the postman had made his delivery, she took out her jotter and saw she'd long ago made allowance for this twice-yearly payment. Now she was making it for the fifth time, but this time there was no John to sign the document; the stiff white sheet in her hand had now been drawn up in her own name.

September was a pleasant month with warm afternoons and chilly evenings, mist rising from the quiet land even before it got dark. Whether she had Mary-Anne's company or not, Sarah got on with her sewing, turning over in her mind the possibility of how she might sell the products of her work directly.

She was well aware that the middlemen who distributed

work to women, like the one who had brought napkins to her sister-in-law, Alice, before the family emigrated, paid as little as possible. The women knew they were being exploited, but had no idea what they could do about it. If women like Alice were to complain about how many hours they put in for a few coppers, they might well lose the only bit of cash income the family had now that so many weavers, like her husband, George, had entirely lost their market for webs of cloth.

The tide of emigration which had begun in May reached a peak as the last summer sailings departed. At many a fireside the only news was of neighbours reporting on an 'American wake'. What was supposed to be a happy farewell party for some member of the family, with music and dancing, often failed to bring the expected pleasure of such a gathering.

While everyone present tried to give the young man, or woman, or family, a fine send-off before escorting them the next morning to the temporary rail terminus a few miles short of Armagh, it was impossible not to be aware they would cross the Atlantic and most likely never come back. The few who couldn't write would disappear immediately as if they had never existed; a worse loss for many a mother or father than if the departed one had died of illness, or in an accident. But there were also others who could write perfectly well but, once away, wanted to forget a hard life with little joy in it and devote themselves entirely to making a better future for themselves. They too disappeared from view and never returned.

Sarah herself wept with relief when within the one week

in mid-September she had letters from both her dearest old friend Helen and Ben, dear Ben Hutchinson, who wrote at length and reminded her of the promise he had drawn from her that she would write to him when he had an address to send her.

Now, after forty-three days at sea and a long stay in quarantine at St John's because his ship, the *Anne* of Donegal, with ninety-six passengers on board was carrying four emigrants who were ill, he had finally been allowed to move on. He'd ended up in a small settlement called Scott's Plains in Ontario where he'd found work with a farmer.

For the moment, he said, it *was* mostly farm work, but the farmer himself was a go-ahead man and had plans to use the new machinery now becoming available. In the meantime, there were horses to shoe and tools to mend and he had dollars in his pocket, apart from a few he enclosed with a request that Sarah give them to Scottie, who had never had any money whatever for himself however hard he worked.

As for Helen's letter, though Sarah was delighted and relieved to have news at last, she was utterly distressed by what her friend had suffered because her own letter, written shortly after John's death in late April, had not arrived until the beginning of September.

Helen explained that the envelope had clearly been immersed in water and then dried out, but neither her postman, nor the local Post Office, could offer any explanation. The ink was smudged and some pages were stuck together, but to anyone familiar with Sarah's well-formed script it was still entirely possible to read her account of John's death and her confession of how much she missed the dear friend with whom she had shared her thoughts and feelings since they'd been children, sitting beside each other in their schoolroom or in her grandmother's own tiny sitting room.

Sarah immediately took out her writing materials and wrote long letters to them both, remembering as she did how much she'd once enjoyed writing letters and how little she'd written since she'd completed the wearying task of thanking people for their condolences and the thoughts and prayers directed towards her after John's death.

As September proceeded, it seemed that the lovely month with plenty of sunshine and none of that humid weather which had so dominated the summer was to be the bringer of good news. It looked as if County Armagh had got off relatively lightly in terms of blight and all the signs were that the harvest would be a good one.

Sarah had to smile when each week the local paper managed a paragraph about some record breaking crop: a single cup potato, something Sarah had never heard of before, had produced seventy-six potatoes weighing a total of twelve and a half pounds and a bean, grown near Portadown, had managed three stalks, yielding a total of one hundred bean pods, 'each containing from three to four beans'.

But the record was taken by neither of these events. That was reported by Mary-Anne in person when she arrived one evening, her sewing in a bag, Sarah's newspaper under her arm.

'Big news from the Archbishop's Palace,' she said confidentially, as she sat down by the fire and handed Sarah her *Armagh Guardian*.

'Oh yes?' replied Sarah, raising an eyebrow.

'Ye'll niver believe this. Sure didn't the gardener bring a carrot inta the kitchen there an' it weighed fourteen poun's.'

For both Sarah and Mary-Anne the autumn was a good time where they could sometimes laugh together after the sadness and anxiety they'd both suffered over the summer. They shared their problems and concerns and gave thanks they'd been spared the dreadful times spoken of with such anxiety by men and women, only a little older than themselves, when the blight had appeared at the end of August.

The weather stayed fair for the harvest and yields were high, all that had been hoped for, especially the crops of flax and wheat. The *Armagh Guardian* reported good trading in the local markets and fairs. The newly founded Agricultural Societies in local villages were holding lectures and hosting competitions. The resident landlords, who'd been active in setting them up, now provided prizes and visited tenants, actively encouraging good practice among them. There was no increase in the number of admissions to the workhouse. This was an item of information reported each week in the newspaper, always a marker of good times and bad.

Until the middle of October, all went well for both women, then within a week they were again called upon to gather up all the strength they could muster and cope with the next set of problems: first, Sam Keenan, and then, Billy Halligan himself, became ill.

Sam hadn't had a day off work in all the years he'd worked at the forge, so said Mary-Anne, but it looked as if he had pneumonia. He had indeed had a soaking one

Saturday night on his way home from work, but that was nothing new. The doctor, who was sent for on Monday morning when he couldn't get out of bed, asked his wife, Selina, if he'd lost weight recently. Selina had replied that he had, though he'd no loss of appetite, in fact these days he was always hungry and looking for more.

The doctor had looked grave, pronounced the need for bed rest and said he'd come again in a week's time. Only later did Sarah find out that the doctor was concerned Sam might have tuberculosis; the underlying condition would make him more vulnerable to the pneumonia which he'd had several times before. Meantime, it looked as if it would be weeks, if not months, before he could come back to work.

As for Billy, chest pains had begun to keep him off his feet and off the land, the latter making him irritable and anxious. Though Jamsey and young Billy were well able to do what was necessary, even without their father's supervision, Billy had never been a man to sit around. Mary-Anne, worn out with his complaints and anxious as to whether it was indeed his heart, sent for the doctor herself and was roundly abused for doing so.

'But what else could you do, Mary-Anne?' asked Sarah, when her friend appeared the next morning with eggs and buttermilk.

'Try tellin' Billy that,' she replied wearily. 'He's afeerd it's his heart, but shure the pain comes an' goes, an' when it goes he's back at work, an' that brings it on again. There's no talkin' to him,' she said, shaking her head, as Sarah lifted the kettle, ready to make her tea. 'No, love, I can't stay,' she said quickly, shaking her head. 'I need to be there when yer doctor man comes fer I can't trust Billy to tell me what he says. I'll come up the night, all bein' well,' she said, as she hurried off.

Meantime, Sarah knew she would have Scottie to deal with as soon as he came back from Sam's home in Ballytyrone. It being Friday and no one waiting with a horse at the forge, she'd sent him over with Sam's wages, knowing only too well as she put them in an envelope that, unlike Sir George Molyneux who was so good to his injured blacksmith, she'd be in no position to go on paying him with only Scottie working unaided in the forge at the quietest time of the year.

Scottie had been distraught when he came to work on Monday morning and found no Sam. It was an hour or two before Sam's oldest boy, a bright-eyed nine-year-old appeared at the front door with a note from Sam's wife in Ballytyrone. No detail in that first note except that the doctor had said bed rest for a week.

Over the long summer months without Ben's presence, Scottie had taken on more of his work. Sam was pleased with his progress in the forge and Sarah had watched him move from being a boy who ran across the fields, squeezing through hawthorn hedges to make a shortcut from Greenan to her back door, to him becoming a young man. Now seventeen and almost as tall as Sam himself he strode round by the lane and the road, whistling to himself and looking around him as if not wanting to miss any detail of bird, tree or bush.

When Monday's note came to Sarah, he stood waiting anxiously while she read it. When she told him what it said, his eyes filled with tears and he shook his head. For what seemed a long time, he was quite unable to tell her why he was so upset, other than his obvious concern for Sam and his family.

But Scottie had never been able, or perhaps he had never wanted, to keep his feelings from her. It wasn't long before she realised that it was not simply his fear of having no work to go to, but the fear of having no contact with her or the life the forge had given him. As Scottie saw it, if the forge went, his whole life – apart from the burden of his grandmother – went with it. The thought clearly appalled him and from what Sarah had heard of his grandmother, she might well have felt the same in his position.

In her solitary hours by the fire that evening she wondered why it was that some older people became so bitter and hostile. She thought often of her own dear grandmother who, even when vexed or overtired, could always say something helpful or even make a little joke to share the current problem.

Evening after evening, for the next two weeks, Sarah puzzled backwards and forwards wondering what she could do if Sam remained unwell for any length of time. If the forge went out of business, then not only Sam's job and Scottie's apprenticeship would disappear, but also her own home.

Without a home she could hardly earn a living by sewing even if her plans in that direction were further on. She *had* taught a small group of children in Lisnagarvey when her grandmother became too poorly to continue, but she had no qualification that would serve in one of the new national schools, besides which all the local ones, according to Mary-Anne, were already well-supplied with teachers.

Time and time again she looked at the jotter that held her calculations. What bills could be delayed, what further economies could be made? There had been no progress on selling the trap though there had been one unacceptable bid for poor Daisy. For the moment, Daisy was out to grass, so was costing nothing to feed, but soon hay would be needed to get her through the winter. Thanks to Ben and Scottie's efforts before Ben went to Canada, she and Scottie would not run short of potatoes, but oats would have to be bought when the crock needed refilling.

Setting aside the costs of running the forge, whether there was any income or not, the only other regular expense apart from milk, buttermilk and eggs from the Halligan's and groceries from Armagh, was the rent to Sir George Molyneux, paid half-yearly and due in October.

There was no way round it. Even if Sam were able to come back in a few weeks' time, the only income foreseeable in the next months running up to Christmas was a weekly withdrawal from the small remains of the savings they'd made before John died. The depleted bank book in the old brown handbag was the last resource. It might just last till Christmas if Sam got back on his feet and there was enough work coming to the forge to pay them both. But what after that?

She was no further on when some two weeks later with no sign of Sam's return to work, Mary-Anne arrived with some good news.

'Ye'll niver guess what's happened,' she began, looking cross, though decidedly cheerful in her manner.

'No, I'm sure I'll never guess. I've got too much guesswork in my life at the moment and not making much headway with it, so please just tell me,' Sarah replied, with a lightness she certainly did not feel.

'Billy's cured. Just like that,' Mary-Anne replied, snapping her fingers smartly. She settled herself by the fire, took out her sewing and took a deep breath. 'D'ye remember me tellin' you Billy's brother said there was a man over by Cabragh way had a charm for pains in the chest,' she began, 'well he finally went over las' night to see him, said he'd tried everythin' else so he might as well try him. An' he came back full o' beans, an' as bright as a button.' She paused and threaded her needle, which needed her total concentration, while Sarah waited, totally intrigued. Sarah herself had heard many a story of people who had gifts or 'charms' before she left Lisnagarvey, but she'd never been close to such a happening herself.

'When Billy arrives yer man says to him, "What's wrong with yer shoulder? There's one up and one down, yer lopsided, man." That was the start of it. The next thing he does is get Billy to take off his jacket and he lays hands on the shoulders. "Tell me," he sez, "was there ever someone a long time ago that would grab you by the shoulder and then beat you?"' Well, Billy has to say yes for his father was a desperit hard man, tho' I was spared ever meetin' him for he died of drink in his forties,' she continued matter-of-factly, 'an' yer man said that *that* was what was wrong with him. The memory was stuck somewhere in his body an' that's why the pain came and went. Now that Billy knew what it was, all he had to do was to tell the pain to go away.'

'And has it?' asked Sarah quickly.

To her surprise, she saw Mary-Anne stop to think. When she did speak what she said was equally surprising.

'Ye know, Sarah, in a wee country part of Ireland like us here, there's an awful lot of old stories and people believe things that are not true at all, but when I go to a woman in labour an' I lay hans on her to see how's she's doin', I know right away whether she'll bear a healthy chile or not. I think till now I thought it was jus' practice and so on and what me mother taught me, but now I can understan' fine well what yer man says. I've done the same m'self though not jus' in the same way, an' diden know I was doin' it.'

'My grandmother often spoke about healing,' Sarah replied slowly. 'She used to pray for people and when they got better she was so pleased. She used to say, "Even if we can't understand, we can still give thanks." Maybe that's all we can do, but I'm so happy for you and Billy. That's the best news I've heard for a long time.'

It was an evening some days later that Mary-Anne came again. She had decided she wanted to make rag rugs like Sarah's. She needed them at home, but she thought making them to sell was a great idea. It was getting a decent price for them that was the problem.

Afterwards, Sarah couldn't remember what it was that made Mary-Anne mention Lily, the bonnet maker. Neither could she remember the story Mary-Anne was recounting about Lily, but suddenly in the middle of what Mary-Anne was saying Sarah thought of Sir George Molyneux and the blacksmith to whom he had been so good.

She made up her mind in an instant and waited for Mary-Anne to finish her story.

'I'm thinking of going to Castle Dillon to see Sir George,' she said lightly, as she cut off the thread she had just woven into the back of her rug and began to rethread her needle.

'Ye are, are ye?' Mary-Anne replied, her eyes opening wide in astonishment. 'And why wou'd ye be doin' that, if it's not a rude question?' she asked, dropping her work in her lap.

'I thought I'd ask him to let me off the rent till the spring and I'll see if I can earn enough to pay him back next summer, if the forge is working again.'

'An' how wou'd ye do that?'

Sarah paused and found to her amazement that another idea had shaped in her mind. Scottie had been teaching her to drive the trap. He said she might as well use it while it was still for sale and it would be good for Daisy to get out and about and moving around again.

According to Scottie, she'd done well at the driving, though he might never have guessed how very difficult it had been not to think of John every time she took up the reins. But now, having set the thoughts of John's accident firmly aside, she was perfectly happy driving. Perhaps it was that which prompted the idea that had come so suddenly upon her.

She thought of all those women sewing napkins, like her sister-in-law, Alice, and all those doing whitework or embroidery. If she could collect their work and sell it in the clothes market in Armagh, she would charge them only a quarter or a third of what the middlemen took and she'd be able to sell her own work and Mary-Anne's at the same time.

Mary-Anne listened carefully, breathed a deep sigh and said: 'Well, I'll tell you one thing, if you do something you'll never fail from want of tryin'. Count me in as one of your clients. When are ye goin' to see yer man?'

'Who?' asked Sarah, preoccupied with the possibilities unrolling in front of her.

Mary-Anne laughed as she gathered up her belongings. 'You were thinkin' of visitin' our local gentry to see if your landlord wou'd let ye off yer rent while ye go inta business.'

Sarah laughed as she walked to the front door with her friend, gave her a hug and looked up at the red glow in the clear dusk sky.

'Tomorrow,' she said firmly. 'Don't they say there is no time like the present?'

'Let me know how you get on,' Mary-Anne called back at her.

She turned out through the gates and made her way down the hill to where Billy had just lit the lamp. It gleamed through the kitchen window as he peered out awaiting her return to tell her that the pain still hadn't come back and he was feeling grand.

CHAPTER ELEVEN

Castle Dillon house was only a mile or two away from the forge on Drumilly Hill. It lay off the road that leads southwards under the new railway line being constructed from Belfast to Armagh.

Beyond the gap awaiting the building of the railway bridge, the road curved round the slopes of Cannon Hill, a local landmark, where an earlier Molyneux had built a monument in 1782 'to commemorate the glorious revolution which took place in favour of the constitution of the kingdom . . . of Ireland'.

Neither Sarah, nor any of her neighbours, had ever seen the house. Though they were very familiar with the pillared gates and gate lodge – impressive structures in themselves – the house lay hidden beyond the end of a long, upward sloping carriage drive and stood out of sight of the road, just beyond the horizon, overlooking a small lake known only to the more daring of local poachers.

Often enough on their evening walks, Sarah and John had passed that gate lodge. Occasionally, they'd see a coach waiting for the lodge-keeper to come out and swing back the heavy, ornate gates of which John spoke so highly. Whenever he saw James Ervine appear, John would move to greet the older man and give him a hand to open the heavy gates, then helping him to close them as well after the departing coach had passed by. Sarah had watched them regularly and smiled, leaving them to their accustomed pattern.

They appeared to exchange a great deal of information in the short time the coach kept both her, and them, waiting, no hardship at all on a lovely summer evening. As they walked on, John would relay the latest news from Castle Dillon, whether any of the family were there at the moment, how the building work was going – for the old house was being completely replaced – though he said the stable block from an earlier period was considered handsome and so was only being refurbished.

Thinking of the stable block, which had its own forge and blacksmith, she remembered there was another entrance to the house somewhere near Hockley Lodge, but as they usually turned for home before that point, the light fading and the air beginning to cool, she'd never seen the entrance itself, nor the different perspective it might have given into the extensive demesne.

Now, as she dressed and prepared to make the short journey, she felt she might just as well be going into terra incognita – the name printed in her old school atlas where it was known that land existed, but, for the moment, known only to a few brave travellers.

Not surprisingly, Scottie was anxious about her first solo outing, but as he had a horse in the shoeing shed, an open-fronted wooden shelter built as a lean-to against the gable wall of the forge, all he could do was raise a hand in salute as he finished fitting the back foot of a good-looking roan filly.

As Daisy stepped out, clearly glad to be on the road again, Sarah herself thought how wonderful it was to be trotting along a dry road. It was such a lovely, warm and pleasant October day, leaves blowing along the side of the road, the hay fields, yellowed after the harvest, now streaked with the vivid green of fresh grass. She was sorry to arrive so quickly at the familiar gates though she was already looking forward to seeing this new building, so much talked about, but till now a completely unknown part of her life.

The gates were shut, no coach in sight, but at the sound of the trap and Daisy stopping alongside, James Ervine hurried out and greeted her.

'Ach, how are ye, Mrs Hamilton? We were heart-sorry to hear about John,' he went on, shaking his head sadly. 'Are ye keepin' well? I sometimes have word of ye from Billy Halligan. Are ye fer the house?'

'Yes, I am, but I was going to ask your advice,' she said, smiling down at him, having collected herself as quickly as she could after his mention of John. Sometimes, she thought, the kindness and the sympathetic comments of people who had known John would never get easier for her to bear. 'Is the other entrance the back one?' she went on. 'Had I not better go in with the tradespeople and gardeners, seeing I'm not visiting in a coach?' she asked steadily.

'Is it Sir George ye want to see?' he asked cautiously.

When she assured him it was, he became very thoughtful. 'Aye, ye might think it the best in the end. If ye go by the front ye'll get his lordship the butler. He'd ask the King of England what his business was and then send him round the back if he saw fit. He's better avoided. If you go in the back, you'll probably see the housekeeper or Sir George's man of business. Have you an appointment to see Sir George?'

'No, but I'm prepared to wait. What I want to ask him won't take long. But it's himself I need to see.'

'Aye,' he replied slowly. 'In that case, definitely the back. Once the butler says he's not at home, you've no hope at all. Whoever you see, don't let them tell ye he's not there, fer I let him in lass night, tho' I hear he's in bad form the day. If somethin's not right he gets powerful upset at times, for all he's a good-hearted man. But I'd say ye had a better chance of seein' him if you go in the back an' they'll see to the mare over at the stables, if yer happy to walk up the last bit up thru' the gardens.'

'I'm always happy to walk in a garden,' she said, smiling broadly. 'I'd love a garden myself, but with horses around I don't stand much chance.'

'Aye,' he said, laughing aloud, as he came and stroked Daisy's nose. 'She might like a few wee flowers for a change from hay, wouldn't ye girl? Good luck, now, ye know yer way, don't you?'

She assured him that she did, manoeuvred Daisy in the wide space in front of the gates, waved to him as he watched her go and drove the short distance to where the road divided, the narrower part winding round the south-west border of the estate.

The entrance wasn't far beyond the stretch they'd known so well, but this time the chestnuts, fat sticky buds and fresh sprouting leaves when they'd last walked, were dropping tattered leaves of pink and gold. 'First to come and first to go,' John always said, adding that 'the first hints of autumn come in the chestnuts as early as August, if you bother to look for them'.

These gates, handsome but much smaller and less dramatic than those tended by James Ervine, stood open. A long, sweeping drive led past the stable block a tall building with its windowless back turned to the road. Above the slated roof, rooks circled and called, rising and falling, black silhouettes against the blue sky. As she drove towards it she caught the first glimpse of the back of the house, the newly quarried stone gleaming in the bright light.

'Good day, ma'am, wou'd ye like to leave her here?'

The man who stood before her she did not know, but the pattern of grime on his face, the bare arms and the leather apron tied at the front told her all she needed to know. He was a blacksmith, whether the one who had appeared in Lily's story or not, he was a robust figure, thoughtful enough to wipe his hand on the backside of his trousers before offering to help her down from the driving seat.

'Thank you very much,' she said, looking round her. 'I've heard about your handsome stables, but that building is even bigger than I'd imagined.'

'But have ye seen the house?' he asked, grinning broadly.

'No, and I confess I'm curious,' she said honestly. 'I just got a glimpse coming in.'

'I'll walk roun' with ye and show ye where to go.'

The driveway was newly gravelled and still untrodden and bumpy in parts, but they were soon at the foot of some stone steps. To her right, three more sets of wide stone steps, with grassed terraces lying between them, rose up to provide a platform for the house itself, the biggest building Sarah had ever seen.

After one long scan of its severe but elegant width she turned her back on it, for to her left, almost beside them, adjoining the driveway with only a grassy slope and no fence whatever between, lay Castle Dillon lake. Only a few yards from where she stood, it gleamed in the light, flat calm, the air full of birdsong, the trees all around its shore bright with autumn colour, the lake which had been made into a bird sanctuary by an earlier Molyneux lay still and peaceful.

'It is quite lovely,' she said, unaware that he was watching her face and taking pleasure in her pleasure.

So absorbed was she in watching a fleet of swans move across the water, she did not notice a small, energetic figure hurrying down the steps from the back of the house. But her escort had seen him.

'Mornin', Sir George,' he said, saluting politely. 'All's well with the grey, sir, but he'll need a day or two's rest.'

'Well that's one less problem, Ross,' he said wearily. 'You've not introduced our visitor,' he added more sharply.

'Sarah Hamilton,' she said steadily. 'Mr Ross was kind enough to walk round with me from the stables. I was hoping, Sir George, I might have a word with you. I'm prepared to wait. You must have a great deal to attend to at the moment.'

'That's the first sensible thing I've had said to me today,' he said shortly. 'Ross, I'm going for a walk by the lake. Will you please take Mrs Hamilton to the housekeeper and see she has some luncheon. There are various others waiting in the library, if you *do* actually want to wait,' he said crisply, giving her a single glance as he turned on his step and marched off.

Sarah smiled. It might indeed seem desirable to have a title and position in the community and no doubt a great deal of money, but like everyone else he had his vexations. James Ervine had said Sir George was 'in bad form' this morning. She had the feeling that beyond the waiting clients, his many public duties and his concern for one of the six greys that pulled the coach when he and Lady Molyneux went to the cathedral in Armagh rather than to nearby Grange parish church, he had some other and more pressing concern.

Robert Ross, who told her he lived with his wife and family at Mullinasilla, only a mile or so as the heron flies from the lake itself, seemed to be in no hurry to deliver her to the housekeeper. He conducted her round the side of the building so that she could view the equally severe frontage of the house and gaze across the existing gardens to the demesne, rolling acres of low green hills extending beyond formal gardens and gravelled walks decorated with statues and small fountains.

The last of the scaffolding had only just gone, he had said, as they began to climb up the sets of stone steps that led, via the broad terraces, from the lake shore to the back entrance. They arrived at a forbidding tall double door beyond the final flight of stone steps and a terrace of local stone.

'What a lovely view to look out upon,' she said, rather wistfully, as they stopped on the doorstep to gaze back down on the lake now spread out below them.

Earlier, before Sir George had appeared, they'd met workmen carrying away loads of stones and debris from the building work. Some had been engaged in sweeping the stone steps themselves. Now, as they stood taking in this new perspective on the lake, gardeners with handcarts and wheelbarrows were arriving from both front and back to begin planting the flowerbeds already laid out and dug over on each of the terraces.

'I hear there's t' be a rose garden an' shrubs,' Robert said soberly, 'but I'm no good at anythin' like that. Me wife sez I wouldn't know a daisy from a dandelion,' he added, laughing.

'No, but you'd know a handsome foot scraper if you saw one,' she came back at him, as she looked up from the pair of wrought-iron specimens she'd been studying, one on each side of the entrance.

'Ah now, ye've said the right thing there,' he replied,

beaming. 'Shure I made that pair m'self to a drawin' Sir George hisself giv' me. I mind he sez to me: "Ross, I want no fancy work, but I want them a good size. There'll be people in an' out all the time thru that door wi' boots full o' mud from the new path roun th' lake. It'll be more than m' life's worth if the housekeeper gets mud in HER house."'

A short time later, Sarah was able to judge the said lady for herself. Middle-aged and comfortable, if not exactly plump, she had iron-grey hair done up in a tight bun and sharp eyes that took in every detail of Sarah's best dress with its soft pale blue fabric and spotless white collar, before holding out a cold hand and inviting her to come in to her sitting room where there was a fire.

She dismissed Robert with a glance the moment Sarah had thanked him for being so helpful and looking after both her and Daisy.

'Daisy?' she repeated, a slight lilt in her voice betrayed the hint of a softer accent beneath her careful pronunciation.

Kerry perhaps, or somewhere on the west coast, Sarah thought to herself, as she obediently sat herself down in the comfortable chair by a bright fire in a sitting room at least three times as big as her own biggest room.

Bridget Carey was not as formidable as she might seem, even if she appeared so to Sir George. Having checked out Sarah's status, discovered she had no groom but was herself driving her late husband's trap, she thawed considerably and spoke about her home in County Clare and her long relationship with 'The family' – by which she meant the various Molyneux families in Dublin, Kerry and Meath and their elaborate connections with the landed gentry in England.

Sarah listened attentively and asked a polite question or two, but had to admit to herself that Mrs Carey's command of genealogy was totally beyond her, however interesting the stories she told about individual members. She did, however, find out a lot about the Molyneux family, especially the very talented ones, like Samuel, who became Secretary to the Prince of Wales, thereafter George II.

'Now, Mrs Hamilton,' said Mrs Carey, pausing for breath, 'I think perhaps you and I might have luncheon here today rather than share the servants' hall. I do make a point of dining there as normal, just to keep an eye on things,' she added firmly, 'but perhaps today . . .'

'That would be very nice indeed, Mrs Carey,' Sarah replied gratefully. 'I was hoping you might tell me a little more about County Clare. Sadly, I've never travelled in Ireland. Beyond Lisnagarvey and Armagh, my knowledge is purely from the atlas and library books, when I get time to read them.'

'Do you like reading then? But you must be very busy with the children with no husband to help you,' Mrs Carey added, as she stood up and rang the bell for one of the maids.

Sarah wondered if Bridget Carey was a gossip or whether she was just lonely. As she herself knew only too well, being surrounded by people did nothing to stop you feeling lonely. Sometimes, indeed, it made matters worse. Clearly, long ago, young Bridget had been taught to defer to 'the family, and the staff who were her superiors', but now she herself had status and had put distance between herself and the servants, while presumably knowing her place with

147

the family. Either way, it didn't give her much scope for companionship, never mind friendship.

It was a long and instructive morning and Sarah was grateful for a much more substantial lunch than she would have had at home. She was, however, relieved when Mrs Carey herself decided it was time to deliver her to the library. She made it clear it was a task she'd entrust to no one else.

As the library door shut behind her, after a suitable thank you had been said, Sarah felt herself relax. She moved over to one of the windows where a cluster of high-backed chairs surrounded a leather-covered desk piled high with books. She sat there, her back to the room, looking out over the gardens until the effort of the morning settled in her mind.

Given the number of people sitting or standing around the large light-filled room – its walls lined with bookcases, some already full, some with boxes stacked in front of them – she decided it would be some time before she was called upon. Indeed she decided she would not be surprised at all if Sir George cherished his freedom and settled himself on the peaceful shores of his lake having given them all the option of waiting if they chose to do so.

In any event, she was right. Hours passed and no one moved from the room other than briefly. She had to confess to feeling tired, though it was seldom she had such a wonderful opportunity to read – and such an amazing collection of books to choose from. Some of the volumes in front of her were in Latin, of which she had only a smattering; a large number were medical works clearly the complete output of one the many talented Molyneuxs before Sir George inherited the title. But alongside these leather-bound volumes were some recent publications, slim volumes by a man called John O'Donovan. These she began to read with interest.

O'Donovan was interested in the meaning of Irish names. He was concerned that with the disappearance of Irish speakers the correct pronunciation of the names – the key, of course, to their meaning – would be lost. She was deep in the origins of names she'd heard of or which occurred locally, when she became aware of a tall gentleman in dark clothes standing beside her chair, waiting patiently till she paused.

'Mrs Hamilton, I presume,' he said, smiling.

'Why, yes. How did you know my name?' she said, looking up at him.

'May I?' he asked politely, his hand on the back of the empty chair beside her.

'Yes, of course,' she said promptly, 'provided you tell me how you knew my name.'

He smiled as he sat down.

'Well,' he began tentatively, 'given a commitment to plain speaking and telling the truth, I am indeed obliged to tell you,' he replied.

She was sure she detected a distinct twinkle in his eye though he was trying to maintain a straight face.

'I encountered Sir George down by the lake, where I had asked if I might walk, and he told me if I wished to speak to him, I must wait in the library. I said I was quite willing to await his pleasure. As soon as I spoke those words, he suddenly said: "I think one of your persuasion is already waiting there. Sensible woman in a blue dress, said her name was Sarah Hamilton."'

Sarah had to laugh. She could just imagine Sir George in his rather abrupt way saying just what he'd said, but before she had begun any reply to the gentleman, he had already begun to speak.

'As I have been honest with you, will you now be honest with me? Are you of "my persuasion" as Sir George calls it?'

'Fair exchange is no robbery,' she said easily. 'Yes, I would say we are both members of the Society of Friends, to give us our Sunday name, but I must confess immediately that however much I respect my Quaker upbringing, I am, and have been for a long time, out of unity.

'As many a good and thoughtful Member has been,' he said soberly. 'Might I be so bold as to ask why you are out of unity when in your dress and manner you are so clearly one of "our persuasion"?'

Sarah looked at him more closely. Older than herself, his face was tanned from wind and sun; a sense of sadness surrounded him despite his ready smile, a gentleness overlain by a strong personality; his voice was pleasant and carried a distinct tone of formal education.

It was a long time since she'd encountered someone like him; probably the last time was when the Lisnagarvey Meeting had a visiting speaker from England.

'There were three reasons,' she said thoughtfully, judging the question to be a fair one. 'To begin with my very dear childhood friend became engaged to someone she had known all her life. They were well-suited, the families were happy for them, but her fiancé was not a Friend. She was visited and warned. Then, my dear brother who was brought up by old friends of my parents after they died ran into financial difficulties with the business he was running on their behalf. It was no fault of his that a number of orders were cancelled leaving him in debt. He too was warned.'

She paused, saddened at the remembrance of something that had been heartbreaking at the time.

'And the third thing,' he said gently, when she looked so sad and it seemed as if she would say no more.

To his surprise, she smiled. 'I was wrong,' she said, 'I should have said four, not three. So, thirdly, I have always loved colour, pattern and decoration, but my sewing hardly qualified for a warning. Then, fourthly, I too married out of unity, but by then I was no longer attending Meeting so my behaviour did not qualify for a visitation,' she said, looking decidedly unrepentant.

'I admire your frankness,' he said coolly. 'I wonder how many of "our persuasion" have reservations about certain restrictions. I once experienced something similar to your brother. The world of business is full of pitfalls. I can see no shame in failing to see what is being carefully withheld from view.'

He paused, as some movement took place by the door of the library. They both watched and saw that a small balding man was surveying the assembled company, clearly waiting till everyone, like themselves, was paying total attention.

'Sir George has been unavoidably detained. Nevertheless, he will be receiving clients in his study in due course. One of the house servants will be in attendance when he is ready to begin.'

So saying, he looked around the room and its occupants as if someone had omitted to do the dusting, turned on his heel and strode off, leaving a distinct trace of hauteur behind him.

CHAPTER TWELVE

It was only moments after the dignified withdrawal of the person James Ervine had described as 'My Lord, the butler,' that a much less pretentious young man appeared at the table where Sarah and the Quaker stranger sat side by side about to continue their conversation.

'I'm sorry to have to interrupt you, sir, but the messenger from The Retreat was most pressing,' the young man said carefully, choosing his words and pronouncing them carefully as if he had learnt them by heart. 'He said I was to give you this immediately.'

He handed over a white envelope and stood discreetly back as Sarah's companion tore it open and nodded sharply.

'Has the messenger gone?'

'No, sir, he was aware you had no transport. He's waiting in front of the stables.'

'Tell him, if you'd be so good, that I will be only a few moments. I'm most grateful. Thank you,' he said, as the young man hurried off.

'I'm afraid you've had bad news,' said Sarah quietly. 'I *am* sorry.'

'And so am I,' he replied, 'both for the bad news and for the end of our conversation. Let me at least tell you my name, in the hope our paths will cross again.'

He held out his hand and shook hers.

'Jonathan Hancock from Yorkshire, manufacturer and enquirer into matters Irish for our Annual Meeting. I shall be here again, but I don't know when. I hope meantime Sir George will treat you well, whatever your business; mine will have to wait,' he said as he stood up. 'Would you offer him my apologies? I shall write to him, of course, but I'd be grateful if *you* would speak a word.'

'Yes, of course I will,' she said firmly, 'I hope your news may soon be better,' she said smiling sadly. She saw a look of great distress pass over his face as he turned briskly away.

Before Sarah had time to collect herself, she saw the young man who had brought the message coming towards her. He stopped, bowed and said: 'Sir George will see you now, madam.'

She wasn't sure whether she felt like laughing or crying. She had so enjoyed talking to Jonathan Hancock, the first person she'd met outside the known figures of her small community. She would have asked him about his enquiries into 'matters Irish', asked him which places he was visiting and what his particular concerns were in a world so much larger than her own.

But now, as she stood up, it was clear that the young man who had addressed her as madam was to escort her to Sir George. The last time she'd been called madam was by the visiting bank manager in Armagh – the one who had explained matters financial to her as if she were totally stupid.

She collected herself as best she could, followed the young man across a wide high-ceilinged gallery partly hung with portraits, then down a handsome staircase. She studiously ignored the rich colour of carpets that seemed to glow in the strong sunlight that fell through tall windows and reflected from white walls and the high ceiling. She tried to remember exactly what it was she had planned to say to Sir George when she'd sat at her own kitchen table, her jotter open in front of her, the columns of figures totalled in pencil, so she could change them as she thought of other possibilities.

'Madam,' said the young man, as he opened a door and held it so she could enter a room somewhat smaller than the library, whose elegant proportions were somewhat offset by the disorder of overflowing boxes of papers and binders spread around a piled-up desk and stacked on another equally beautiful carpet.

'James, come here. A chair for Mrs Hamilton.'

Sir George's tone was peremptory and James was so hasty in his response that he caught the hem of her dress as he placed the chair behind her. She wondered how she could release it discreetly before some slight movement she might make would create a tear in the soft fabric. All thought of what she was going to say to Sir George now went out of her head, yet again.

'How many more are there up there, James?'

'No more, Sir George. Mr Hancock was called away by a messenger from The Retreat.'

'So Mrs Hamilton is the last. Well, thanks be for that,' he said, not troubling to disguise a sigh of relief.

He waved his hand and James beat a hasty retreat.

'Jonathan Hancock asked me to apologise for him,' Sarah said steadily. 'The message appeared to be urgent and was clearly bad news. He said he would write to you.'

'Was he the man I met down by the lake that I thought was of your persuasion?'

'Yes, he was,' she replied, nodding.

'Was which?'

'Both, in fact,' she said, his irritability making her smile. 'Both the man you met and the man you thought was of "my persuasion".'

She could see now why James was so upset by his shortness of manner and why he had a reputation of sometimes being 'in bad form', but she could not dislike the man. To be honest, he was behaving just like a fractious child, but having spent most of her day in his almost completed home she had begun to have a great deal of sympathy for him.

'Well that's one less thing to do as well. Now what can I do for you?' he said, his irritability somewhat concealed beneath a habitual courtesy.

'I have a bill for half-yearly rent which I can pay, but if I pay it I may not be able to carry on through the winter.'

'And your property is . . .'

'Drumilly Hill, house and forge with garden.'

'And you lost your husband earlier this year,' he said, his voice softening marginally.

'I did.'

'And you are still there and the forge is not working?'

'Yes, I'm still there,' she said quickly. 'The forge *is* working, but somewhat reduced in capacity. One apprentice got the opportunity to go to Canada and now the journeyman is ill so only the younger apprentice is at work.'

'But why don't you just give it up and find something smaller, or go back to your family?'

'I have no family apart from a brother who has difficulties of his own,' she began, surprised that he didn't just say yes or no. 'If I had given up the forge last April, I would have taken away the livelihood of three men: one supporting a family of four, the others two elderly women. I would have lost my home as well and then I'd have no base from which to work to find a way of earning a living myself.'

'And you have some prospect of that?' he asked, his curiosity glinting through his sober question.

When she outlined her plans for collecting and selling needlework from women working at home, he began to fire a string of questions at her: how would she do this? Where would she sell her products? What commission would she take? – and so on.

Sarah answered all his questions but progressively she began to wonder why he should really want to know. What possible interest could he have in her simple project to make herself independent from the variable earnings of the forge? It could hardly be relevant to her ability to pay him the arrears of rent in due course.

'You would, of course, have to learn to keep accounts,' he said, looking at her very directly.

To her own surprise, she laughed.

'If I hadn't been able to keep accounts, I would never have managed the last six months,' she said cheerfully.

'And why was that?'

'The income from the forge is strongly seasonal, so it's important to make savings in the spring and summer to balance the continued outgoings in the quieter part of the year. Funerals are costly and the loss of a key worker is a major financial blow,' she continued, managing to keep her voice steady. 'Overheads continue, wages have to be paid . . .'

'And then there was the blight. Was that a factor?'

She was slightly startled by this unexpected question, but she now stopped speculating on what he was trying to find out and simply explained that the two apprentices had made a special effort with the late crop and opened some extra planting. The potato garden had indeed been smitten, as almost all the crops in the area had been, but the loss of about a quarter had been entirely offset by the extra crop. She had not had to write in any overall loss.

'So you can feed your surviving apprentice and yourself over the winter and, assuming your journeyman recovers, the forge will remain viable?'

'Yes, on the predictions I've made that is a real possibility,' she agreed.

She felt suddenly weary and was glad that it now

looked as if he was about to say yea or nay. To her surprise, he stood up, went to the mantelpiece and pulled on a tasselled rope.

'You are looking tired, Mrs Hamilton, and I still have some questions to ask you. I hope you will take tea with me.'

'Thank you, Sir George; a cup of tea would be very welcome.'

He walked over to the window and stood staring out. After a few moments, when she was sure he was preoccupied with his own thoughts, she moved carefully and released the hem of her dress from the foot of the chair, sat back more comfortably and wondered what he would ask her next.

She still had no idea why he was questioning her at all. Of course, he had a perfect right to do so, given she was asking him in effect to lend her money, his rent money, to tide her over the worst months of the year and help her get on her feet again, financially speaking. But the sum was so small when one thought of the enormous sum invested in this very beautiful new house, she could not make sense of it at all.

Sure time will reveal all, be patient a little longer and it will come to you.

As clearly as if she had been standing behind her chair, Sarah heard the voice of her dear grandmother and saw the light in her eyes, a small smile playing round her lips. What would her grandmother make of this enormous house and this hard-pressed man who had just invited her to take tea?

Sir George turned abruptly, came back to his desk, searched through the tottering piles of paper and finally found the item he wanted.

'Listen to this,' he said without more ado. He began to read a convoluted text about the purchase of some land and the provisions and conditions made for its sale.

She listened carefully, noting one or two terms with which she was not familiar.

'What do you think of that?'

'Of the proposition the writer is making or the terms in which he is putting them?'

'Both,' he said shortly, as there was a knock at the door accompanied by a rattle of tea cups.

'Come,' he said, raising his voice, 'over here by the fire and put some more logs on before you go.'

'Go on,' he said, turning his back on the trolley as the two housemaids wheeled it carefully across the room, avoiding the obstacles as best they could. 'Tell me what you think.'

'I think it is unnecessarily complicated. He is making three main points. They could easily be made in half the time and space and in simpler language.'

'How would you reply to that?' he asked, poking the offending text.

'If it were me or if it were you?'

'Both.'

For a moment, Sarah was completely taken aback, but there was no doubt what her answer should be.

'I would apply plain speaking, ignore the flourishes and pretensions and reply as if it were simply a courteous request for a response to a proposition.'

'Come to the fire, Mrs Hamilton. It is not cold today, but I find a fire cheering and tea more enjoyable with the flicker of flames. Do you agree?'

'Very much so,' she said, amazed at the sudden change in his tone. 'However vexatious the day, it always seems better if one can watch the flicker and glow of flames and catch the smell of wood or turf. Definitely one of life's joys,' she said, as she sat down gratefully in the armchair opposite him and took the cup of tea he offered her.

Yet again George Molyneux surprised her. Throughout tea, which he insisted she needed, he encouraged her with sandwiches and cake, while entertaining her with stories of his family, the problems presented by the unfinished house and those being dealt with on the committees in some of the public bodies on which he served. Without criticising individuals or revealing anything of a confidential nature, he made her laugh over the elaborate comings and goings that surrounded some of the most basic of problems.

At one point, he mentioned a lengthy meeting in which the Workhouse Committee, of which he was chairman, was required to decide whether the purchase of ribbon for certain girls in their care was an appropriate expenditure. Sarah immediately remembered the stories told by Lily, the bonnet maker, one evening by Mary-Anne's welcoming fire and thought how Mary-Anne would react were she to tell her that she had heard a version of the same story from Sir George himself.

Much recovered in spirits, Sarah resumed her chair opposite Sir George who now surveyed her across the broad, leather-topped desk with its leaning towers of paper.

'Mrs Hamilton, I have not forgotten the errand which brought you here, but I have one further question which has a bearing on the way that problem can be resolved. You are aware, I am sure, that I have been somewhat overwhelmed by my various duties,' he said, waving a hand at the nearest top-heavy pile. 'I came back from a business trip to Dublin and found that my so-called man of business had departed, leaving me his resignation without any explanation,' he said, glaring at the offending piles of letters and documents.

'That was over a week ago and although I have interviewed two young men who sounded promising, I was not impressed by their personality, despite their glowing references and their education.

'I need someone with common sense, as well as education. I've met no one at all suitable for the position until today. I am sure we can agree a suitable salary and conditions of work to allow a certain flexibility for your other commitments, but first I must ask for your answer. Will you take over this task? You will have all my support and co-operation, but I have great need of your obvious skills.'

Sarah laughed, put her hand to her mouth and apologised immediately. 'My dear grandmother always told me that when I was puzzled or couldn't understand all I needed was patience,' she explained. 'All would be revealed if only I applied patience.'

She was pleased to see him smile and wondered if she should ask him for time 'to consult her conscience', to wait upon insight as to what she should do. But before the words had even shaped in her mind, she knew there was no need. She knew she had already made up her mind. The answer was yes.

CHAPTER THIRTEEN

Despite the fact that it was only a little after five o'clock, Sarah felt as if she had been away from home for several days. It was clear that both Scottie and Mary-Anne felt the same.

She had barely turned in between the gate pillars before Scottie was taking the reins and helping her down, while Mary-Anne appeared in a flurry of skirts from the swirling smoke of a new fire, well made up against her arrival, the kettle now down at the first sound of Daisy and the trap.

While Scottie ate his supper and Mary-Anne and Sarah downed large mugs of tea, the events of the day were tumbled out and shared, one thing leading to another, a name, a word, a person, opening up a whole new train of thought.

It wasn't just that Scottie and Mary-Anne had difficulty

in grasping all that had happened, Sarah was having trouble herself. While she was easy enough answering their questions about the house, the stories they'd heard about it compared to what she'd seen and what Sir George had said about paying the half-year rent, she found she was just too tired to give them a full account of everything else as well.

When Mary-Anne saw Sarah droop in her chair and announced that she'd come back up first thing in the morning, Sarah was grateful. What she missed was the look that Mary-Anne gave Scottie that had him on his feet in moments, but she sat back in her chair, closed her eyes and gave thanks when they both said, 'See you in the morning. Sleep well,' and she heard them pull the front door closed behind them.

No visitor ever knocked at a closed door unless it was a matter of known illness, for a closed door meant either absence or a need for privacy.

For a long time Sarah simply sat looking into the glowing heart of the fire, cherishing the smell of the applewood logs Billy Halligan had brought her by way of thanks for mending his best jacket so the tear it had suffered was totally invisible.

Time passed and she found herself thinking about John. What would he say if he knew she had acquired a position with Sir George? She could almost see him on the opposite side of the hearth listening to what she told him, nodding his head and agreeing that indeed he was right, sure wasn't she far more reliable than any young man, and just as well educated, even if she hadn't been to some expensive school?

But if she still had John, she would have no need and

certainly no wish to have any other job than making a life together and running the forge accounts to help them make their living.

She found herself arguing with herself. Of course, John would congratulate her if she was on her own; he would understand she had to pay the rent, he would back her on keeping the forge going, in hoping that Sam Keenan would recover and be able to come back to work as soon as he could. But what John would do was not relevant; the real problem was what she herself felt about this strange change in her fortunes.

She sat for a long time, the fire making her drowsy. Then she found herself alert, replaying the conversation she'd had with Sir George after she'd said yes to the task of looking after his affairs, answering his letters and keeping his accounts.

To begin with, she couldn't quite keep up with him. When he started laying out his side of the bargain, he offered her a weekly sum that was as much as the takings for a good week at the forge in summer. He made it clear that he needed extra help in the coming month, but in return for extra hours this month she would subsequently have a day off every week until Christmas so that she could pursue her plan to collect finished pieces of clothing and embroidery from home workers for sale in the market in Armagh.

He also made it clear that she would have her meals with the senior staff and receive a share of leftovers with the rest of his staff whenever there was entertainment for a large number of guests.

She'd had trouble at the time, taking it all in, but he

was so clear and confident in his offer that he might as well have been reading a set of indentures written out in a clear copperplate in front of him. It all came back to her as she sat by the dying fire, too tired to make it up, but too reluctant to go to bed.

He left out nothing. Daisy would be fed as if she were at home. If circumstances meant Sarah had to stay late, or the weather was severe, one of the outside staff would drive her home in one of the smaller carriages and pick her up again the next morning.

He even mentioned her dresses. Having assured him that what she was wearing was her best dress, he suggested that she needed at least two more to see her through the winter. Whether she chose to make them herself or preferred the house's dressmaker to make them, he would pay for them. She remembered smiling when he added: 'As I pay for uniforms for the house staff, I don't see why you should not have the same consideration. Your appearance is an appropriate part of your work.'

She wondered what he meant by that, but by this time her eyelids were drooping and her eyes prickling with tiredness. She had to remind herself that it was still only Monday, the first Monday in October and she had said she could make a start on Wednesday. In forty-eight hours she would have completed her first day at work, a work which she could never have imagined at any time in the last years.

Her grandmother was right, as she usually was. Time would reveal all. However interesting, taxing or boring, the task she had to perform only time would reveal. The only thing she was sure about at this moment was that Sir

George Molyneux, however irritable he might be when provoked by circumstances, was a good, kind man, and from all she had now seen and heard, one whom she would willingly support in his many and various enterprises.

Sarah was up early on Wednesday morning knowing she had bread to bake for Scottie's evening meal and herself to wash and dress after she'd done all the dusty and dirty morning jobs.

But there was more to do than she'd expected. She needed a fresh collar for her best dress and found her fingers were all thumbs when she took out her sewing things to secure it with a few stitches. Scottie arrived early for breakfast and asked for cleaning materials, clearly wanting to polish up Daisy's harness before they went. She spent longer over their bowl of porridge and pot of tea than she normally would for Scottie seemed to be anxious at her being away all day, not only today, but Thursday and Friday as well.

In many ways, it was not surprising that he was anxious, though he'd been managing well in the forge. He'd been completing any tasks that came in where he had the relevant experience, as well as shoeing all the various horses from the breadman's heavy draught animal to the fine-boned hunters kept by the Cope family. His skill in shoeing seemed to parallel his gift of making horses feel comfortable which he'd had since his very first weeks in the forge, now over five years ago.

But today he seemed remarkably uneasy. It looked as if it was because she was going out all day, when he'd become used to knowing she was only yards away in the house, doing her everyday work or sitting by the fire sewing small garments.

Until now, he'd never seemed troubled if she went into Armagh with the Halligans or walked down to Mary-Anne to collect eggs, or milk, if they were running low, but she'd never been away for a whole long day, like Monday. That, it seemed had really upset him, so Mary-Anne had told her on Tuesday morning. Now it would be four long days in the week and the fifth day would join them in November when they started selling in the market in Armagh.

Given he was not yet in his last year of apprenticeship, there was nothing surprising in him being anxious about being left on his own, but if that really was the problem what could she possibly do to reassure him? It would be a different matter, of course, if Sam Keenan was back at work, but there was no news yet this week of that happening. His wife had said last week that 'he hadn't the energy of a good fly', and Sarah knew from many such stories she'd heard that if he tried to force himself it would be a bad mistake. But that was hardly going to help Scottie.

As they sat drinking their tea, Sarah was only too aware of time moving on and things she still needed to do before she left. Try as she might, she could think of nothing she could say to him that might reassure him in her absence.

'Which way d'ye go in to the demesne, the front or the back?' he said suddenly, just as she was beginning to think she must get moving whether she liked it or not.

'Oh, I think I'll stick to the back,' she said smiling. 'I might bump into a coach if I went the front way. The back way is only carts and gardeners and they're not in a desperate hurry like the coaches sometimes are. At least so says James Ervine.'

She'd spoken lightly, but she saw the colour drain from his face. 'What's wrong, Scottie? What have I said to upset you?'

He shook his head and she saw tears in his eyes. 'I'll niver forget that day I waited on the pillar to see the boss comin' home and him dead on a door wi' the Halligans carryin' him,' he said, his voice choked by a great sob.

She stood up and put her arms round him. 'And you think I might go and die on you as well?' she said gently.

He nodded, tears dripping on to his dusty working trousers and marking them with dark wet spots.

'Now how could I go and do that when it was *you* taught me to drive?'

She was amazed at the lightness of her tone and she had no idea where the words had come from, but their effect was magical.

'Aye and there's no stone walls that way either, only ditches,' he said, wiping his eyes, as if the ditches would provide complete protection for her in the event of an accident.

'And how could I go falling in a ditch in my best dress when it's the only one I've got at the moment?'

She saw him smile and some dark shadow moved away.

'You're not anxious about being here on your own till we get Sam Keenan back?' she asked quietly.

To her great relief, he shook his head, 'Ach no. People are all right if ye're honest wi' them. If I'm not sure I can mend somethin' I say so. An' if they ask about Sam I tell them what his wife tole me las' night: "He's grand in hisself but he still hasn't the energy of a good fly." He was in his bed already whin I called to see him, but shure everyone says it's jus' a matter of time, maybe only a week or two. He's over the worst.'

'Oh that *is* good news,' Sarah said happily. She'd not expected to hear again from Sam's wife till payday and this fresh news was a further relief. 'If you're ever anxious about anything, you know you could go down to the Halligans, don't you? They'd always help out,' she said, wanting him to feel easy.

'Aye. Ah know that,' he replied promptly, 'but it was only *you* I was worried about.'

She did her best to suppress a smile at his unconsidered honesty. 'Well, if I promise to drive carefully, will you make sure you eat what I leave for you? So that I don't have to worry about you, now that I've Sir George to look after. I'm not even in my work dress yet and it's nearly time to go,' she added quickly.

'Never worry,' he said, beaming at her as she turned towards the bedroom stairs. 'I'll tell Daisy yer a wee bit late. She'll not let you down.'

Scottie was right. Daisy herself seemed to be delighted to be harnessed up again. She needed little encouragement to set off at a good pace and very little guidance at the sharp turn that took them towards Hockley Lodge and the back entrance. They drew up outside the stables a few minutes before nine o'clock and were greeted by Robert Ross and a tall, blonde youth called William.

'Good morning, ma'am. I've heered the news about you comin' to work here an' it seems Sir George is in much better form than whin you last come. Long may it last,' he said, raising his eyes heavenwards. 'Now, William here is going to look after Daisy. Tell me, do you ever ride her?'

Sarah laughed and shook her head.

'I'm afraid horse riding was not on the curriculum of the wee school I went to. It was Scottie who taught me to drive.'

'Aye, an' yer a right han' at it, if it's new to you,' he replied, nodding vigorously. 'Now I've a favour to ask you. Wou'd ye mind if William here got Daisy ready for a saddle and rode her when she's ready? Sometimes we hafta take letters to local folk and we've only a couple o' the young ladies' horses we can use. If Daisy wou'd help us out it wou'd be company for her while ye're at yer work. An' ye might give it a go yerself when she's broke in. Though there'll be no trouble there for she's used to people and is good-natured forby. What dy'e say? Fer I know I'm keepin' ye back and I'm sure yer man is waitin' on ye.'

'By all means go ahead,' she said nodding happily. 'I'm sure Scottie would ride her even if I didn't. I certainly know she likes company. She really stepped out this morning when she knew where she was going.'

'Aye, they can tell these things,' he said, as he fell into step beside her, leaving William and Daisy to their morning's work. 'Yer man, Sir George, was powerful pleased when he came to see me about Daisy. That's how we know'd about yer new job. Ye'll find everyone knows now. Things go round this house faster than grooms on horseback,' he said, laughing as he rang the doorbell and waited till Bridget Carey opened the heavy door.

'Good luck,' he said, saluting her as Bridget took her arm and drew her inside.

She was grateful that Sir George was nowhere to be seen, so she propped her bag with her own pens and paper, her jotter, rubber, and a comb and mirror, by the side of the desk and studied the towers of papers built with loose sheets. Some packets were tied with tape and others with string, the whole lot covered with a fine film of dust, presumably from the log fire burning merrily in the grate.

She stood and looked at the desk and its burden and wondered where to start. The sunlight was beaming through tall windows, pulling out the rich colour of the carpets. In contrast, far above her head, the smooth white ceiling was decorated with an elaborate plaster centrepiece which matched the architrave running round the whole room. It was full of flowers and intertwining leaves that created a sense of order and pattern in complete contrast with the room below, a room full of disorder, piles of books and overflowing boxes of paper heaped up on chairs and on the floor, making it difficult to move around even though the room itself was so large.

She made up her mind. What must come first was the surface of the desk, for it was clear that letters had been deposited for so long that, like sodden slopes in winter, it would need only a very little more deposited on top to start a landslide.

It was perfectly obvious the letters at the bottom of the

piles had arrived before those in the middle, or at the top. She began creating new, less unstable, piles on the floor, a scribbled note from her jotter recording the dates of the arrival of items at the bottom and at the top. Some of the items went back a long way.

She had just revealed half of the handsome leather covering on the surface of the desk and was wondering where the nearest duster might be, when she heard the door open behind her. To her surprise, the person who entered was not Sir George, as she thought it might be, but a thin, pale girl in a black dress with her dark hair almost completely hidden under a crisp white cap. She carried a tray gingerly in both hands. It bore a silver teapot, a pretty china cup and saucer with a motif of garden flowers and a matching plate displaying a pretty arrangement of shortbread biscuits.

'Your tea, my lady,' the girl said, bobbing a curtsey, as soon as she had put the tray down on the newly revealed surface of the desk.

For a moment, Sarah was quite overwhelmed by the desire to laugh, but then she saw the painful unease on the girl's face.

'I'm not that sort of lady, I'm a servant just as you are,' she said gently. 'My name is Sarah Hamilton, what's yours?'

'Annie,' she replied baldly, clearly still defeated by what to call this person in front of her.

'And have you been at Castle Dillon long, Annie?' she asked patiently, aware the girl was close to tears, though for what reason she could not guess.

'Since yesterday.'

'Then *you* are a day ahead of me,' said Sarah, smiling.

'This is my first day and I don't know who anyone is, except Sir George and Mrs Carey and Robert the blacksmith.'

'Mrs Carey said if I diden mine me manners they'd sen' me back,' Annie said, her voice wavering.

'Back where?' Sarah asked.

'T' th' workhouse.'

The look of devastation on the girl's face made Sarah think of all the negative things she had ever heard about that institution. What could she possibly say about it?

'And are your mother and father still there?' she asked, totally overwhelmed by the sadness and anxiety in the girl's face.

'No,' she said, shaking her head. 'I've no mother an' no father. I've no one belongin' to me. I'm all on ma lone.'

For a moment, Sarah thought she heard steps approaching the door. She wondered if someone might appear to scold Annie for idling, but just as she'd had to find something to say to Scottie, she knew she had to do, or say, something to help this poor girl.

Once again, like both Scottie and herself, with only his elderly Granny 'belongin'' to him, was someone else with no sheltering arms to hold them, to enfold them and comfort them when they were in distress. No mother, no father, no sister, no brother, no husband, no wife. As Annie had put it so simply, they were 'on their lone'.

'Here,' she said quickly, 'put these in your pocket and we'll see each other tomorrow. Call me "Mrs Hamilton" when anyone else is here. Call me "Sarah" when I'm on my own,' she added, as she handed over two of the shortbread biscuits from the pretty china plate.

To her great delight, she saw a wisp of a smile as the fingers closed on what was clearly a rare treat. The thin, pale face was transformed for a single moment and in that moment Sarah saw Annie had the makings of a very pretty girl.

Time moved on and Sarah was summoned to lunch by the young man called James she'd met on her last visit. He escorted her to her place beside Mrs Carey at the top of the long table in the servants' hall. The food was good and plentiful, but Sarah found it hard to enjoy while replying to Bridget Carey's stream of questions above the noise of the large assembled company. She was so glad to get lunch over that she said a polite 'No, thank you' to tea in Mrs Carey's sitting room on the grounds that she'd not managed a quarter of what needed doing today.

She was grateful for the enfolding quiet of Sir George's study where the fire had been made up in her absence and someone had left a basket containing wax polish and cleaning materials probably in response to her question to James as to where she could find such things.

She sniffed the polish appreciatively and applied it sparingly to the half of the desk that stood empty and dusty. She was so encouraged by the wonderful effect it had on the leather surface she was sure she got through clearing the second half much faster than the first.

For the moment, she was not opening letters and looking at them unless they'd already been opened in the first place. Her sole concern was to create order, to have piles that were not so high they'd fall over. Sorting them for content, or urgency, she tried not to think about. Some of the envelopes looked very battered and worn as if they'd been around for a long time, but clearly all of them remained unanswered.

What could they be about? she wondered. She knew there were no letters in what she'd sorted from family and friends. These would be marked private and probably would be delivered straight to the family breakfast table, not stacked up in Sir George's study. So what were all of these?

Finally, overcome by curiosity, she opened a letter that still looked fresh and recent. Despite its very small copperplate, she found the text consistent and legible. The writer began by insisting that it was a true copy of the minutes made this day of our Lord, 13th September 1845 at the request of Sir George Molyneux, Chairman of the said Committee of Governors of the Armagh Workhouse.

Fascinated, she read on and found that one of the topics under discussion was the eleven-year-old who had applied for permission to go and live with a Mr Hamilton. It seemed that Mary-Jane Gray had returned to the house rather than live in the country with the Hamilton family and it was proposed that the shoes and stockings given to Mary-Jane Gray on her going out to service were now to be given to this new applicant.

Sarah paused, wondering if Annie had had such a 'going out' present. Then her eye caught a list of punishments. Three young men were to have no supper for a week, two of them to have twenty-four lashes as well.

Distressed by the punishment for not working hard enough, Sarah was reluctant to read any further, but an item about illegitimate children caught her eye. Sadly, she read it and was reminded that Annie was only one of a large number, fifty-three in this report who had no one to protect them apart from the officers of the workhouse whose rules seemed harsh indeed.

The fire was burning low by the time the desk was clear and the piles on the carpet arranged chronologically. Sir George had not appeared and no one she'd spoken to in the course of the day seemed to have the slightest idea where he was. It was almost six o'clock when James appeared once more with two small bundles of post on a silver tray.

'Mrs Carey said to tell you: "These came yesterday and these today and she knew there was no point sending them round till you'd sorted out the desk."'

He bowed and placed the two small bundles on the wide stretch of gleaming leather.

'Shall I ask for your conveyance to be brought to the servants' door, ma'am?' he asked, as the clock struck six.

'No, thank you, James. I'll walk down to the stables when I've checked everything out. I'll be going shortly,' she replied, wondering why this young man always made her feel so uneasy.

She stood looking down at the desk. Clearing it had been her long day's work. She touched the two small bundles, each tied in a bow with string from the kitchen. The earlier one had a white envelope on top.

She removed the string from both packets and picked out an envelope that looked somehow familiar. Suddenly it came to her that the message from The Retreat had arrived in such an envelope, bringing to an end her long wait in the library and her conversation with a Quaker man.

She turned it over but did not open it. She knew right away who it was from. He'd told her he would write to Sir George and he had. A man of his word, as all Quakers had been brought up to be.

'Jonathan Hancock,' she said to herself, smiling as she thought back to their meeting on Monday. 'I wonder what business *you* have with Sir George Molyneux.'

CHAPTER FOURTEEN

The colour was wonderful – a deep, rich plum – but Sarah couldn't be sure what the fabric was. Not linen, or wool and certainly not velvet which would not wear well. She stood in John Wilson's shop in English Street and stroked the rich fabric, totally absorbed with its intense colour and the possibility of making from it one of the new dresses she so badly needed.

After her first whole month as Sir George's assistant she knew a great deal about many things previously unknown to her, but what she did not know was how she was going to find the time and energy to make the two extra dresses Sir George had suggested she would need.

'Nice bit o' cloth, Sarah, an' good value inta the bargain.'

'Hello, Lily, I haven't seen you for ages,' Sarah said, smiling warmly at the small figure who had so often amused both her and Mary-Anne by the welcoming fireside at the foot of the hill.

'I'm afraid my new job keeps me busy,' Sarah added apologetically. 'I have to catch up with Mary-Anne in the evenings so she comes up and tells me the news while I bake or give myself a clean collar for the morning. How are you, Lily?'

'Oh, busy as usual,' Lily grinned, twisting her face in a wry smile. 'There's anither lock o' girls settin' up for Australia an' I've the bonnets to do as per usual.'

Sarah laughed.

'Yes, I thought you'd be busy. I have to copy up the minutes for the Workhouse Committee for a contact of Sir George so I thought about you when I saw that. And, of course, Wilson's as well for the dresses.'

'Aye, ye'd know all about it. An' yer man,' she said, dropping her voice to a whisper, 'makes a nice wee bit out of it wi' the stuff fer dresses, an' shawls forby. Oh aye, they set thim girls up well. Shure I suppose it's cheaper than havin' to feed thim fer years if they've bin deserted. Shure most of thim has nether far'er nor mor'er.'

Sarah nodded her agreement, but did not say that at the last count there were fifty-three illegitimate children in the workhouse, as well as a number whose fathers had deserted them, knowing their mothers would have no option but to go to the workhouse. The Guardians were pursuing the fathers but without much success.

'That's a good price,' repeated Jilly, fingering the material. 'I'd say yer man has bought out the stock from some puir soul goin' broke. He'll make a bob or two on it, that's for sure.'

Sarah detected a note of hostility towards John Wilson, of whom she herself had never heard a bad word, so she changed the subject by asking Lily's advice.

'Do you think it would make up well?'

'Aye, I'm sure it wou'd. Are ye makin' it yerself?' she asked sharply.

'Well I'd like to, but if I can't, I've been told there's a good dressmaker at Castle Dillon.'

'Aye, but ye'd hafta pay her,' she said dismissively.

Sarah agreed that she would and was glad when John Wilson himself appeared at their side, looking amiable and asking if he could be of any assistance. To Sarah's surprise Lily disappeared so quickly she had no time to say goodbye to her.

'I'm admiring this lovely fabric, Mr Wilson. I hadn't got as far as the price tag yet,' she said laughing.

He nodded agreeably, told her the name of the mix of fibres, of which she had never heard and then added promptly: 'We might, of course, make a special discount for a regular customer like yourself.'

Sarah smiled to herself. It was true, she visited the shop often on a Saturday if she came to town to buy groceries. But when she looked at fabric, mostly it was to see what she could buy for herself, or for Mary-Anne, to turn into garments they could sell in the market.

Since the late summer, they had both worked hard to build up stock ahead of next Thursday, when the first of her promised days off coincided with the cloth market held in a market yard at the back of the Scotch Street shops.

She made up her mind. The colour was lovely and she

was now reassured that the fabric was robust enough for everyday wear.

'Well that always helps, Mr Wilson,' she said, as he took a pencil from behind his ear and made a scribble on the sales ticket.

'Glad to be of service,' he replied, signalling the young assistant to measure and cut as required and make up a parcel in strong brown paper.

As there was no sign of Lily anywhere, Sarah set off for the Charlemont Arms Hotel in English Street where she'd been able to leave Daisy and the trap, her other shopping already loaded earlier, to give her the chance to move freely in the crowded streets and to look rather than buy.

She was just about to turn down the side entrance to the stables behind the new inn when she heard her name. Surprised, she turned quickly and saw Jonathan Hancock hurrying towards her.

'Greetings, Friend Sarah,' he said smiling, and using the conventional greeting between Quakers.

She paused only a moment before returning it. He knew perfectly well since their first meeting that she was out of unity with the Quakers, but in no way out of love with the principles she'd learnt from her grandmother.

'I got such a surprise when I got your letter on behalf of Sir George,' he said, reaching out to take her parcel. 'It's almost lunchtime,' he went on quickly. 'Will you eat with me, please? There are so many things I want to ask you and the dining room here is quiet.'

She could think of no good reason why she should not,

183

so they went together into the new dining room with its raftered ceiling and open fire.

'Did you go to Sir George to ask for employment?' he asked, his eyes bright, a small smile playing round his lips.

'No, I went to ask him to forgive me my rent for six months to see if I could earn a living and keep my husband's forge going.'

She saw the smile disappear as he registered that she must have been bereaved, but he paused only for a moment, and then went on.

'And you ended up as his "woman of business". How on earth did you manage that?'

She laughed and told him the whole story, watching with amusement the changing expressions on his very mobile face. He seemed younger than when they'd last met, but then, on that occasion, he'd been waiting to see Sir George for a long time, just as she had, but unlike her that very long morning, he'd probably had the journey by coach and ship from Yorkshire somewhere in the previous days.

Suddenly, she remembered the hand-delivered letter which had brought an end to their first conversation in Sir George's library and the envelope of the same kind that appeared on a silver tray as she was about to leave after her exhausting first day in the study. She'd been so tired she'd not had the energy to open it. When she did apply the engraved, silver paper knife next morning, she found it was his courteous request to Sir George that they might speak about the Armagh Workhouse of which Sir George was now Chairman of the Guardian's Committee.

Replying on behalf of Sir George, who said, somewhat

to her surprise, that he would do all in his power to assist him 'in such an admirable project', was one of the very first tasks she'd undertaken at the handsome desk assigned to her, the one Sir George himself resolutely refused to use.

She'd wondered at the time exactly what the 'admirable project' was. Clearly Sir George had heard of it, but she assumed she'd just have to wait for a further exchange of letters to find out. Now, here she was, able to ask Jonathan himself any question she wanted.

They talked easily and at length while Jonathan explained how he'd been commissioned by their Yearly Meeting to join a group making a survey of the causes of poverty in Ireland. They had begun their work in 1838 during a period of famine. Now, in 1845, they felt that many of the causes of famine then were still present and not fully understood, even though the building of workhouses had been a step towards helping the poorest of the poor.

She understood now why Sir George had been so positive in his response. However irritable he might be about the paperwork which he so disliked and the people who regularly called upon him for both his time and his money, he was, as she had guessed after their first meeting, a kind-hearted man who was generous to both servants and tenants.

'But why did you come to Armagh, Jonathan, or is it not just Armagh that you visit?' she asked.

'No, not just Armagh,' he said, pausing visibly to collect himself. 'I was already visiting Armagh regularly to see my wife, so they thought I might be able to extend those visits for the benefit of the ongoing work.'

'Your wife?' Sarah repeated, taken aback as she tried to make sense of the situation.

'My wife lives at The Retreat. She's been there for many years and no longer knows who I am.'

Sarah felt relief sweep over her. His behaviour had been so easy towards her, proper and yet very warm that, for a moment, she just couldn't take in the fact that he could be married. As everyone knew, The Retreat was an alternative to the Armagh and District Lunatic Asylum, if you were wealthy enough to afford its charges.

'And had she been taken ill that day we met and you had to leave immediately?' she asked gently, remembering his distress and his hasty parting words when he said he hoped they would meet again.

'Yes, you could say that,' he replied soberly. 'At times she has violent phases. I had visited her in the morning and she seemed quite stable, but as soon as I left there was a dramatic change. They thought I might be able to help.'

'And were you?'

'No, I'm afraid not. If anything, my presence made things worse. They asked me to leave and were sorry they'd sent for me,' he said wryly.

'And has she been at The Retreat for long?' she asked cautiously, seeing how little he wanted to have to speak about it.

'Since the second year of our marriage,' he began, collecting himself. 'Her family are landowners in Richhill. They said it would be more homely for her to be in care here, rather than in Yorkshire. I felt they wanted to be near her, so I agreed. She's been there ten years.'

'And you've been visiting all that time?'

'Yes, I have,' he admitted wearily. 'To be honest, having work to do for the Yearly Meeting when I come makes it easier for me. I've cousins in Lurgan and Lisburn, and another one in Donegal. I'll be visiting them all while I'm over to seek their help with information from their own localities. Then I'll be writing reports for the Yearly Meeting.'

'But what about your own work?' Sarah asked promptly. 'You said you were a manufacturer.'

'Yes, that's true,' he agreed with a slight smile. 'But if you can have absentee landlords then you can have absentee manufacturers,' he said lightly. 'I *am* privileged; I have good people, many of them fellow Friends working for me. The business is a large one and has always been diversified. Even in these hard times the productive ones can subsidise the weak ones, so no one is thrown out of work. We try to find ways of adapting.'

'Like getting your women workers to turn to making cheap clothing from fabric you can't sell?'

'How did you hear about that?' he asked, looking totally amazed.

'I didn't. But when I was trying to think of a way of making a living for myself and keeping the forge going, it came to me as an idea. My brother, Charles, runs a workshop in Lurgan for the elderly couple who brought him up when our parents died. He's in the process of trying to sell up, but he gave me cloth when I told him what I was planning to do. He said it was a good idea, but he was so short of capital that he couldn't do it himself. He's thinking of going to America, but he hasn't even got the money for his fare. I've started saving up for him.'

They paused as a skinny girl in a black dress came and took their empty plates away. Sarah smiled encouragingly at her, thinking of Annie back at Castle Dillon, wondering if this girl too was an orphan who had been found a place where she'd 'hafta mine her manners'.

'There are so many in such need,' Sarah said sadly, without quite thinking about it, as he offered her the menu to choose a dessert.

'Does it sometimes burden you?'

'Yes,' she said, promptly. 'Here am I with a lovely lunch and apple crumble as a treat, when many hard-working people will be lucky if they get a bowl of porridge tonight.' She paused and then went on, 'Even as a little girl, I worried about other people. My grandmother tried to help me because I got so upset when I saw great need and couldn't do anything about it. She used to say: "Do what you can, do it in love and be sure that it will be more than you ever imagined."'

'Did she indeed?' he replied immediately. 'That was one of my mother's sayings too. Do you know where it comes from?'

'No. I've often wondered. I know it's not the Bible. Could it be Shakespeare?' she asked, as the thought struck her.

'I don't know Shakespeare well enough. There are plays like *Coriolanus* I've never even read,' he said honestly. 'But it doesn't really matter where it comes from, does it? If something helps you on your way you just give thanks and use it, don't you?'

* * *

Although Sarah was always glad to see Mary-Anne, she was grateful she didn't come up the hill that Saturday evening. When Scottie came to collect bread and a small casserole she'd made the previous day with a meal for herself, she did confess to him how tired she felt. He'd delighted her by the way he came back at her with a big grin and said that his news could keep as it was all good.

It was not so much that she was physically tired, though she would admit that as well. It was more that she had so much on her mind after the hours she had spent in the Charlemont Arms. She just needed to be by herself in the quiet to let the events of the day settle.

She moved slowly but made a beginning on the jobs left over from the morning. Then she brought out an old winter dress to wear on Sunday while her best dress was being ironed and freshened for Monday. She became aware that all the time she was working she kept thinking of 'Do what you can . . . do it in love . . .'

Like a catchy tune, or a well-loved verse of poetry, it repeated and repeated in her head, even when she finally got into bed and stretched out her weary body, ready for sleep.

It was such a long time since she'd had a conversation of any length with a man. She tried in vain to think who there had ever been in her life, besides her own dear John, to whom she could speak as freely as she had today with Jonathan. Women, yes. Her dear friend Helen, and now Mary-Anne, but that was something different.

She could say anything she wanted to John, any thought that passed through her mind. He would always respond.

In the dark of the night, she could see the concentration on his brow, a slight movement of his lips, as if he were repeating her words, his total focus on her face. But John had not been educated beyond the local school and the age of twelve. He wrote a good hand and read his few books, but he was often so tired from the hard physical labour of the forge that he had little time or energy for broadening his mind, alert as it might be.

The ache of longing for his presence came upon her, as it had so often in the long months since April. It had been a lovely spring day when he went to Armagh for supplies for the forge and now, tomorrow, Sunday, was the first of November. The dark of winter would rule for at least three months and perhaps far more.

She shuddered at the thought, as if she was being asked to face those months without warm clothing or a bite to eat. But now, she reminded herself against this bleak prospect, there was someone else to whom she could talk. Not often and usually only by letter, but there was someone with whom she could share words and thoughts, if nothing more. It was a gift, totally unexpected, but still to be cherished.

There were other gifts too and in the quiet of a dim, misty Sunday morning, Sarah stood at her ironing board and gave thanks. Sam Keenan had now fully recovered from his pneumonia and tomorrow there would be two hammers echoing from the forge as she left for work.

Scottie had not only shot up in height during the summer but he seemed to have grown up disproportionately as well. To Sarah's great surprise, he told her that he now kept in touch with Ben, who had made his way to Peterborough, Ontario, where he was working with a farmer anxious to promote mechanisation on his farm.

Sarah had received some dollars from Ben many months back to be given to Scottie, but now it seemed he sent them direct whenever he could. He'd also introduced Scottie to the former teacher in Loughgall he'd visited so often himself. It now seemed a new friendship had been established and Scottie had an older man to support and encourage him, as well as having the support of Sarah herself.

A gleam of sunlight penetrated the dim, low-ceilinged kitchen, catching the pile of papers she'd been sorting, among them her jotter and bank book. The still open page now showed the first deposit from her monthly salary cheque. The balance was still very low with winter to come but when she wrote to her brother this afternoon she would ask him for some more fabric and tell him that this time she would like to pay him for the previous lot as well. She would also tell him that, all being well, she could send him the price of his ticket. He'd need the money before the ice melted so as to get a passage once the St Lawrence Seaway was free of ice next May, if by then he still wanted to go.

CHAPTER FIFTEEN

'Shure we can but try,' said Mary-Anne, as they sat at Sarah's kitchen table drinking tea after a long evening checking and folding the garments they'd worked on since midsummer when Sarah had first put the idea of the clothes market to her friend.

'Of course, you're right,' Sarah replied, yawning deeply and then laughing at herself. 'I'm sorry, Mary-Anne, at this moment I'm so tired, I couldn't give you change of a sixpence.'

Mary-Anne nodded ruefully, drained her mug of tea and stood up. 'We've done our best an' if it doesn' work out shure there's no great harm done. Ye'll be as right as rain in the mornin'.'

At the front door she paused, put her arms around Sarah, hugged her and kissed her cheek. 'Jamsey will be up here in good time the morra an' Scottie can give him a han' t' pack the trap. You can pick me up on the way past. I'll be ready and I'll have a bit of lunch in a bag; you'll have enough to do without doin' that as well. Now away to yer bed, like a good wumman,' she said briskly, as she drew her shawl round her and stepped out into the damp and misty night.

Sarah yawned yet again as she looked round the cluttered room. Garments were stacked, neatly tied up with strips of torn fabric or string to keep them in manageable bundles. They weren't heavy, but they had to fit into the trap with both Mary-Anne and herself, as well as Jamsey, who'd offered to help them load and unload and take care of Daisy until whatever time they were ready for the homeward journey.

Most of the garments were their own work, but some had been made by friends or neighbours. Those were the items Sarah was most anxious to sell. But standing looking at them wasn't going to help. She could almost hear Mary-Anne scolding her as she stood staring at their stock when she should be seeing to the fire, laying the table for breakfast and getting herself off to bed.

The next morning even the irrepressible Mary-Anne was quiet as they trotted briskly into town, Daisy clearly surprised at this change in direction. By nine o'clock, they had laid out their stall, chatted briefly to the traders on either side of them and were awaiting their first customer. They were both surprised and somewhat taken aback when a red-faced man came up to them and without any acknowledgement or greeting, started turning over garments and examining some of them.

Sarah had just made up her mind to speak when he glanced at them dismissively. 'I suppose the pair of you have a licence to sell this stuff?'

'Of course,' said Sarah calmly, knowing without even looking at her that Mary-Anne was getting cross.

'An' where might I ask did ye get all this stuff?' he went on, dropping a child's dress in a crumpled heap on top of a row of neatly arranged garments.

'You may indeed ask,' said Sarah, 'but we're under no obligation to tell you,' she said, picking up the child's dress and refolding it neatly.

He scowled at them, turned his back and walked away. A few minutes later their first customer arrived. She was impressed with the quality of the work and pleasantly surprised when they told her the price.

She bought five items and Mary-Anne could hardly wait till she was out of earshot to say: 'Diden I tell you so?'

'Who does thon fat-faced fella think he is?' she demanded, after their next customer had gone.

Sarah herself had been wondering the same thing. Clearly, his nose was out of joint and if he wanted to know who they were it could only mean he must somehow see them as competition. In one respect they were indeed competition if he were one of the 'drapers' who handed out cloth and collected garments from home workers, paying them a pittance for their long hours of labour. Anyone else selling similar work would of course be a threat.

They didn't have long to wait for an answer to their questions. Around noon, although they'd remained busy all morning, there was a sudden lull. When Mary-Anne and Sarah observed their neighbours taking out their lunch, they produced their own.

'I hope you had as good a morning as we've had,' said Sarah, addressing a young woman far gone in pregnancy, who was sitting down gratefully on one of the rickety chairs provided with the stall itself.

'Yes, it was good enough but I'm hoping the afternoon will be even better. I've my eye on your baby clothes if we make enough,' she said with a smile.

'Ye'd be welcome to choose what ye want now an' we'll put it by for ye, till ye see how things go,' said Mary-Anne promptly. 'Come an' have a look when ye've had a bit of a rest. It's hard work standin' an' ye might miss what you particularly wanted if ye leave it too long.'

'That's very good of you,' said a tall young man, clearly her husband, as he refolded heavy-duty work trousers and took dark-coloured linen shirts from a battered cardboard box stacked under the equally battered wooden stall itself. 'I think Rachel here took a fancy to the baby's dress your first customer didn't buy.'

'Did you know the gentleman in question?' Sarah asked promptly.

'Oh yes, we know him all right,' said Rachel, looking up at her husband. 'My mother used to do work for him until her eyes got bad. She used to say "he's as mean as get out."'

Sarah had never heard the expression before but it was clear when Mary-Anne laughed aloud that she was entirely familiar with the comment. Clearly, it was not complimentary.

Rachel and Joe were selling seconds of work clothes from a factory near Antrim. They worked on commission, but that was paid weekly in cash. It wasn't a lot, they admitted, but they saved it for the rent which otherwise made a big hole in what Joe earned as a home weaver.

Much encouraged by the friendliness of the young couple, Sarah and Mary-Anne brought out all the baby clothes they still had left and let Rachel choose what she wanted. Joe insisted that in another hour he'd know how much they could spend and there'd still be time to sell anything she'd chosen but couldn't afford.

'Isn't it nice to meet nice people?' Mary-Anne whispered to Sarah as they tidied up their lunch bags, straightened their stock and observed the people who were now reappearing from various eating places as well as shops and offices nearby.

'Well now, will you at least take credit for the idea?' said Mary-Anne, nudging her friend as they sat once again at Sarah's kitchen table. 'Wou'd ye have believed that much if I'd told you?'

Mary-Anne waved her hand at the piles of coins they had just counted and put in saucers and bowls on the table, while Sarah made her notes and added up the total.

'I couldn't have done it without you, Mary-Anne. Are you sure we can keep going?'

'Sure what's t' stop us. I ken see we've got t'fine more stuff in a hurry for next week, but sure when we deliver the money to the women that was tryin' us out can't we ask them if they'd do a bit extra this week till we see how much we'll be needin'? If I know some of them, they'll be only too glad to have the chance, especially those with husbands on short time or out of work. An' I can do extra m'self. I can leave most of my jobs to the boys and do far more than I was doin'.'

'Yes, but every week?' Sarah said cautiously.

'Every week we need stuff till we get a whole team together. Now we've shown we can do it, I'm tellin' you they'll be queuin' up for a decent rate of pay. They've not had that before. Didn't ye hear yerself what young Rachel said about what yer man giv' t' her mother whin she was workin' for him? Sure it was next t'nothin' an' with a red nose like that, he must be on the bottle. Drinkin' poor folks' earnin's!' she ended up furiously.

In spite of herself, Sarah laughed. Mary-Anne was so forthright, she seldom paused to think, but she was also so kind-hearted that it was only the likes of Mr Rednose, as they'd christened him, that got the rough end of her tongue. Sarah knew perfectly well that Mary-Anne was quite capable of finding women in need and getting them organised, provided Sarah herself did all the calculations of their earnings. Mary-Anne had confessed freely she was no good at sums. Her own housekeeping she managed with money in different sized jam pots so she could see where she was and which jar needed the egg money when it came.

They agreed that tonight it was too late to make any more plans, but they'd made a start, had learnt a lot and made a tidy sum from both their own work and the modest commission they were charging to cover their expenses. Sarah was sure they would enjoy the activity even more when they'd had a bit of practice and a proper team they could rely on for creating their stock. Cheered as she was by their success, she couldn't see how she could make time to sew, as well as all the other things she needed to do for the house or forge. But the pencilled figures in her battered jotter could not be argued away. The first day had been a great success.

November proceeded damp and misty but with no hard weather. Sarah and Daisy were able to get to work without problems and once back in Sir George's room she slowly began to get order into the piles of documents she'd now found in cupboards and drawers. To these new piles, she had to add a suitcase full of documents which Sir George presented her with after one of his visits to his Dublin house.

Among the most welcome items to emerge from the Dublin suitcase was the Armagh out-letter file in which the letters Sir George had sent from Castle Dillon had been copied up in a flowing hand with a great many flourishes and squiggles.

Sarah rather wondered if the young man who had abandoned Sir George without notice, leaving his letters and papers in such a state of disorder, had artistic pretensions. But she was still enormously grateful. The presence of the out-letter book meant she could now trace back letters and ongoing negotiations and tell Sir George what he'd said on previous occasions.

She'd come to enjoy the way he smiled at her when she told him about a newly arrived letter, one of a sequence whose predecessors she'd read in the out-letter book. 'Well you know what to say to *him*,' he'd say, washing his hands entirely of the matter.

He was seldom irritable with her and often asked her advice as a 'disinterested bystander'. Sarah was seldom disinterested in any matter touching the management of his estates, his responsibility for tenants or servants, but she knew what he meant. He needed to try out his ideas and she enjoyed their discussions, just as she had enjoyed talking to Jonathan Hancock.

Christmas came and with it the annual supper for staff. Sir George lent her to Mrs Carey so that together they could organise both the family gathering and the purchasing of suitable gifts for all the staff. She'd already found Bridget Carey to be a sensible and practical woman, now she found that she was indeed rather lonely and came to enjoy her company even more. She was sharper and more demanding than Mary-Anne, but with the same quality of forthrightness and a quickness of wit that took Sarah by surprise until she'd got to know her better.

It was only when the family went back to Dublin in January that she realised the winter that she had been dreading had been busy and productive and was now moving forward at great speed. There were times when she felt she missed John even more as the months went by, but the loneliness she had imagined was certainly mitigated by all the new friends she had made.

Often, after a taxing morning, Sir George would insist she left for home before it was fully dark, so she indeed had the long dark nights she had dreaded. But when she'd been dreading them, she hadn't been able to think that those same long evenings would give her time to make a third new dress, to sew small garments for the Thursday market and to write to her friends, particularly Helen in South Carolina, Ben in Peterborough, Ontario, Jonathan Hancock in Yorkshire and her brother Charles in Lurgan.

Charles had never been a keen letter-writer, unlike Jonathan, who had asked her permission to write to her privately as well as via Sir George and their correspondence over the workhouse, but Charles had now become a regular correspondent for the happiest of reasons.

Sometime after Sarah's meeting with Jonathan and her telling him about her plan to encourage women to make garments for sale, she had a long and very cheerful letter from Charles. He said he'd had good news, but it had been totally unexpected and he hadn't quite taken it all in as yet.

He explained he'd been advertising in a local Lurgan paper to try to sell surplus stock and he'd been contacted by a prospective buyer. What emerged from their meeting was that rather than simply buy the stock, this gentleman wanted to rent his workshop, use the existing stock and then bring in fabric from a source he already had in order to give employment. What he needed, he said, was a skilled labour force, stock to make a beginning and someone to manage the process.

Charles was clearly delighted. It was obvious that he didn't want to go to America and leave his elderly adopted parents, but that, as he explained subsequently, was the only way he'd been able to imagine of supporting them, albeit from afar.

Sarah had never known Charles so animated or so full of

ideas. He seemed genuinely interested in her own efforts to sell clothes and to give women the chance to earn a decent wage from their work. He plied her with questions and kept her up-to-date with both his successes and frustrations.

It was when he told her that his well-spoken and mature gentleman had contacts with some charitable society in Yorkshire that Sarah felt sure it was thanks to Jonathan that this project had been put in hand, a project which benefitted not only Charles, but all the weavers and finishers who had lost their employment in the Lurgan workshop over the last failing months.

But her suspicions could certainly be kept secret, even if she did share Charles's good news with Jonathan in the regular letters they now exchanged.

The winter was tedious at times with grey skies and misting rain but there was never any need for Sarah to stay overnight at Castle Dillon or even to be prevented from getting there on time in the first place. Only on one morning did a sudden flurry of snow catch them on an exposed part of the road. She slowed down immediately, but Daisy seemed indifferent to the unexpected white flakes that swirled around them, melting as they touched the rough surface of the road. On the hawthorn hedges, the light flakes settled, creating a crisp dressing that then melted as suddenly as it had come, when the sun reappeared from behind the passing cloud.

'Jewels on the tree,' Sarah said aloud, thinking of her grandmother as the drops shimmered, catching the light, hanging suspended in the still air until they grew too large, then dropped, still shining, into the tangled grass of the hedgerow.

But that was the only snow to come in what was to be a mild winter leading into an early spring. Sarah was grateful for the harmless weather. She knew it made life easier for everyone – she was especially aware of the cost of keeping a fire going and how hard it was for poor people who could sometimes buy food but could seldom pay for fuel as well.

Reading her *Armagh Guardian*, a part of her work now, as well as something she would have chosen to do, she read of the increasing distress in areas where the textile industry was failing. She had never been to Belfast, but a report on the state of the weavers of fancy goods in Ballymacarrett was perfectly intelligible to her even if she didn't know either the Queen's Bridge, Conn's Water or the lanes on both sides of the Holywood road.

Out of 411 looms, 266 were unemployed, while of the remaining 175, a considerable number will be idle this week, for there is little or no prospect at present of webs being procured.

She copied out the extract carefully into a letter she was writing to Jonathan.

Tears sprang to her eyes completely unbidden. Yes, it was the sad plight of these families with no income but also, she admitted, she had seen in an instant her beloved John, a web of cloth on his shoulder after he had bumped into her in the main street of Lisnagarvey – an unromantic first meeting which had become a joke between them.

She dried her tears and tried to go on with her letter, but

her eyes misted over yet again. It was not simply the stark message of the newspaper she was copying into her letter:

The people (194 families, over 1,000 people) are in positive want – in absolute danger of starvation, perhaps before another week unless effective relief be procured.

It was the thought that she had a comfortable home, more friends than ever she'd had in her whole life, and that she had enough to eat and money in the bank. How could she return in love and give thanks for all she had without John, whom she had loved so dearly?

And yet again she thought of her grandmother. 'Do what you can, do it in love . . .' Yes, there were things she could do, but she didn't have to do it all herself. The important thing was to do what she could. She should give thanks every time she counted a pile of money to go out to women sewing by their own firesides.

Mary-Anne had been doing most of the collecting of clothes for the market and the delivering of money from their sales, but then Scottie had offered his help. He would drive her to work on a Saturday morning, take Daisy out of the shafts and fit her up with a saddle lent by Sir George from the stables. Then, thanks to Sam Keenan who said he could always manage a day or two on his own, Scottie would deliver little envelopes of money to all the women on this side of Armagh, while Lily and Harry Magowan did the same job for the women in the city.

'Ask and it shall be given,' another of grandmother's sayings.

She smiled suddenly, her sadness passing as she thought of Sam Keenan's more robust version. 'Well, if ye niver ask, ye'll niver get!'

He had a point, and perhaps it was one she should pay more attention to. Being self-reliant was one thing, but not accepting graciously your own limits was another. Perhaps there was more she could do to address the ocean of need she knew existed if she asked for help.

Smiling again, she went back to her letter to Jonathan and asked him what he thought could be done for the weavers of Ballymacarrett, and indeed all the textile workers in Ulster at present in such distress.

CHAPTER SIXTEEN

Sarah could hardly believe that even before the end of April she could no longer wear either the plum dress or the newer sage green one which had sustained her through both autumn and winter. Both of them were already too warm, even in the large rooms and airy spaces of Castle Dillon. Everyone agreed, 'Sure we've had no winter this year.'

Taking out her much-loved blue dress from the chest in her bedroom on the last Saturday in April 1846, Sarah shed tears. This was the dress she had made for her wedding in early April, three years ago. It was also the dress in which she'd driven to Castle Dillon to ask Sir George if he would allow her to postpone her rent for six months.

It was, of course, the dress in which she'd been approached by Jonathan Hancock in the library of Castle

Dillon when Sir George had informed him that there was a woman 'of his persuasion' already waiting.

That was when he had first spoken of her as a 'sensible woman'.

She smiled as she stood at the ironing board gently coaxing away the creases in the light fabric. She thought of both Sir George and Jonathan, now good friends in different ways. Sir George had refused her delayed payment when she'd offered it to him this very week. He'd said promptly that she could enter it in her records as a 'bonus for effort beyond the call of duty'.

More than once, Sir George had insisted she'd saved his sanity and she'd had to admit when she thought back to those towers of papers and the missing documents to which they referred, that he did have a point. It would be wrong not to give thanks for her achievements and the appreciation it had brought her.

But on this lovely, warm April day, she still had to face the anniversary of John's death. This year, the date fell on a Sunday, but whether it was the day or the date on the calendar, she doubted if she could ever forget that sunlit spring day he went off to Armagh, smiling and waving goodbye, and his return, a white-faced figure sprawled on a door carried by colleagues and neighbours.

She knew how that image had haunted poor Scottie who'd kept lookout from the pillar with the best view down the road. He had wept in her arms more than once, as the memory came back to him. There was little comfort she could give him except an attempt at reassurance that she would look after him.

Now Scottie, inches taller than this time last year and growing in confidence all the time, was part of the team running the marketing of handmade clothes. He had even found some women in need of work living in Loughgall, near the old schoolmaster who now enjoyed his visits as once he'd welcomed Ben.

Dear Ben. That was another event she'd never forget, when he'd found his voice and then amazed both Scottie and Sam Keenan. Ben wrote regularly both to her and to Scottie and sent what dollars he could spare to help Scottie take care of his granny. Ben's own old nurse, whom he'd supported as best he could on an apprentice's allowance, had indeed died shortly after his departure.

Things change and one must move with change, she reflected, thinking of her brother, now hard at work again in the Lurgan workshop and Jonathan Hancock, now very much her friend; Jonathan, who was currently in north Donegal looking at the possibility of improving the diet of the poorest people. Fish, he said, in his most recent letter, were very plentiful around their coasts, but only accessible in the best of weather when their flimsy curraghs were able to be put to sea. He'd told her then how he was looking for some Scottish fishermen who would come and teach them to use the new boats being bought for them by one of the wealthy landowners.

Suddenly, weary of being indoors when the sun was beaming golden shafts of light on the well-swept kitchen floor, she put her iron back to heat on the hearth and went and stood at the door, her eyes dazzled by the bright light.

'Good mornin', Mrs Hamilton. Are ye enjoyin' the sun?'

The voice was familiar, the figure indistinct through watering eyes, but when she shaded them she beamed with pleasure. Paddy McCann, the good-hearted man who had offered her a good price for the mending of the damaged trap. And an impressive job he had made of it.

She insisted he come in for a mug of tea and a bit of cake while the edgy black stallion who pulled his own trap was shoed by Scottie, to whom Sam left all the shoeing these days.

He told her he was glad to see her looking so well, that he'd heard about her job at Castle Dillon as well as the good work she was doing for the home workers. He asked, predictably, if the trap was going well and she was glad to be able to tell him that in all honesty without his work on the trap the clothes market on a Thursday would never have happened, never mind her daily drives to Castle Dillon.

'Ach, sure isn't that great,' he said beaming with pleasure. 'D'ye mine you were lukin' to sell it after poor John went? Isn't it a mercy that no one was after it when you were a bit short o' money? You couldn't do either of yer jobs now wi'out it. Now, if it ever gives ye a problem, yer to send young Scottie straight over on Daisy an' I'll either come and fix it here, or I'll lend ye my trap to put Daisy in, till I can see m' way to do it. An' there'll be no charge,' he added vigorously, as he drained his mug and stood up.

'One good deed deserves another, an' I'd not be much good with a needle an' thread,' he added, laughing, as Scottie appeared at the door to tell him he'd taken his horse for a drink at the trough and had left him tethered in the shade behind the forge.

* * *

Within days of Paddy's visit, the weather had settled even finer and drier than in April. Already in the first week of May, the hawthorn blossom was weighing down the branches of the hedgerows and filling the air with its sweet perfume. When a brief, pleasant shower began to settle the dust round the entrance to the forge early one Sunday evening, Sarah put down her sewing and stepped outside to feel the warm rain on her face. She laughed at herself. When in her life had she ever celebrated a shower of rain?

But she was not the only one to celebrate. Two days later, the *Armagh Guardian* reported the brief shower of Sunday night saying, 'more of which would be very desirable to the farmers'. It then went on to do a round-up of news from surrounding areas saying that the crops around the district of Moy and Charlemont looked remarkably well and healthy, and so 'forward' in that district was the season that a field of upland hay had already been cut and cocked.

Provisions of every sort are abundant, they added, and are comparatively cheap: potatoes three and a half pence to four and a half pence a stone, several samples of new ones having been brought to market. At Aughnacloy, the potato market on Wednesday was so very large that room could scarcely be found for all the carts.

Sarah reported this heartening news to Jonathan in Donegal adding that her neighbour, Billy, said he'd never seen such vigorous growth so early in the year.

Jonathan replied immediately saying it was splendid news – for with a generous crop the merchants could not afford to store potatoes till the price went up as they had the previous year. Provided the markets were full of sound potatoes, there was at least a source of food, the problem being the lack of the wherewithal to purchase for those with no cash income.

He had noted, he said, in the last set of minutes she'd copied out for him that the number of admissions to Armagh Workhouse had gone up. Despite the good weather and hopeful predictions, free emigration schemes were again being advertised by landowners who saw no prospect of receiving their rents.

Sarah read his letters avidly both for the information he shared with her and in the hope of getting some clue to his well-being. Although he wrote most regularly and with apparent enjoyment, she'd noticed at times a distinct hint of sadness in his letters. Perhaps, like herself, he got very tired and then could not lift his spirits. She wondered if he might have had bad news about his wife, of whom he never spoke, but she was almost sure that she'd not find out unless they could meet and talk face-to-face. She hoped they might meet sometime in May or June before he went back to Yorkshire.

In the meantime, the long, light days were filled with activity at Castle Dillon. For the first year, the extensive gardens around the house were in production. Fruit and vegetables were so prolific that the kitchen staff were overworked with bottling, jam-making and preserving. The outside staff, organised by Robert Ross, were responsible for delivering cartloads of produce to churches and chapels who had offered to deliver to those in greatest need.

Many of the gentry who sat on the Guardian's Committee with Sir George made similar arrangements for simply giving food to those in need in their immediate area, despite the contrary arguments that charity did not solve the problems and only public works providing labour for men would resolve the situation.

As Sarah copied out details of discussions and disagreements to be sent to colleagues of Sir George, she felt her spirits falter. The more she knew about rents, and cess, and presentments, the more she saw the complexity of the situation. The ocean of need would not be resolved by the exceptional fine stems of heavy-eared wheat and oats brought into the *Armagh Guardian* office, nor the bumper crops they so happily predicted.

The whole situation however changed one Friday evening when Mary-Anne arrived so red in the face from hurrying that she had to sit down at the table and lean on its worn surface till she got her breath back.

'What *has* happened, Mary-Anne? Is Billy or one of the boys ill? Tell me what I can do to help,' Sarah said, pulling out the wooden chair beside her and catching at her hand.

Mary-Anne shook her head as tears welled up in her eyes.

'Billy went out t' mend a hole in one of the hedges where the cattle could push out an' get inta the next field where some o' the new potato rigs are. They were all lookin' as right as rain on Wednesday but when Billy went to the hole in the hedge t' mend it about an hour ago he cou'd see it's got the blight. An' it's not just that field but all what they've put in this year. The whole lot of it was just startin' ti' smell. I think Billy an' the boys are heartbroke. Shure I couldn't get a word outa one of them.'

There was very little Sarah could say. After Billy's very slight losses the previous year, this was a whole different situation. With his cows producing milk and butter, and Sarah earning commission as well as selling her own work, they would certainly not starve, but that was not the point. Like being put out of work, there was still the dislocation and disruption of what had happened and the burden of paying the rent when there was so little cash coming in.

Sarah made tea, but neither of them could manage even a small slice from the fruit cake she'd made the previous evening.

Even before the *Armagh Guardian* published its report, the news had already circulated around the whole district. This time the failure was complete. None of the schemes for retrieving the good portions from damaged tubers the previous year would be of the slightest use this time. With this crop, the rotten tops led down to equally blackened and disintegrating messy potatoes.

This year there was nothing but a stinking mass, with a smell so distinctive it could not be mistaken.

For the next few weeks, people might still have some of last year's potatoes stored in straw-lined clamps or dry potato houses, but they wouldn't last long. Worse still, merchants who had good supplies they'd been holding for that period between old crop and new could now put up their prices even further. Once those were gone, the chances of getting another crop in the infected soil were exceedingly unlikely.

* * *

June, a month Sarah particularly loved, was very enjoyable as far as the weather went. There were none of the hot, humid days that had driven her in April to bring out her coolest dress. The long light evenings with still, golden sunsets and pleasant showers kept the ground moist but did not damage the growing crops. Sadly, however, the news of the spreading blight in every part of Ireland seemed to depress everyone, even those who had both money and food to feed their own families.

Sarah began to dread the arrival of the newspapers: the *Armagh Guardian* fetched by whichever of the Halligans had business in town on a Tuesday and *The Times* and *London Illustrated News* provided in Sir George's library for anyone, visitor or servant, who chose to read them.

She read them all dutifully, fully aware that Sir George needed her to be well informed, but she found little comfort or prospect of help in any of them, for what was happening all around her, as poverty increased and the government increasingly argued, delayed and disagreed about ways of providing relief.

There were, however, more urgent pressures upon Sarah herself. Sir George, having agreed to accompany his wife to her parents' home in Warwickshire with the children, left a note telling her that provided she acknowledged any incoming letters and quoted the date of his return to those requesting the favour of an immediate reply, she was free to spend the remaining time as she wished, whether at home or in his library.

He did ask, however, that she would oversee the financial side of the management of the household, paying staff and household bills as usual. He referred her to yet another pile of papers, sadly in need of sorting and filing, but the only records available to help her. Except, as she discovered, the incredible memory of Bridget Carey for even the smallest household items and a neatly copied-up notebook kept by Robert Ross detailing the needs of the stables.

The first week of Sir George's absence was the most taxing she had ever spent, even remembering those first days when she had struggled to clear the backlog left by his departing man of business. She was so exhausted by the time she got home that she found two letters from Jonathan and had not the energy to respond to either.

When she read them for a second time the next day before setting out for Castle Dillon, she discovered that he'd been called to Dublin to report to the Yearly Meeting there. He said he would enclose his address in tomorrow's letter. She read the second letter yet again but found no address. Sadly disappointed, she set about her morning chores with only half her mind upon them.

But the taxing week was not yet over. Halfway through the morning James, the footman, arrived with a note which had just been delivered. A young man was waiting for her in the stables, he said, and he had already spoken to Robert Ross and asked him to fetch Daisy.

'Oh, no,' Sarah said, as she scanned the hastily written message. 'James, I'll have to go home. Will you please apologise to Mrs Carey for me? We were to work together this afternoon but my neighbour has died.'

'Ach dear, I'm sorry indeed. I'll tell her all right. D'ye want me to run down and tell the young man yer comin'?'

'Thank you, I've some papers to collect to take with me. But I'll be as quick as I can,' she said, noticing, despite her distress, that James had abandoned his usual formality and had spoken with a soft southern accent.

She concentrated on gathering together the documents that needed to go to the bank and putting them in her shopping bag. 'Oh Mary-Anne, my dear friend,' she said, as she picked up her notebook, 'Whatever has happened, what's happened at all?'

CHAPTER SEVENTEEN

Despite Daisy's willing co-operation, the short journey to the foot of Drumilly Hill seemed to take such a long time. Sarah felt tears run down her face and didn't bother to wipe them. Only when her nose began to do the same, did she drive one-handed and take a handkerchief from her pocket to mop herself up.

The road was deserted, but as she came close to Halligan's farm, she met a man on horseback riding in the opposite direction. She didn't know the man himself, but from his neat dark suit and white shirt, she assumed he was the doctor.

Jamsey, hearing Daisy's hooves on the hard-packed earth of the farmyard, came out to meet her.

'How is she?' Sarah asked, bending down towards him.

'Waitin' fer ye,' he said shortly. 'Go on in. The doctor's just away,' he added, as he took her reins, helped her down and moved the trap round the side of the house.

'Sarah, thank God you're here. I jus' don't know where t' start.'

Mary-Anne, dry-eyed and wearing her working clothes, jumped up from her chair, came and threw her arms round Sarah and hugged her fiercely. She held her for a few moments as if she would never let her go.

'I jus' can't think right,' she said, shaking her head. 'Jamsey's no better than meself and young Billy's away into Armagh an' dosen' even know yet. How am ah goin' ta tell him? Sure he an' the father were two peas outa the one pod an' not just in looks ither.'

'What happened, Mary-Anne? Just tell me.'

Mary-Anne put the kettle down and poked up the fire, adding turf and small pieces of coal to hurry it up. Then she took a deep breath and began telling Sarah the whole story, her voice perfectly steady, her hands folded in her lap.

'We were up at our usual time an' Billy away out to see t' the cows, while I went to wake the boys. He hardly said a word to me afore he went, but then he niver does. That's jus' his way an' young Billy is jus' the same,' she added, drawing breath. 'The boys like their porridge afore they go out, but my Billy is always out first thing and I wait an' make his porridge with me own after I've put the place straight.'

Sarah nodded encouragingly, trying to be patient, knowing that by telling the story Mary-Anne was probably trying to get things sorted in her own mind. She tried to sit perfectly still though the tension she was feeling made her want to leap to her feet and do something.

'Well, I looked at the clock an' thought to meself, "time I had the porridge on", so I gets it all ready an' was jus goin' to put it in the bowls when Jamsey came in lukin' for somethin' or other he needed. "Where's yer father?", I sez. "Does he not want his breakfast?"

'Well, then he tole me he hadn't seen him at all this mornin' an' I sez to him: "Well, where can he be?" It's not as if we had a big farm o' land. Shure its only twenty acres or so,' she added, for Sarah's benefit.

'So the long an' the short of it is the pair of us went out to look for him, for young Billy was away to Armagh, an' Jamsey went one way and I went the ither an' I found him lying dead in the hedge where he'd mended that hole a couple of weeks ago, that Friday night when he foun' the blight. He musta been lukin' over that bit that he'd mended, like he did on the Friday night, and he jus' dropped down dead inta the hedge. The doctor says it was his heart. It must jus' have give out. An' sure I shou'den be surprised for he was heartbroke when he saw all that hard work on the potato fields lost, an' not knowin what worse was in front of us,' she said, standing up and bringing the teapot and mugs from the dresser to the table. She made tea from the steaming kettle which had been rattling its lid furiously as she finished her story.

'Now drink up, Sarah, for you're as white as a sheet. I'll be all right now yer here. I know what we hafta do, I was jus' all through m'self an' I'm better now.'

Mary-Anne was as good as her word. She was not overwhelmed by grief but clearly the shock had affected her. Now she set too in her usual practical way, her only problem being money. She didn't know if they had any, apart from what she kept in unlabelled jam pots in the bottom of the dresser, the different sizes holding sums for the various expenses she herself dealt with.

'Does Billy keep money and papers somewhere safe?' asked Sarah, remembering the brown handbag.

'Aye, he's got a blue folder tied with a bit of string. It nearly fell apart one day it was that full when he took it out from behind the Bible to look for somethin'. So I got him the piece of string an' said maybe he needed anither folder for them to share the load. But sure he niver bothered.'

'It'll be up there,' she went on, waving to a wall-hanging bookcase with a cretonne curtain to keep out the smoke from the hearth. 'Don't for any sakes try to move them books, they're heavy as lead and dirty forby, for I can't stan' on a chair to dust them, me head gets that light,' she explained, as she drew Sarah over to the alcove on one side of the hearth.

Sarah was taller than Mary-Anne and feared neither heights nor a wobbling chair on an uneven floor. The bulging blue folder was clearly visible behind a pile of Bible commentaries, the massive Bible itself and some account books with marbled covers.

Getting it out was hard on the back, but Sarah managed it and brought the cardboard folder to the table.

'Do you mind if I look to see what I can find?' Sarah asked cautiously.

'Ach, away with yerself,' replied Mary-Anne dismissively, 'sure you an' me has no secrets. I just hope you fine somethin' so I can send for the undertaker. I'd not be one bit a good doin' what hasta be done.'

The bulging file looked intimidating but on closer inspection the pieces of paper, many torn or discoloured at the edges, were actually in strict chronological order. They went back to the point where Billy's father had signed over the farm to him some twenty years earlier. Most of the tattered papers were receipts, but leafing steadily through so that she would miss nothing, she found a Friendly Society paying-in book – just the same as the one she'd found in the brown handbag after John died.

Mary-Anne had disappeared at the sound of a trap, so Sarah stood up, stretched her aching shoulders and breathed a sigh of relief. She'd been wondering how she could help Mary-Anne from her own savings and whether what she could manage would be enough, but now there was no need. The Friendly Society would pay for the funeral and the small collection of large papery fivers she'd found sandwiched together, all in the one place, between the receipts, would keep Mary-Anne's jam pots topped up for a long time – even longer, if they went on selling clothes in the market as successfully as they had so far. Billy had no bank book. His life's savings she held in her hand.

She felt totally overwhelmed by sadness. Billy was somewhere in his forties, a bit younger than Mary-Anne. He had worked hard all his life, asked for little and done his best for his sons. She wondered if it was actually the failure of the potato crop that had caused his heart failure; the sense of something he could not deal with by hard work defeating him completely.

Sarah went outside and, as she expected, she saw young Billy leaning against the trap, silent and white-faced.

Mary-Anne stood near him, but did not touch him. Like father, like son, she'd once said, neither of them could give you a kiss or a hug. It just wasn't in them.

They both looked at her, even Mary-Anne's mobile face stiffened like her son's.

'I'm so sorry about your father, Billy. I didn't know him that well, but John valued him highly. He said he couldn't want a better neighbour.'

Billy glanced at her momentarily and then stood looking at his boots.

'What should we do now, Sarah?' Mary-Anne asked quietly.

'Perhaps Billy and Jamsey could go to the undertaker in Armagh and bring us back some bread and cake at the same time, till we get our own baked tomorrow morning. I'll write a notice for the *Guardian* while you make them a bite to eat now. If I put "funeral details to follow", is that all right?'

'Aye, as right as rain,' said Mary-Anne.

To Sarah's surprise, Billy managed to glance at her and nod his agreement.

Sometimes in the next three days, Sarah couldn't quite believe what was happening. She had been through it all before. She thought at one point that the wake and the funeral was like a play in which everyone knew their lines: when to come and when to go, when to accept food and drink, when to decline politely. She realised she'd been given the part of Mary-Anne's sister, so she did everything that a sister would do, just like the night after John's funeral. Then, Mary-Anne had been a sister to her when she'd lost their unborn child.

Apart from a brief visit to Armagh with papers and rents from Castle Dillon for the bank and the task of opening of an account there for Mary-Anne, Sarah was seldom out of the house at the foot of the hill, except late at night when she went home to sleep and change her clothes. After four days, it was Mary-Anne who said, 'Yer worn out, Sarah. Away home an' forget all about me for a bit. I'll come up when I'm more meself. I'm all right. After all ye've done fer me, I won't be going back on meself. That's a promise.'

Sarah smiled to herself. Mary-Anne's word was as good as any Quaker yea or nay, and she knew she was longing for the quiet of her own fireside.

She set off up the hill hardly noticing the calm, golden evening now fading somewhat earlier into a soft and quiet dusk. The month had moved on. Tomorrow, Friday, would be the last day of July. She'd have to go into Armagh for groceries and money to pay both Sam and Scottie, who'd thoughtfully assured her there was no hurry.

The front door was closed, the house stuffy, but she was glad to find the fire carefully smoored and not out. She left the front door open, stirred the fire and put the kettle down. How long had it been since she'd had tea by her own fireside, since she'd sewn for her own pleasure, or read a newspaper? It had been four long days but it seemed longer; they were so full of people, and talk, and activity.

She took a great deep breath, eased her shoulders – which always ached when she was tired – sat down in her usual place and watched the stirred fire till it threw out tiny flames and set the kettle murmuring gently before it started to sing.

She sat for a long time drinking her tea and thinking about the life she now had. She missed John in so many ways and she wondered if she always would. When she was sewing, she could almost imagine him watching her as he'd always done. When she handed someone a mug of tea, she thought of his thank you, always in terms of some homely phrase rather than the bare words themselves. She dreamt of him often and couldn't quite believe he wasn't there when she woke in her empty bed.

Yet, despite her loneliness for John, she now recognised that she knew more people than she'd ever known in all her thirty-odd years: the staff at Castle Dillon to begin with, from the eminently practical Bridget Carey, to the good-looking, but uneasy, James, once the newest footman. All of them were on easy terms with her, as she was with them.

She was aware, too, that in the last four days she'd been treated as if she'd always been Mary-Anne's friend and neighbour. She'd been given a place in the community so that, at one level, she was no longer on her own or 'on her lone', as Annie the housemaid had said to her on her first day in Sir George's study, a day that now seemed a very long time ago.

She now had so much to make her happy, not least the work she did for Sir George and her contact with Jonathan: their regular letters, both public and private, and their occasional meetings. She had so missed his letters in this last week or so, and wondered if, for some reason, he'd sent them to Castle Dillon and they'd be waiting for her tomorrow. Even more, she'd missed writing to him, always knowing that he would read with attention whatever she laid in front of him and that he'd reply directly to any question she asked him.

It surprised her that she could miss someone so much when she hardly knew them and had spent only hours in their company. She stood up and peered at the clock, the room now dim and shadowy, except where the flicker of flames reflected from the glass doors of the dresser and bounced off china and glazed ware sitting on open shelves.

She had just trimmed the new wick in the lamp and had satisfied herself with its performance, when she heard a knock at the front door. Startled, because the door was still standing open and no one ever knocked it when it was open, she stood for a moment, trying to identify the dark figure that stood there.

As she moved towards the door, the figure became visible in the spill from the lamp.

'Sarah, are you all right? I've been so worried when you didn't write. Tell me you are well,' he said, stepping towards her.

For one strange moment, she thought he was going to put his arms around her, but then he drew back a little and stood looking at her.

'Jonathan,' she said, as if she couldn't think of anything else to say. 'I'm perfectly well, just very tired,' she added, collecting herself.

'But you haven't been at work for several days.'

'How do you know that?' she asked, even more surprised, as she waved him to the armchair opposite hers.

'I went looking for you at Castle Dillon and the blacksmith told me you'd had to go home several days ago.

I've been so concerned. I kept hoping for a letter so we could plan to meet,' he went on hurriedly. 'There's nothing wrong between us, is there? You would tell me, wouldn't you, if I said or did something to upset you?'

'Yes, of course I would,' she replied easily. 'We've both been brought up to speak what's in our heart and say what we think to be true. I was so sad not to be able to write to you, but you forgot to include your address. You said you would in that second letter you sent from Dublin but you must have forgotten and I haven't got a Yorkshire address where it might have been forwarded to you.'

'And would you have written if you'd had my Yorkshire address?'

'Yes, of course I would.'

He sighed and took a deep breath, the lines of stress moving from his face. 'You're not angry are you, that I should feel so bereft when deprived of your letters?'

She looked across at him, sitting in John's chair and was reminded of John's phrase: 'He's not sayin' the half of it.' He was, however, saying as much as he deemed proper, but only someone totally unthinking and insensitive could fail to see the warmth in his manner, the affection in his eyes. To her surprise, she had a sudden urge to put her arms around him and reassure him.

'I'm delighted to see you,' she said honestly. 'I'm just so glad I was here; I've been with Mary-Anne for four days now. She's lost her husband, Billy, which is why I had to come home from work on Monday. I'll be back at work tomorrow.'

'And Saturday?'

'Only to collect the post to bring home,' she said easily. 'When Sir George is away he leaves me free to come and go as I please, so long as I check for anything urgent. There seldom is – just the same kind of things all the time, most of which I can handle for him.'

'So you could come and have lunch with me in the Charlemont Arms Hotel on Saturday before I go back to Yorkshire?'

'Yes, I could,' she said smiling. 'I've had news from Toronto, which might please you. I can tell you all about it then.'

He smiled and looked her straight in the eye. 'I've never seen you tired before, you must go straight to bed and sleep well,' he said, standing up.

'Jonathan, how did you get here? Have you a driver waiting?'

'No, there were none available,' he said easily. 'All needed, I was told, to collect people for some event in the Tontine Rooms. So I walked,' he added, as they reached the front door.

He turned towards her, touched her hand lightly and said: 'But I shall enjoy the walk back with a lighter heart. It will probably seem to be no distance at all.'

CHAPTER EIGHTEEN

Sarah woke early on Saturday morning; a shaft of sunlight fell, like a pointer across the floor, through the gap left in the curtains where she'd drawn them wearily the previous evening. She admitted freely as she got to her feet that she was still tired after the long days of Billy's departure and the unexpected pile of letters and queries that had awaited her the previous day at Castle Dillon. There were some items she still had to deal with but she smiled as she drew the curtains back on sunlit fields and thought of Jonathan and their meeting at lunchtime in Armagh.

There were household tasks from yesterday to be completed as well as those that waited on the desk, so she did her morning chores, ate breakfast with Scottie and told him she'd be going to work at the usual time. When he just nodded, she wondered why he was so uncharacteristically silent. Usually, over breakfast, he told her about the people who'd come to the forge the previous day or gave her an account of his most recent visit to his friend in Loughgall, old Mr McMahon, who had been a teacher all his working life.

Harry McMahon, she had discovered, now spent his time and his small pension on whatever books he could lay his hands on when he made his visits to Belfast. His younger sister lived within walking distance of Smithfield, a market where you could find a strange and varied collection of things to buy. Harry was well-known in all the second-hand bookshops and well accustomed to bargaining, so his very limited means would stretch further. Scottie, like Ben before him, was now working his way through the library Harry had managed to accumulate.

But Scottie continued to drink his tea in silence. He stood up as soon as he had finished with a muttered 'Thank you', as he went out to harness Daisy and make sure the trap was ready for Sarah's departure.

Sarah washed and changed her clothes with half her mind on Scottie. She decided that when he handed over the reins she really must ask him if all was well at home.

But it was Sam Keenan who was standing tightening the girths on Daisy's harness when she was ready to go. As he helped her up into the trap, she asked him where Scottie was.

'Ach, ah think it's the oul lady, the granny. He ast me if I'd mine if he went back home for an hour or two to see to her. I sez it was all right with me but shou'den he away an' tell you. But he jus' shakes the head an' says "Sure she'll understan'." Ah hope I did right,' he added, looking uneasy. 'We sometimes do be busy of a Saturday.'

'You did the right thing, Sam,' Sarah replied reassuringly. 'Scottie is no good at asking for what he needs. If there's a horse comes you'd rather not shoe yourself, let them come back on Monday. We're not so hard-pressed we can't risk losing a job if the poor woman isn't well. I'll be back early, sometime this afternoon. Make sure you take a rest and go and make yourself tea at lunchtime,' she said, shaking the reins, much to Daisy's satisfaction.

Sam smiled, much relieved and amused by the way Daisy tossed her head. They both knew she was not an animal that liked standing waiting once she was in harness.

The August morning would have been warm, but for a robust breeze that caught up dried leaves from the side of the road and blew them swirling from one grass verge to the other. Some of them were papery and dry already. The season, which came early and brought harvest a month ahead of what was usual, was continuing to come early. As she turned along the now familiar stretch of road leading to the back entrance, she looked up, saw gold and pink leaves on the chestnuts and immediately thought of John and how he used to say the signs of the coming season were always there well in advance if you had eyes to look in the right places.

It would be the second autumn without John. She wondered if she would always remember the sayings they'd shared, the trees and hedgerows they'd scanned on their walks together, enjoying the quiet and the fresh air after the long day's work, looking for familiar things: the tangle of honeysuckle working its way along the top of a hedge; the stone-built gateposts; the entrance to a long-abandoned farmhouse, wreathed in a prolific rambling rose now grown wild from what was once the small front garden; a young tree growing out of the decaying chimney stack, getting bigger each year.

Knowing the enormity of need since the failure of the potato crop, not just on Billy Halligan's farm or merely here in Ulster, but all over Ireland, she sometimes felt that the only comfort to be found lay in plants and flowers that went on blooming: a symbol of hope, that when growth began again there might once more be enough food for everyone.

It was a pleasant thought but she had to admit that most of the time she felt the weight of information coming into Castle Dillon, by way of newspapers and documents, was simply reinforcing the view that Ireland would never be the same again, whatever happened next. The prospects for the coming year looked grim in the extreme with little in the way of relief works underway and no outdoor relief other than the generosity of individuals and small groups.

As if a great black cloud had obscured the sun, her memories of John, instead of being gentle and fond, became an aching sense of loss. She wondered if all widows kept somewhere in their hearts the idea that one morning they would wake up with the dear, familiar figure still asleep beside them. She knew perfectly well in her head that it could not be so, but a part of her heart still ached with longing for something she felt she could never have again.

The morning's work challenged and absorbed her, but the sense of loss that had come upon her on the way to work did not dissolve. It only moved away until a further challenge presented itself.

'I've brought yer tea . . . Sarah,' Annie said, as she held the tray one-handed, closed the door behind her with the other and walked steadily across the room to the desk.

Sarah smiled. After many months, Annie had finally managed to call her by her first name when she was alone, but neither of them had forgotten their very first meeting when Annie had addressed her anxiously as 'My lady'. For Sarah, it was one of the pleasures of coming to work: seeing the way the anxious and lonely girl from the workhouse had gained in confidence and skill, very much as Scottie had. She had come a long way from the emaciated and trembling girl in the ill-fitting black dress and the starched white apron.

Annie put the tray down carefully on the one remaining space on the desk and stood watching her, knowing that sometimes if she was in the middle of a document she'd have to finish it before she lost track of what it was saying. She stood now waiting patiently until Sarah put the piece of paper down, looked up at her and smiled.

Sarah was taken aback, not only was Annie looking well-fed, she was positively blooming, a kind of radiance glowing all round her.

'I missed you on Monday and every day after, till I heard what happened to your poor friend,' she began. 'I was waitin' for you to tell you somethin' nobody else knows. I'm engaged t' be married,' she said, beaming.

231

'Oh Annie, how lovely,' Sarah replied, anxious about just what age Annie might be. She certainly couldn't be more than sixteen. 'Do I know the lucky man?' she asked, wondering if it was wise to encourage what might be a real problem to Bridget Carey, who could dismiss her if she thought fit.

'Aye, surely ye know him. James, the footman. He's three years older than me but he says we'll have to wait a while and it'll be better to keep it secret. Except fer you. He said I could tell you, but no one else. And I was disappointed on Monday when you'd had to go home,' she added, her smile disappearing.

'My goodness, Annie, this is a real surprise,' said Sarah, touched by the confidence, but anxious lest there was disappointment to come. 'Can I ask what age you are?'

'I'm almost sixteen, but Jimmy . . . I mean, James, says I'm sensible beyond m' years. I don't mind havin' t' wait, or to keep it secret, so long as I know I'll have someone belongin' to me one day. I'm not on m' lone any more an' nor is he, even though he has a father who has nothin' to do with him, except gettin' him this job. He niver speaks to him except to correct him in front of others, an' he lets no one know he's anythin' to do with him.'

'You mean James's father is here on the staff?' Sarah asked, wondering how such a secret could ever have been kept.

'Aye, he's the big bossy butler,' she said sharply, 'but James is not one bit like him. He mus' take after his mother. The poor wumman died when he was born, jus' like mine,' she said sadly.

'How little we know about each other,' Sarah said thoughtfully, thinking of John and his phrase about 'not telling her the half of it'. 'But perhaps, Annie,' she went on, 'some secrets are better than others. Do you think you and James can keep your secret? How will you meet? If you even go for a walk, it'll be all around the servants' hall by the morning.'

To her surprise, Annie grinned happily.

'We've foun' somewhere nobody knows about. It's in one of the old barns, a loft that's empty an' had no ladder up. James foun' it an' got a ladder an' hid the ladder nearby. We never go together an' we always go by different ways, but once we're there we can talk till our heart's content. James is learnin' me how to write so he can leave me messages when he gets kep' back, if yer man says he's needed,' she added crossly. 'But I don't hafta worry about him. I know I'll see him at work an' know he's all right, even though we niver look at each other unless there's no one about.'

Sarah shared her biscuits as she always did and finished her tea, knowing that Annie would be missed the moment preparations were begun for lunch.

'Give James my congratulations,' she said smiling. 'I wish you joy,' she added quickly, motioning for Annie to hurry away.

The second the door closed behind her, she took out her hanky and wiped the tears that had spilt down her face the moment Annie picked up the tray and turned her back. She wondered what might lie in store for two young people with so little to help them beyond the status and income of very junior household servants.

But at least they had that, she told herself, as she set about clearing her desk and leaving it ready for Monday morning. They would not starve like the millions of others throughout Ireland no longer able to afford the last of the surviving potatoes held in store by middlemen waiting to get the best possible price. Nor would they die of neglect were they to become ill, for Sir George would never tolerate that. But life could be so hard for those with no sheltering arms to protect them. She would do what she could and hope against hope that life would be kind to them.

The stiff breeze had dropped to a whisper as she turned out of the back entrance and drove the three odd miles into Armagh; the sky a vivid blue except where the heat of midday had built up huge castles of white cloud beyond the low, green hills. All was quiet on the road but she expected it to be busy in Armagh, for despite the increase in poverty, there were still many townspeople and larger farmers who had enough for their needs, and gentry who had always shopped locally.

It was these people who had patronised the stall she and Mary-Anne had set up in the weekly clothes market, missing out only this last week in almost a year of successful trading. That work would go on giving Mary-Anne a much-needed income along with the network of women, now well-established, who were happy to produce whatever they asked for.

It was still but a drop in a sea of poverty, but it was as much as she could manage for the moment.

She told herself she ought to give thanks and take

strength from the good things: for the happiness of Annie and James, for Sam Keenan's complete recovery from an illness that had carried off many a more robust-looking man, for her own regular income and the many friendships she had made. She was lonely only for John, but she could not now say, like Annie had once said, that she was on her lone with no one belongin' to her – that simply wasn't true any more.

Determined to cheer up before she met Jonathan, she took Daisy to the stables behind the Charlemont Arms and greeted Davy, the stable boy, whom she'd got to know on her regular visits to buy groceries or go to the Ulster Bank for Sir George.

'Here you are, Davy, your friend Daisy,' she said, as Davy took her reins and helped her down.

'Do you know how long ye'll be?' he asked politely, eyeing the full stalls and parked traps.

'Not as long as usual, probably. I've just come for lunch with a friend,' she said honestly.

'We're busy today, Mrs Hamilton,' he explained. 'Ah don't think I can take any more. Ye'll certainly be the last one yourself if it's anither trap that comes,' he went on. 'I could fit in a horseman, but ye see yerself I couldn't do a trap. Would yer friend be comin' in a trap or maybe a carriage?'

'Do you know, Davy, I've no idea. He's staying in the hotel here but he may well have hired a trap. What would he have to do then?'

'Well, if he's stayin' here I'll hafta to fit him in somehow. Maybe if someone's had their lunch early, they'll be goin' home soon,' he said, beaming at her as she gave him a small coin, knowing he always took good care of Daisy.

She smoothed out her skirt and walked slowly round to the front of the hotel. English Street was busy and there seemed to be something on across the road at the Tontine Rooms. As there was no sign of Jonathan, she decided he must be waiting for her in the dining room.

The dining room was crowded and noisy, stuffy with the heat from the traditional fire. She'd heard from one of the waiters that if they left the fire unlit in summer some regular was sure to complain, so the best they could do was not bank it up with logs as they did in winter.

It was still unpleasantly warm and as she looked around the crowded tables, she could see only one small table unoccupied. Of Jonathan there was no sign at all.

Poised uneasily at the open door, she wondered what could have happened. Like reliable yeas and nays, they both knew that the time of a meeting required strict punctuality even if it had not been plain good manners.

'I'm sorry, ma'am, we don't seem to have a table for one left.'

'Actually it's for two,' she said, smiling patiently at the young waiter who was sweating visibly. 'I'm meeting a friend, but I think he must have been delayed.'

'Would that be a Mr Hancock from York, ma'am?'

'Yes, indeed,' she replied, surprised and wondering how he could possibly know.

'He asked me this morning to ensure that the small table by the window was available for 12.30 p.m. He said he had dined there before and particularly liked it. We don't normally accept bookings,' he added, as he led her between the tables by the most uncongested route. 'Will you order, ma'am, or would you prefer to wait?' he asked, lowering a large menu into the space in front of her.

'I'll wait, thank you,' she said, sitting down gratefully.

It was somewhat cooler here by the window but, as she relaxed a little, a small party of well-dressed men just beside her burst out laughing and proceeded to address each other as if across a large field rather than a modest table for six. As well as the amount of noise they were making, they were so close by she couldn't avoid hearing every word they said.

'Well, to my mind Sir Norman's right. He says these relief works are a waste of money. Over by Blackwater, they're shaving the tops of hills and filling up valleys, so he says, and he's been to look. What use is that? Why not put the money into drainage? We've enough wet land that needs it and there'd be something to show for the labour and the money we're having to shell out, but try telling that to your man Trevelyan at Dublin Castle. You might as well spit into the wind.'

'Yes, Henry, but they don't want hard-working landlords to benefit. Landlords are wicked and exploitive. Surely you know we're all a bad lot, even if we do live here and are not sporting ourselves in Bath or London. Did you see the cartoon in the *Illustrated*?'

There was raucous laughter as one of the gentlemen suggested that an older member of their group wouldn't know what to do with a wench like the one portrayed.

The noise now distressed her more than the heat had done and she wondered if the best thing to do was go and wait outside. She was sure Jonathan would come, or would send her a message, but she knew she was growing more exhausted by the minute.

Suddenly, there was silence. She could hardly believe it, until a discreet glance revealed steaming plates of roast beef and vegetables being placed carefully by the waiter in front of each of the well-nourished gentlemen.

A few moments later, Jonathan appeared, clearly distressed by the delay.

'Sarah, my dear, forgive me. It was the last thing I expected. I promise I'll tell all, but please let us order our lunch and perhaps if you can spare the time we could go and walk on The Mall. After my adventure this morning, I have need of both your company and your good advice.'

Lunch was pleasant and became even more pleasant when the noisy party at the next table decided to have coffee in the smoking room.

'Have you heard, Jonathan, about levelling hills and filling valleys?' Sarah asked, when the last member of the group disappeared.

'Who's been saying that?' he replied, raising his eyebrows.

She told him what she'd overheard and he nodded sadly. 'I'm afraid there's an argument going on about so-called productive and unproductive relief works. The intention is that landlords should not benefit if they are not contributing, but that doesn't apply in every case. Outside Ulster, there are many absentee landlords, but that is not the case here in the north. There are landlords here who have sold land on their English estates to fund help for their tenants here. Some have set up schemes for assisted emigration, but the detractors then say it is for their own benefit.'

'And is it?' asked Sarah, aware that she had not heard this criticism and was not informed at all in this area.

'There are always those who are self-interested,' he began, 'but most of the landlords I talk to are simply trying anything that might help. They know the land is overpopulated, it simply cannot support the number of people it does from agriculture. An industrialised country *might* support eight million, but Ireland is a long, long way from being industrialised. Besides, as you know from Ballymacarrett and Tartaraghan, even industry is subject to change. Industrial workers can lose their livelihood just as randomly as those depending on potatoes if there is blight.'

'Tartaraghan, Jonathan? I know where that is, but I don't know anything about it,' she replied apologetically.

'Oh sorry,' he said, looking puzzled. 'I thought maybe it was you that told me about Tartaraghan. I know it's not very far from you at Drumilly. Sometimes I speak to so many people and read so many papers and journals, I don't know who told me what,' he went on, looking so dejected that Sarah laughed and asked him if he wanted apple pie.

'You know, Jonathan,' she said, as the waiter removed their dinner plates, 'I get upset too when I hear some of the things that are happening. The situation is bad in places here in the north, but so much worse in Cork and Limerick and down the west coast. I have to keep telling myself that allowing the bad news to disable me means I can't even do the tiny little bit I *can* do.'

'Yes, my friend, you are right. "Do what you can, do it in love and be sure it will be more than you ever imagined." Did your grandmother say that to you, or did you say it to me? I think it's true by the way. You've done more than you know and I don't just mean setting up your sewing project to let women earn money. Have you ever heard of the Choctaw Indians?'

'Yes, I have actually,' she said, totally surprised by the question. 'My dear friend Helen in Charleston told me about them. Apparently, they've collected money for people with no food in Ireland because they've suffered famine themselves, but they didn't know how to get the money to Ireland. Helen's husband sits on a committee that has also raised money from all sorts of people, not just Irish emigrants and they had the same problem. Helen wondered if I could help, so I told her to contact the Quakers. I reckoned you'd have links with the Quaker community in America and they could organise something.'

He smiled gleefully and tapped the table.

'Well, you'll be glad to hear that the Dublin Yearly Meeting has just received donations from both the Charlestown Committee and the Choctaw, both very generous amounts even before dollars are converted to pounds.'

'Oh Jonathan, doesn't it give you heart when you see the kindness of strangers?' she said suddenly, as he told her the amounts.

'Yes, it does. It really does. I'm afraid I do lose heart at times. I'd be much worse if it weren't for you,' he added, as they got up together and moved towards the door.

He paused to drop a coin on the waiter's plate by the door.

'You'll make sure my bill is ready by six, won't you?' he said, when the waiter thanked him.

'I'm booked on the early evening coach for the crossing at high tide,' he explained, turning to her as they stepped out into the sunshine. 'I'll not be back till December and there seems so much to say,' he added sadly. 'Sarah, dear, do say you can stay with me and we can go and walk together this afternoon.'

CHAPTER NINETEEN

The streets were less crowded now but they were still grateful when they reached the foot of College Street and turned across the broad roadway opposite the courthouse to walk under the shade of the trees. They sat down on the first available seat and breathed more deeply in the cooler air.

'It was a lovely lunch, Jonathan. Thank you,' she said quietly, 'but I'm rather glad to be away from everyone. I can think better down here,' she said, laughing briefly. 'Perhaps I'm a country girl at heart,' she went on, glad to see him relax a little, though it was clear to her that something was on his mind.

'Do you want to tell me what happened before you arrived at the Charlemont Arms?' she asked cautiously. 'You did say you would,' she added encouragingly.

'No, I don't want to tell you at all,' he said, with a wry smile, 'but I must. Honesty is required for my dear friend.'

He paused as if he were not sure how to put it, then suddenly making up his mind, he began. 'I'd had the idea that I might buy you a little gift, some flowers, or a plant in a pot that you could take care of. I'm sure you'd have green fingers if you had a little garden. So I went up to the market, but I was disappointed. There was nothing that looked right. As I was walking back down again, in plenty of time to meet you, I found a group of men just ahead of me. They were very rough-looking and had sticks and cudgels in their hands; they were pushing their way into a bakery through the people just coming out.'

He stopped, looked her straight in the eyes and went on: 'I nearly passed by on the other side. They did look so fierce: unshaven, wild-eyed, ragged. I knew I had to do something, but what was I to do? I really hadn't the slightest idea. But I found myself following them into the shop. There were a couple of women inside who'd obviously been waiting to be served and when I looked at them I could see they were really frightened. There was a young assistant behind the counter and he wasn't much better.'

'So what *did* you do, Jonathan?'

'How do you know I did anything except turn tail and disappear?'

'Because I do know a bit about you. Not as much as I could know, but enough to know you'd have done something. Do tell me, please.'

'I turned and spoke to them. I couldn't believe I was doing it. I said something like, "What's the matter my friends, can you not ask for what you need? Ask and it shall be given." And one of them put down his stick and said, "Sir, we need bread, our wives and children are starving."

'It was then that the baker appeared from the back of the shop, at least I assumed he was, certainly he was dusting flour from his hands. "Can you provide these good people with bread?" I said. "Have you enough for all of them and the two ladies over there?" "I have, sir," he said, counting the heads. "You'll be wanting large loaves then, sir." So I agreed that I would, though I didn't know how much money I had in my purse.

'Well,' he said, taking a deep breath, 'I took it out and found I had two sovereigns, so I gave them to him and he handed me one of them back. "You might need that if you're travelling in these parts," he said, and turned away from us and went away into the bakery. He came back loaded up with the largest loaves I have ever seen. He gave one to each man and one to each of the two women.

'Sarah, I don't think I shall ever forget what happened next. The thought of it makes me weep,' he said apologetically. He paused, took a deep breath and went on. 'One of the women handed hers back. "Baker, please share this out. I still have food at home," she said, and the men stood back to let her pass. And the other one did the same and followed her. So the baker carved the two loaves into big pieces and they shared them between them, giving the biggest pieces to the one with the most children. Then they wished the baker and me good day and one of them said "God bless you, sir" and I was really hard-pressed not to weep tears of relief and joy.'

Sarah looked at him gently and took his hand. 'Well done, Jonathan. Now you know the courage you have, you must treasure it. That's what my wise grandmother would say, so I'm saying it for her.'

He nodded gently, clasped his other hand over hers and said: 'I need even more courage now for what I have to tell you. I hope you'll not be angry with me, but I won't see you again till almost Christmas and it seems such a long time to hold this pain in my heart.'

'What pain, Jonathan dear? What's troubling you? Tell me what I can do to help.'

'Sarah, my dear, when I met my wife, she was very young and beautiful and full of a gaiety I had never known in all my life. I was not so young, but I was enchanted by her. I was welcomed by her family because they knew I could provide well for her and it seemed as if our marriage would bring such happiness to everyone. The liveliness and gaiety, the "disinhibition" as the doctors now call it, was an early sign of her mental illness. Within a year of our marriage, she had to have professional care. Now she doesn't know who I am. Sometimes she is angry when I visit, throws my gifts on the floor or tramples on them. I cannot recognise even the shadow of the young woman I thought I loved. But she is my wife and so I cannot therefore confess the love of a mature man for the woman I truly love. And the pain of concealment is truly hard to bear. What am I to do, Sarah? There is no one else I can ask but you.'

'But you had your answer earlier today, Jonathan. Have you forgotten what you said to the men in the baker's shop? You said, "Ask and it shall be given." You must ask this woman whom you love to tell you what to do,' she said gently, as she drew her hands back from his.

'You are the woman I love, Sarah. I shall never love anyone else while you live, but I cannot ask you to marry me, even if I knew you loved me too.'

Sarah had but little doubt that she was the woman he was referring to, for Jonathan's face was always so revealing. He could not be deceitful even if he tried. But what was she to say to him? She had loved John so dearly, would have gone on loving him, but now he was beyond her love and this man was dear to her, she had no doubts at all about that.

'What would you like me to say? What would comfort you? You know I care for you. You are my dearest friend and yes, I have love for you. Were you not married, I could indeed give you my promise.'

'To marry me?'

'Yes.'

'But that, my dearest, is all I need to give me courage. If you find someone you want to marry, I must release you and wish every blessing upon you, but if you do not, then all I have is yours to deal with as you wish, whether I am able to marry you or not.'

They walked all afternoon, moving from one sitting place to another on the tree-lined walk that circled the green of the racecourse lying at the centre of the small city of Armagh. They walked side by side as if they had always walked together, not touching or holding hands, merely being as close as it was possible to be, looking at the same falling leaves, at the nursemaids pushing prams outside the handsome new houses in Hartland Place, at the detachment of cavalry who went jingling past in the direction of their barracks.

They talked about all manner of things, sharing details of their very different lives in a way that letters could seldom convey; easy with each other, a great burden lifted from Jonathan, and for Sarah, the pleasure of seeing the distress fall from his face. Their only sadness was that time was passing so quickly. It was hard to believe they must go back to the hotel so soon and say their goodbye in the stable yard where Daisy would be waiting and Jonathan's luggage stood ready for the evening coach.

'Will you write to me tomorrow, Sarah dear, so that I have something of you to come and comfort me in my empty house soon after I get back? Please.'

'Indeed, I would willingly, if I had your address,' she came back at him, laughing, reminding him of the omission that had caused him such anxiety only a very short time ago.

He had to dash into the hotel, beg a sheet of paper and write down the address for her while Daisy was being brought out of her stall. They clasped hands just for a moment in the busy stable yard and then he handed her up into the trap, passing her the reins when she settled herself.

'I will write tonight, on the ship, but you will probably not get it for a day or two. But you do know I'll be thinking about you.'

She nodded vigorously as Daisy fidgeted.

'Be of good cheer. It's been a wonderful afternoon,' she

said, trying to smile and not quite managing it, knowing how sad he was they'd had to part so soon.

'See you at Christmas,' she said, as easily as she could manage. 'I hope you have a good crossing.'

'My luggage is heavier, full of papers and problems, but my heart is much, much lighter,' he said, looking up at her and raising a hand as the trap clattered slowly over the cobbles.

Sam Keenan was watching for her as she came between the large stone pillars. Only when she saw him did she remember she'd said she would be back early. A good thing Scottie was nowhere in sight. He'd become more confident in her driving but she knew he would never forget what had happened to John on that lovely spring day. It was often clear that he still feared he might lose her as well.

'You should be away home, Sam. I'm sorry, I got delayed,' she said, as he helped her down. 'Have you seen Scottie?'

'Aye, the old lady's gone but he's left you a note. I think there's somethin' else wrong but I thought I'd not ask him whit it was till he tole you first.'

'Sam, go on home,' she insisted. 'Whatever's in the note will keep till Monday. Your good wife will be wondering what's kept you. I don't want her worrying.'

'Aye, well. Women do be worryin' but sure amn't I the lucky one that she pays that much attenshun. Some men's wives don't even notice them.'

'Yes, you have a point there,' she said, as she watched

him unharness Daisy ready to be led out to her field. 'Now away on, as they say. I'll see you Monday, all being well.'

The house was warm but the fire was out. It was a very long time since the fire had been out, for Scottie had always watched over it, whatever else was happening, since she'd been going to Castle Dillon. It reminded her of stories John had told her about hearths that had never cooled in fifty years or more, someone always taking over, until finally some old person died with all his family in America and there was no one left to carry on.

She was reluctant to set it going again while wearing one of her work dresses. But then she caught sight of the envelope on the table. Scottie's note, addressed in his swirling hand. 'Mrs Sarah Hamilton. By hand.'

She sighed as she picked it up. Another death, but an old lady sadly failing for many years. A merciful release, some would say, but Sam seemed to think there was something else as well as the old lady's death. She tore the envelope open, scanned the carefully written sentences quickly and took a deep breath. Another problem, another person in need. This time it was her dear Scottie. It would take more than a fresh fire and a mug of tea to work out what to do about this one.

She changed her dress and lit the fire. After a good lunch she wasn't hungry, but the thought of a mug of tea was very appealing. As the tiny flames moved from dry sticks to small pieces of turf, and then on to carefully placed pieces of coal, she finally put the kettle down and brought the teapot and caddy to the table.

What comfort there was in the familiar things of every

day. How many pots of tea shared with John, with John and Scottie and Ben, with friends and neighbours and welcome customers at the forge. She thought of Paddy McCann and the trap he had repaired, a critical part of her everyday life now. And on Thursday evening, Jonathan had sat by the fire with her for the first time.And now they had what one might call an understanding. If circumstances changed to leave him free then she knew she would marry him.

What a different life she might have if that were to happen. No fires to make, no stone floors to sweep, no bread to bake, or food to cook. Jonathan was a wealthy man though he chose to live simply enough and to use much of his time – and no doubt part of his fortune – to help those in the greatest need. But would the change in her life matter if she loved the man?

Marrying John had also changed her life, but they had been so happy together. What was new to her, he'd helped her with: explaining patiently what she didn't understand, whether it was the rules relating to apprenticeship that meant she had to provide food for Ben and Scottie, or the secret of baking bread on a griddle.

She had no doubt in her mind that if you loved someone then the tasks could be shared and the problems resolved. Whether it was a country blacksmith or a wealthy manufacturer made little difference when in both cases there was love and trust.

She sat for a long time, quite glad to be alone, knowing that Mary-Anne was visiting Billy's elderly parents and that she would see her tomorrow. Now, she could no longer feel lonely. Sad, yes. Missing John's presence in the life they had made together, yes, but lonely? No.

To have even one person with whom one could be oneself was richness, to have more than one was true wealth, and she had many friends. And now there was Jonathan. Whatever hardship the future might bring, and there was indeed much to fear as the depth of poverty increased, she nevertheless saw that she was steady in herself and was valued by those with whom she worked. She still had the capacity to laugh. She was truly blessed and must give thanks.

She stood up and went to the open door. The evening was windless, the light lingering though the nights had already begun to drop down. Jonathan would have a calm crossing. They had never spoken about his journeyings, whether he was a good sailor or not. She knew he had often slept in barns or lofts, when he found himself in places with no inn and no one who could offer him a bed. He accepted what he was offered and was thankful. That was something else that they shared.

Suddenly weary, she decided it was time she went to bed. It had been a long day. She remembered her morning at work and Annie and her good news. What an age away it seemed, and how little she ever expected to have good news of her own.

At this moment, she could not think of anyone, other than Mary-Anne, with whom she could share it. Perhaps not even with Mary-Anne. She would have to consider carefully in case it might cause her pain, though she knew that Mary-Anne, in her usual generosity of spirit, would never grudge her any possible happiness. She would have to think about that tomorrow.

* * *

There was no surprise in Scottie's note when he'd asked for a few days' leave to help with his grandmother's burial. Rereading it on a quiet, rather misty Sunday morning, she saw that he planned to come and see her when he had the chance, but he couldn't come to work, at least not till Uncle Edward arrived to take charge of what had to be done.

Last night, she'd been so relieved when she read that his uncle was coming over from Scotland. The thought of being part of another wake and funeral, so soon after her days helping Mary-Anne, lay heavy upon her, but as she reread his letter she was reminded of the different and more serious problem she'd set aside when she knew she was too weary to make decisions.

Scottie explained that his uncle would have to pay for the old lady's funeral for no provision had been made during his granny's lifetime. Not entirely surprisingly, as a result, Uncle Edward had told him he would have to come back to live with him in Ayr and find a job nearby. Scottie couldn't stay in Ireland with rent to pay for the cottage and his uncle said he was no longer able to help with feeding and clothing him for the rest of his apprenticeship. Perhaps if he saved his money, he could complete his apprenticeship at some future date at a nearby forge in Scotland.

'Poor Scottie,' she said aloud, thinking of how Scottie had changed and developed in the last year. The last thing he'd want to do was go back to Scotland, leaving his friends to go and live with his uncle whom he hardly knew and to set aside his apprenticeship, just when he'd found his feet and his confidence and the strong support of Sam Keenan.

He had worked so hard all the time he'd been in the

forge. Now that he'd grown several inches and filled out a little he looked much more like a blacksmith, but there was still over a year before he could be classed as a journeyman. What a disaster to have to give up all that he'd achieved.

She laughed to herself as she laid out her jotter and writing things, even before she'd made her breakfast. So many things in life could be resolved by money. It was true that money by itself would seldom create happiness, but without it the opportunity to be happy was very limited. What Scottie needed was money and, after she'd had some breakfast, she'd set herself the task of finding it.

CHAPTER TWENTY

Sarah was grateful for the reassurance her calculations provided. Even her half of the very modest commission she and Mary-Anne took from the women who provided the varied garments they sold had accumulated in the year to a useful sum. That was good news, but even better was something she had completely forgotten about. She had to go and check with her bank book to convince herself she was not now misremembering.

No, she wasn't imagining it. She was quite sure she had paid the half-yearly rent, but while Sir George had taken what she owed for her current six months' rent, he had vigorously refused the sum owing since the day she had first come to Castle Dillon. She'd asked him then if she could delay the payment in order to try and get an income to support herself and help her keep the forge going. She had no idea what was going to happen on that day.

So, she had a year's tiny weekly earnings made up of the various payments for her own sewing and the six months' rent she had expected to pay. She added it up and smiled. She could now give Scottie a salary for the work he did distributing fabric from her brother's factory, collecting finished goods from the women who sewed and taking them their earnings as soon as she'd them made up. Now, he could both look after himself and pay his rent. She'd have more than enough left to give Sam a small pay rise to make up for some extra hours he might need to work during Scottie's occasional absences to collect or deliver. She would also be able to ensure now that Scottie had some decent clothes for when he was not at work in the forge.

Suddenly delighted with how unexpectedly easy it had been to find what she needed, she took out her writing materials and began her promised letter to Jonathan. She thought of him now, after his night crossing, travelling by coach from Heysham to the outskirts of York, a long journey she knew even without taking out her battered atlas to work it out in miles.

Somewhere on the outskirts of that city he would finally arrive home, welcomed by an elderly housekeeper and her son, who worked in the gardens. He so seldom spoke of his home that she wondered if White Hill House was a family residence he'd been obliged to take on when his elderly parents died, or whether perhaps it had sad memories of some kind. Not something to ask him in a letter, or at least not now. But since yesterday, it looked as if there would be time and opportunity for sharing much more than they'd already shared.

She was absorbed in her letter when she heard a knock at the door. To her amazement, it being Sunday, it was Sam Keenan, looking distressed.

'Sam, what's wrong?'

'Ach it's the wee lassie. She's taken some sort of a fever. M'wife's trying to keep her cool but we don' know what to do. I don't like to ask, but wou'd you lend me the trap or let me ride Daisy? By the time I would walk to the doctor in Armagh sure we might 'ave lost her, she's that hot you cou'd feel the heat of her wi'out even touchin' her.'

'Take whichever you want, Sam – I'll go down to Mary-Anne. She knows more about children than I do and she and I can go over to Selina in her trap. At least we could keep her company till you get back with the doctor. Mary-Anne might know what to do.'

She picked up her purse from the dresser as she walked to the door with him.

'Sam, it might help if you had the doctor's fee to hand to him when you see him, it being a Sunday. Take this,' she said, giving him more than he would need. 'You may need medicine as well. Now, not a word,' she added, as he looked for a moment as if he might protest. 'On second thoughts, take Daisy and the trap in case Halligan's horse is out at grass and will have to be caught and saddled. You can drop me at the foot of the hill on your way.'

While Sam was harnessing Daisy, Sarah collected some milk and fresh bread and looked around the kitchen to see if there was anything else that might help. Selina's children would be properly fed but might not have had any supper. She remembered a half fruit cake in the tin and wrapped it up for the other children. She knew little about these childhood fevers but Mary-Anne was a different story. She was often called upon by people with sudden illness.

There was nothing on the roads and lanes around Greenan and Mary-Anne's young mare was clearly glad to be out, so they'd spoke of nothing except the youngest child on the short, speedy journey. Sarah reckoned the child must be about fifteen months old and remembered that Sam had once told her she was bonny.

She was indeed. They arrived to find her with her eyes closed, long eyelashes dark against dimpled cheeks, soft damp curls sticking to her head. The little face itself was beaded with sweat which Selina, torn with anxiety, kept wiping with her handkerchief, holding her as if she would never let her go. The older children stared wide-eyed at their mother from under the kitchen table, where the eldest girl, only seven years old herself, had told them to sit so they wouldn't be in anyone's way when Da came back with the doctor.

Sarah, her eyes filling with tears, looked at Mary-Anne and prayed there was something she could do. She looked around the clean and tidy kitchen, hopeful she could find something she herself could do. Were there any words of comfort to offer to Selina and what about the little girls and their older brother?

'Perhaps, Selina, you've an old sheet I could use,'

Mary-Anne said, after one brief look at the child. 'We need to wet it and wrap it roun' the wee un, then maybe my friend, Sarah here, could make us a cup of tea. Sarah has brought us some cake. Do any of you like cake?' she asked, raising her voice and looking down at the children under the table, as she took the child from Selina while she went and got a sheet.

The three pairs of eyes were taking in every detail of what was going on, as Sarah fetched the water bucket from under the dresser and helped Mary-Anne to soak the sheet and then wring it out. Selina wrapped it round the little one and said she could still feel the heat of the child through it.

All Sarah could think of was Sam coming back with the doctor, but she let Mary-Anne tell her what to do. She cut cake and talked to the children, who now seemed more interested in the cake than in the baby being wrapped in a wet sheet. Selina was silent but dry-eyed, her face pale with dark circles.

Time passed slowly. They changed the sheet three times whenever Selina felt it dry below her hands and then they heard the sound they'd all been waiting for: Daisy and the trap.

Selina stood up, looked through the window and handed the baby to Mary-Anne.

'And no doctor in sight,' she said to them both, as she went out to tell her husband that their youngest and bonniest was still with them, but still had her eyes tightly closed.

Some hours later, by which time the children had been

put to bed and Sarah was aching from sitting patiently on a hard kitchen chair, Mary-Anne and Selina unwrapped the sheet once again. Sarah got up and she and Mary-Anne soaked it once more, squeezed it out ready to rewrap the inert child, when suddenly the little one began to cry and wave her arms around.

'That's good news, Selina,' Mary-Anne said, feeling the small body all over. 'One more damp sheet and we'll see how she is.'

Half an hour later, the sheet still moist, the little one opened her eyes, looked around her, put her thumb in her mouth and promptly fell asleep.

'Put her in her cradle now, Selina, and keep her warm, and don't worry if she shivers. The fever has broke and she'll likely mend but she might sleep the clock round. There's no more any of us can do the night. It's up to the man above,' she added, as Sam and Selina crossed both themselves and the child.

It was not until they were back in Drumilly that Sarah was able to ask Mary-Anne what had happened to little Kathleen. Did she know what it was? Had she met it before when helping mothers before or after giving birth?

'Ach, dear aye. It's common enough but there's no big medical name for it bar "fever". It comes on sudden-like. Most doctors say there's nothing they can do about it. They do all agree for certain there's nothing to be done for the first night. If the child gets through that, there's a chance for them, but a lot of them don't. That's why yer man in Armagh said he'd not come till tomorrow, tho' no doubt he'd take his consultation fee handy enough if he'd come and he'd had a death certificate to sign.'

She paused and looked at Sarah who was listening attentively. 'It just depends on the chile,' she began, 'if they're poorly, or skinny, or jus' not well fed, then they've no great chance, but that wee one was as bonny as Sam told you. He's a good father is Sam and Selina thinks the world of them all. She tole me she was an only chile herself, and neglected forby. So she's never goin' to do that, is she?'

Sarah was so tired the next morning that she wondered how she would ever get through the day. Scottie didn't appear for breakfast but she wrote him a short note to reassure him that he didn't have to go back to Scotland unless he wanted to. She left his bowl of porridge over a saucepan of hot water in case he was just late. Though possibly he simply couldn't come if his uncle had arrived.

Sam Keenan arrived as she was putting her note on the table under a fresh pot of jam so Scottie would be sure to notice it. Sam was wreathed in smiles.

'Sure the wee one ate her breakfast with the rest of them but she fell asleep agin the minit Selina put the spoon down. Wou'd you mine if I walked down to Mrs Halligan to tell her the good news? Ah don't know what we'd have done lass night wi' out ye's.'

'Sure, Sam, she'll be so glad to see you. Go ahead. I won't be ready to go to work for a while. I need to bake bread for tonight in case Scottie comes for his meal and I have to change my clothes,' she said, smiling, as she brushed ash off her skirt – the one she wore in the mornings till the fire was restored, the hearth swept and the coal bucket filled.

'Aye,' he replied, with a great beaming smile, his joy spilling out all around her. 'There's the quare difference in yer work clothes an' mine, but yours wouldn't do well in the forge with the soot and dust, an' mine wou'den do well with the nice desk an' all those clean pieces of paper!'

Sarah was grateful there was still no word of the Molyneux family's return to Castle Dillon. She could manage her work perfectly well, but she was grateful not to have to answer questions or give an account of a document over which she'd had to puzzle.

She'd long ago got used to the way in which the gentry filled up the pages with courteous expressions of gratitude or good wishes for Sir George's health, but she still found it just as tedious to have to extract the actual content of the letter, as it was to decipher the swirls and curlicues of the writer's man of business.

She often thought of Jonathan's clear copperplate and his direct way of speaking. Perhaps it was no surprise that there were now many successful Quaker businesses with a reputation for honest trading and an approach to their success that meant many less favoured individuals benefitted from their efforts.

It was only on Wednesday, after a second good night's sleep that Sarah begin to feel more like herself. She managed a smile and friendly words for both Annie and James when they appeared separately with her morning tea and the day's letters, and then she went and shared the lunch break with Bridget Carey, as she often did, instead of asking for her meal on a tray which she'd been so glad to do on the previous days.

'It's good to see you, Sarah. There's not many I can talk to here, as you well know,' Bridget said, welcoming her into the housekeeper's room, the most spotless room Sarah had ever encountered. It was full of old, lovingly polished pieces of furniture, each piece with a story of who had given it to her, or how she'd rescued it from an attic, or even a bonfire.

'Have you seen yesterday's local paper yet?' Bridget asked, pointing to the neatly folded *Armagh Guardian* in the magazine rack beside her own chair.

'I glanced at it last night,' Sarah replied, laughing, 'but to tell you the truth I was so tired I had only looked at the front page when I decided I needed to get to bed.'

'Aye, and there wouldn't have been anything on that page to encourage sweet dreams,' Bridget commented sharply. 'Did you read the letters from Limerick and Kerry and the post-mortems on the two poor men that died from starvation? If the government don't do something to help, they'll soon be dying by the thousand. Sure there's no food left. The people have no potatoes and no money for meal,' she went on bitterly. 'We don't know how well off we are up here. I was born in Clare and things there are going from bad to worse. There are very few resident landlords to organise any help, not like our Sir George, just a few priests speaking out. But what money do priests have to give away?'

Sarah listened attentively. There was nothing new in what

Bridget was saying, but hearing her soft Southern accent Sarah became more aware of the vast areas of countryside, far from any of the villages or towns, where there might be some help to be had. One of the men who had died had walked miles for some free food. Exhausted by the long walk, he had collapsed and died before he received it.

'We're all right, Sarah, food and plenty to spare and cartloads going out every day to people in need, but did you see this report about the gang of men in Armagh itself, last Saturday?'

Sarah shook her head as Bridget lifted up the paper, unfolded it, rifled through the inside pages and proceeded to read out an item about a group of men armed with sticks and cudgels, of menacing appearance, who had entered a bakery, threatened the baker, but gone away quietly when provided with bread.

'What do you think of that, Sarah? And it can only get worse. There's no cold in August or September, though you and I enjoy our fire in the evenings, but then between the linen going down and the blight finishing off the potatoes and winter yet to come, can we expect there to be any improvement in matters?'

There were indeed lovely autumn days in both August and September and even in October, but both August and September were stormier than usual, with a number of gales and sheet lightening, unusual in the Armagh area. It caused much distress at a time when many poor, hungry people were beginning to feel that 'the wrath of God', as preached to them by the more extreme evangelicals, both ministers and priests, was now being seen at work, his wrath cursing all around them.

By the end of August, the last hope of the late potato crop was gone. This time, unlike the previous year, it was not a partial failure. When Mary-Anne came up to see Sarah and to help prepare goods for their Thursday market, she admitted to her that at times she was almost glad that Billy had died when he did.

'Sure I know it seems an awful thing to say, an' I was heartbroken in m'own way when he went, but if he'd lived to see those fields he and the boys brought over from pasture juss las' year, it wou'da been even harder to watch him. He'd juss have giv' up. Young Billy wou'd be like that himself, but Jamsey is more like me; he's not goin' to lie down under it. He's read that there's organisations giving away seed for next year, turnip and swedes an' suchlike, that can grow where the soil still maybe has the taint of the blight. Jamsey'll turn his hand to anythin' an' where he goes Billy will follow. Billy's a good worker, but he can't find his own way. He's been doing a lot o' my work for me so I can do more sewing. D'you know he even baked bread lass week? And not much wrong with it, just a wee bit too hard in the crust.'

Mary-Anne was unambiguous in her support for marketing the handmade items. Jamsey and Scottie between them were now visiting the women in their homes, collecting and delivering as needed, and although the volume of garments continued to grow, the volume of sales more than kept pace. Sarah was always on the lookout for any drop in demand, but as she read somewhere, the poor had to rob their belly to clothe their back, and in fact she saw no drop in sales. It even went up when the first snow of what was to be a hard winter arrived towards the end of October.

In other parts of Ireland, there had been heavy emigration, especially in areas where landlords, knowing their rents would not be paid, simply evicted their hungry tenants so they could turn the land over to grazing and increase their acreages of oats and barley.

The *Armagh Guardian* reported regularly on the sale of firearms and there were frequent attacks on both rent collectors and carters taking grain to the ports. Relief committees were formed everywhere but many of them spent much of their time arguing about the nature of relief to be given. Even when a project was proposed and adopted, it could take months before any money was forthcoming to pay the wages of the men queuing up for paid work.

Meanwhile the weather worsened, so even where supplies of cheap grain were available, there was little chance of getting it to the remoter areas where they were needed.

True to his word, Sir George allowed Sarah to continue to take Thursday off each week and, if the weather was bad, to take work home on a Friday so she need not make up half a day or so on Saturday. He no longer chaired the workhouse committee but he still insisted on a copy of the minutes. He now brought her the news that fever had broken out in all parts of the house.

It was not till Lady Molyneux herself paid for the construction of fever sheds on some land she owned, nearer to Armagh than to Castle Dillon but a little distance from the workhouse itself, that the gross overcrowding of that building was eased.

But the success of the fever sheds in easing the pressure on workhouse staff was short-lived. Before the autumn turned into what Sir Norman Stronge called 'the first real winter we've had', a number of doctors, including the workhouse's own doctor, died of the fever despite being well clothed and well fed. Now it seemed that no one was to be spared; no one was safe, not even the privileged owners and servants of the large Castle Dillon estate.

CHAPTER TWENTY-ONE

Drumilly Hill,
Ardrea
12th October 1846

My dearest Jonathan,
I admit, I have been so anxious, even when I kept telling myself that the dreadful gales this week must have disrupted the sailings between Belfast and Heysham and therefore delayed the post. When there was no delivery on Friday or Saturday, presumably because my robust postman had nothing to deliver, I knew I shouldn't worry. But, nevertheless, I confess I did!

Now I have not just one letter from you, but two, and I do not know where to start. I am so relieved, so delighted by your cheering news and so grateful that you are well that, like a child with a bag of sweeties, I am overwhelmed by choice.

But, as you are always so good about reassuring me that you are well in body, however challenged in spirit, then I must begin by doing the same.

I can say honestly that I have been at work today as usual; the signs of storm damage are obvious all along my way. Sadly, one of those lovely chestnut trees I know I've mentioned to you had come down, right across the road, completely blocking my access to the house via the back entrance.

I had to turn around and drive back to the front entrance and ask the lodge-keeper if he could look after Daisy and the trap for me while I walked up and round to the housekeeper's entrance, as we all call it. I assumed one of the outside staff would come and collect her but he refused completely to allow me to walk up the main drive. He said I was a valued member of staff, not a mere tradesperson. He was so fierce with me I had to laugh at the dear man and do as I was told. So Daisy swept me up in the trap, past the front door and around to the stables as if she lived there, which I suppose in a way she does while I am at work.

There is a fair amount of damage to trees and wooden fences on the estate but as Sir George said: 'No one's hurt, that's all that matters.'

He is the kindest man. I can never be cross with him when he's being irritable. It must be hard when *everyone thinks you are there to solve their problems, especially when it is money. Just because he is a major landowner does not mean he has unlimited resources. And at the moment, he so misses his children. I don't know why Lady Emma is so anxious to remain in Bath after their family holiday in England but I know Sir George is devoted to the little ones. I've seen him out walking with his eldest son in particular. He is just nine, very like his father in looks, and I know Sir George would so love to have him here.*

I do hope we don't have such dreadful storms when you come over for your December visit, especially as you are going up to Donegal where the weather is often more severe than here in Armagh.

Although I do read my newspapers carefully, even if I have been known to fall asleep over them after a long day, I did not know about the Belfast women's group who have formed a committee to raise funds for destitute people in Connaught, nor did I know about the generous gifts from both the Indian army and the Sultan of Turkey. What you say about the flow of funds from America and from all parts of the community there, not just from Irish emigrants, is such very good news.

I must now tell you that Ben, our senior apprentice who emigrated last May, has been sending dollars regularly to me 'to use as I see need'; that is why I have asked among the women who sew for the Thursday clothes stall if they have any family or friends in Tartaraghan.

It is only a few short miles away from Ardrea, but until you mentioned it to me, I was not aware of exactly where it lay and I had no idea it had one of the highest densities of population in any rural district in Ireland – over 7,000 souls and poor boggy land in an area only three miles by five miles. The people are, of course, mostly weavers working in their own homes and they are having great difficulties.

One of my neighbours on the market stalls tells me that a web of cloth, sixty yards long and three and a half days' work, is fetching only two shillings and sixpence – and that is if there is any demand! Weavers with children would need at least five shillings a week for meal and flour along with potatoes to provide even a minimal diet. I've been told that a local doctor often called out at night, reports he has seen men still working at 2 a.m. in the morning. The potatoes, as you know, are a complete failure this year, unlike last year when it was partial and there was a good grain harvest as well.

I just hadn't realised that women cannot join the relief committees that are springing up everywhere and I'm heartened by those Belfast women who have formed their own. What I'm hoping is that if I can find a few women in Tartaraghan to sew for the stall, I can encourage them to form their own committee as well. I'll then use Ben's dollars to buy meal and flour in bulk so they can better afford to buy it from their earnings. If I can buy in large enough quantities the committee can then provide, without charge, to those who have no money whatsoever.

My dear, what a practical letter I have written and so little of the thoughts and feelings we've been sharing recently, but I am now so overcome by tiredness I cannot begin to speak of other things. I shall, however, send this to you with Sir George's mail tomorrow afternoon and I promise to write again in the evening.

My loving thoughts are with you,
Your sincere friend,
Sarah

Sarah was sadly aware of the drop in temperature as the month of October moved on. The days were cold and a sharp breeze brought wintry showers and flurries of snow. She got used to travelling home in the now early dusk, knowing that Scottie would be waiting anxiously if she was still on the road when it became fully dark. The only good thing about the flurries of snow, he said, was that it helped to keep the light for a bit longer.

Some of the old people with a reputation for predicting the weather had already said it would be a hard winter. As if the loss of jobs in both towns and in the countryside and the total failure of the potato crop were not burden enough, there was the question of trying to keep warm.

In one of the many reports and documents that came to Sir George's desk, Sarah had read that the cost of keeping up even the most miserably small turf fire for a week was sixpence. It had also become clear that with no money at all coming in, many people had already sold items of clothing in order to buy food; now, dressed in rags, they were exposed to cold as well as hunger.

Work at the forge was quiet, but not much beyond the normal pattern for the short days when there was so little work on the land. There were still horses to be shod and tools to mend and Sam and Scottie had tackled a couple of orders for farm gates from some of the gentlemen farmers in the area. Given two workers instead of four and her own reliable income to subsidise their wages, Sarah was not immediately concerned about either Sam and his family, or about Scottie.

As for her good friend Mary-Anne, she and her two sons had a small, regular income from her sewing and from the farm, where they produced between them milk, butter, eggs and vegetables as well as hay. Jamsey had bought two piglets early in the year and hoped to have them fattened for Christmas when there was always demand for pork from the big houses.

'My goodness, missus, that was a treat indeed,' said Sam, putting down his knife and fork after cleaning his plate and licking his lips. 'It's the quare while since we've had spuds. If it's not a rude question, how did ye come by them?'

Sarah laughed as she watched Scottie scrape up the last vestiges of the tasty champ she'd made with some of Mary-Anne's butter and chopped scallions from the garden. Sam breathed a great sigh of satisfaction as she finished her own portion and then shared the small remains from the saucepan equally between Scottie and him.

'You've Sir George to thank for those, as well as for giving me today off, "for overtime" as he always says. He had a big delivery of potatoes and vegetables earlier in the week and all the day staff got some to take home. I've a few more left and I'm watching like a hawk in case I see them begin to weep or start to smell, though I must admit they do look very robust to me. I'm wondering if they came from abroad. It's hardly manners to ask, is it?'

'Indeed no,' said Sam quickly, as his small second helping disappeared as rapidly as the first. 'Shure isn't it good of the man to share what he has – there's manys that wou'dn't, an' cou'den care less.'

'I'm afraid so,' she said, piling up their very clean plates. 'We've neighbours enough getting no help at all. Do you know Tartaraghan, Sam? I know it's not very far away but I didn't know anything about it till I read a letter to Sir George from one of their clergy.'

'I know Tartaraghan,' said Scottie abruptly, 'but only from Mr McMahon,' he added, looking from Sarah to Sam and back again. 'It has over seven thousand people in a rural district, five miles long by three miles wide, running from beyond Loughgall down to the shores of Lough Neagh,' he began, his voice flat and featureless, his eyes focused on the grain of the well-scrubbed table. 'It's poor, boggy land with great patches of woodland and no real villages,' he went on, still not looking at either of them. 'The man who owns most of it, I forget his name, Sir Something Obre, lives in Belgium at a spa for the good of his health. He has a factor to collect his rents,' he said, his feelings clear in his tightened lips and

273

over-bright eyes when he finally looked up at them.

'Well, ye certainly know more'n I do, though I know there's many like him,' said Sam, looking at his young workmate sharply and seeing his distress. 'The wife's granny comes from Milltown, down towards the shore, but she an' her fam'ly up an' away t' Belfast a good while ago, some place called Ballymacarrett. Her ones were all weavers, even the childer worked at windin', whatever that is,' he said honestly, as he sat back in his chair and crossed himself, as he always did after he had eaten.

'Two of the women who sew for the market are from Tartaraghan,' said Sarah, looking at Scottie. 'Do you not go there to collect from them?'

'No, that must be Jamsey,' he said, shaking his head. 'We have to divide up the jobs between us. He has to do the further away ones because Mrs Halligan doesn't need their trap as much as you need yours.'

Sarah nodded as she stood up to make them mugs of tea. One of the two Tartaraghan women, Sophie Lawson, had come to the stall at the Thursday market last week simply to thank her for taking their work and selling it. She'd looked so tired when she arrived and made herself known, that Sarah wondered if she'd had to walk all the way to Armagh, seven or perhaps eight miles if she hadn't got a lift.

What Sophie had said to her then, Sarah had reported to Jonathan in a letter that very evening. Without the Thursday market, Sophie would have no money at all coming in, she'd told him. Like most of her neighbours, her husband was a weaver: there was no market for his unfinished webs of cloth with cheap cloth already dyed and finished coming in from overseas at a lower price. There was no other kind of work to be had in the neighbourhood, apart from a bit of extra farm work at the harvest, and that was now long past. They'd heard about relief work being started in other parts of Ireland but there was nothing like that where she lived. They had five children and only a bit of a garden for potatoes. The potatoes were all lost and the few turnips they'd had were now all used up.

Although Sarah knew Jonathan would use what she'd sent him and report their plight immediately to the Quaker Relief Committee, she also knew the central committee was so pressed by requests for help it might take some time for them to set up soup kitchens in Tartaraghan. In the meantime, she had Ben's dollars and a contact with a trader who was known to be very fair.

Last week, she'd bought as much meal and flour as the dollars would cover and then, with some of her own earnings, bought a few pounds worth of heavy fabric from her brother in Lurgan. He said he'd managed a specially reduced price for her, but she was perfectly sure that some of the reduction had been a subsidy from his own money. That fabric would give some more women a start making clothing for the stall. Hopefully the money it brought in would keep them going till some further help arrived.

'Sam, I wonder if you could manage tomorrow without this young man,' she said, as she fetched the teapot from the dresser.

'I'm sure it wou'd be for a good reason, comin' from you, Mrs Hamilton,' he said, nodding his head.

'Well, we can't do much but it's better than nothing. I've bought meal and flour with Ben's dollars,' she explained, 'and I want to take it to Tartaraghan and get Sophie Lawson to help share it out to those worst off. The problem is it's so heavy. It was cheaper to buy in big sacks but I'll need Scottie to help me – if you don't mind, Scottie,' she said, glancing at him.

He just looked at her. It was a look which said that he would always do whatever she wanted.

The last Saturday in October dawned bright and cold, dazzling sun beaming from an icy blue sky as Scottie and Sarah manoeuvred the heavy sacks delivered by a carter earlier in the week. Even with their hard work struggling to get the heavy sacks up into the trap, they both felt the cold as they prepared to set off towards Tartaraghan. The Tartaraghan Road is not well known. It is only signposted on the outskirts of Loughgall. Sarah drew her old woollen shawl around her as she squeezed into her seat between two sacks of meal and let Scottie take up the reins.

The sunlight didn't last, but as the sky clouded over they were grateful that the biting wind eased somewhat. They drove through familiar territory and soon passed Mr McMahon's house on the outskirts of Loughgall. Scottie pointed it out to her before they turned north and then west on the Tartaraghan Road, following Jamsey's careful directions.

Although there were thatched cabins dotted randomly along the road, the faint light from a now overcast, grey sky revealed little sign of human beings, only a dim, green, low-lying area with little sign of cultivation or people working. Beyond great stretches of boggy fields, dark patches of woodland stretched to the horizon. They obscured any sight of the wide acres of the biggest lough in the British Isles, one which Sarah had never visited but had seen gleaming in the sunlight from below the monument on Cannon Hill, one of John's favourite Sunday walks.

Somewhere they must have taken a wrong turn, but one road seemed little different from any other and there were few landmarks to guide them, apart from a square church tower which appeared briefly and was then obscured by yet another patch of dark woodland.

Jamsey had mentioned the church which was near to Sophie Lawson's home and Sarah was aware that it was the rector of that church who had written to Sir George asking for assistance. It was the obvious place for them to start their morning's work. Finally they got there, directed by a woman ill-clad for the damp cold, carrying a basket of turf to a neighbour's cottage.

There was no room in the trap so they couldn't even offer her a lift, but Sarah leant down and told her to be sure to visit Sophie Lawson when she had done her errand, so she could carry home some meal in her basket.

Sarah would never forget the look on the woman's face as she blessed them and gave thanks for the offer. So many people, cold and hungry, hiding in their cabins to escape the even more miserable cold of outdoors was a stark contrast to the indifference of a gentleman in Belgium: warm, well clothed and well fed, pressing for his rents and threatening them with eviction if they didn't pay up.

They did manage what they had planned to do, delivering a large sack to each of the churches, then being warmly welcomed by Sophie who had a wood fire that smelt of pine branches. They stood over it, hands extended over the cheerful blaze, noses twitching with the scent of resin, while Sophie made them tea, asking them exactly what they wanted her to do with the sack they had brought for her.

'Just use your own judgement, Sophie. Ask for a penny a pound from people if they have any income at all and keep it till you see Scottie here or Jamsey. Any money you can collect means we can buy more. But if you know they have no money give them what they need for a week and we'll see what we can do for them then.'

Sophie nodded as she made the tea and offered some bread, apologising that she had no butter or jam. They both thanked her for the offer but Sarah insisted she had their lunch in two paper bags.

'What d'ye want for the fabric, Sarah?'

'I thought maybe a penny a yard, but not to be paid until something sold for them on the stall. Same reason. If we can bring in some money, however little, we can buy more. And someone might send us a present of money like Ben did. We can only hope, can't we?' she replied, grateful to feel warm again.

Sophie's house was spotlessly clean and there was a glass jar with a handful of late flowering dahlias on the kitchen table. With her children gone to visit her mother, she'd been working on her current piece of sewing: it sat on a stool by her chair in the window, wrapped in an old but clean piece of torn linen.

She looked at Sarah and said, 'Sure hope is all we've got, if we let go of that we're finished.'

'Well, we'll not do that if we're still fit to stand, will we, Scottie?' she said, turning to him, as he looked round the bright room, his eye lighting upon some books.

'Are you a reader then?' Sophie asked.

He nodded shyly and then plucked up the courage to ask if he might look at them.

'Surely, go ahead. I want Sarah to meet the other woman who sews for the stall. I didn't actually know her till we found out about the stall. She lives a wee bit down the road,' Sophie said, as they moved towards the open door. 'We'll call back and collect you to take Sarah home,' she said over her shoulder, laughing when she saw Scottie promptly choosing one of the books and sitting himself down by the fire.

They were struck by a chill air as they went out together but the wind had dropped away completely. It was more damp than cold. They talked easily, Sophie speaking about her father who had been a teacher but who had died of fever when she was only a girl.

'So who brought you up, Sophie?' Sarah asked, wondering if children who had lost their parents always recognised each other.

'A kind neighbour with no children of her own,' Sophie replied promptly. 'I married her son, but he was jealous of the children when they came along and he used to beat me. In the end, I was glad when he left me. I don't know where he is. I sometimes tell people I don't know, that he's a weaver looking for work, but I couldn't tell you that, could I?'

'Why not?'

'Because you always tell the truth about things. You tell it the way it is and you expect the same in return. My father told me always to trust Quakers for their yea was yea and their nay was nay. And I've noticed you always mean what you say . . .'

Sophie broke off as they stopped by the closed door of her neighbour's house.

'Oh Sarah, I'm sorry. I've taken you away from the fire and I should have remembered Rachel goes to see her mother most mornings once she gets her own work done. That's probably where she is now,' she said apologetically.

She was about to say something else when they saw a woman hurrying to meet them. She appeared to be carrying a bale of cloth in both hands, but as she got nearer they could see it was not a regular bale, it was something wrapped in layers of white linen.

It became obvious what the burden was as she came up to them. The well-wrapped parcel was a dead child, its tiny face white as marble.

'Mrs Lawson and you, lady, who iver ye are, can ye help me? I don' care where I die or where they put me, but I want a coffun for this wee one an' I haven a ha'penny to m'name. I'm no beggar. I'm not askin' for food or anythin' else, just a wee coffun for the chile so she'll rest aisy. I'll follow her soon enough. But they'll not put her in the holy groun' if there's no coffun – they'll put her under the hedge.'

Sarah had to swallow hard and try not to cry. What had she to cry about, she that had food, and fire, and friends, and a man that loved her, albeit it far away and not able to marry her.

She took out her purse. 'Do you know how much it would cost?'

'Maybe two shillings, maybe three. She's very small for two years old. I couldn't bring meself to ask the man who makes thim, when I knowed I had nothin' to give him.'

Sarah opened her purse and found three shillings and a single penny. She gave the silver to the woman and the penny to Sophie.

'If you go to Sophie's house, she'll give you meal,' Sarah began trying to avoid the woman's profuse thanks. 'Have you a fire?'

'I have whin I collect sticks.'

'Can you sew?'

'Aye, I'm a brave han' at that. Work clothes and trousers an' suchlike,' she said, looking puzzled. 'But sure what use am I, wi' no husban' an' no childer left . . . I'd be better dead. If I saw me wee love inta the churchyard, I'd go willin' enough.'

'Would you not stay and give us a hand?' said Sophie abruptly.

'What d'ye mean?'

Sarah listened as Sophie outlined the plan they'd just put together to get food into the area until the soup kitchens could be set up and, still talking together, the three women walked back towards Sophie's house which was on the way to the church. As they passed Daisy and the trap, tethered to a fence post, Sarah got up on the step, leant into the body of the vehicle and pulled out a paper bag from under the driver's seat.

'Here, that'll keep you going till you cook some porridge,' she said, putting it into her hand. 'Will the little one lie in the church till the coffin's made?'

'Aye. He's a good man, the rector. He'd not say no now that a coffun is comin'. That's why I've swaddled her, but I can't lay her in a manger like our Lord. She cou'dnt lie in church if I hadn't a coffun. I can't thank ye's enough,' she added, her voice suddenly thick with emotion and relief.

'Don't thank us, just give us a hand after you've been to the rector. Sophie will help you, and you'll help others. We must keep up hope,' she added, as she handed over the paper bag with some bread and jam for her lunch.

CHAPTER TWENTY-TWO

White Hill House,
Mill Road,
Somerton,
York
18th October 1846

My dearest Sarah,
I must confess that I was grateful to be alone in my
study after breakfast with neither my good-hearted
housekeeper nor her inquisitive son in any way likely
to require my attention or guidance while I read your
most recent letter. Your description of the situation in
Tartaraghan was heartbreaking and when you spoke
of the child in swaddling clothes looking like a web
of cloth, I have to confess to tears.

That poor woman, who in one year has lost not only her husband, but four children one after the other, is not to be criticised in any way for her lack of hope. I know that we are taught that despair is a sin, but how many of us have ever had to bear such heartbreak?

I feel sure that between you and Sophie Lawson some hope may have been kindled and I pray sincerely she will not be exposed to any of these ministers and priests, who I hear have taken up preaching that the famine is 'the wrath of God'. I cannot possibly agree with their reading.

If I partially managed to control my tears over the coffin-less child, I certainly did not manage when you gave the woman your modest lunch. I was, however, somewhat cheered when you confessed that Scottie had lectured you firmly and insisted you eat half of his portion. You must remember, my dearest, that if you do not take care of yourself, you will not be able to help others. Apart from my own selfish wishes to know that you are in good health, I must point to all the so-called 'tiny' offerings you make – not simply the market stall which helps both seamstresses and purchasers, but the example you set: working yourself, encouraging young people like Scottie, Jamsey and Billy as well as Annie and James at Castle Dillon and not-so-young people like Sam Keenan and Mary-Anne, not forgetting Sir George himself. It is common knowledge he tells everyone that he'd be lost without you.

Like a ripple in a pond, even small acts can spread out in widening circles and touch others, who themselves create new circles.

There are times when I do have to confess to you my feelings of distress, when the help that is needed is lacking for a whole variety of reasons: if there is no active person in an area or if an area is remote, which usually means a lack of roads and any means of transport, and then saddest of all the indifference of some landowners to their tenants, like the gentleman in Belgium whose Christian name Scottie can't remember.

But I try hard to gather up in my heart the small signs of hope. For example, did you know that the coastguards all around the shores of Ireland have been active in bringing in supplies by boat, especially in the areas I've just mentioned? This is something I shall be exploring when I come in December and visit my cousins in Donegal. Parts of that county, however beautiful, are rugged and trackless; approaching from the sea may achieve more than working from the villages accessible by road.

You ask about my own work as a manufacturer. You are quite right, I do owe it to my brothers to make sure I share with them the problems of the textile trade at the moment.

There is no doubt the competition from India in particular has created serious problems, but so far we have been able to maintain our labour force by dropping our prices and diversifying the goods we manufacture. The cheap clothing project, which I insist you inspired, flourishes. Profits are slim, but I am fortunate to have three brothers who are like-minded. Sadly, the fourth one is not, but for the moment he is willing to accept his share of the income and leave all the work of running the mills and factories to the four of us. It is a small price to pay for the freedom to do what we think right.

It is snowing here at the moment and you mention 'wintry flurries' in your letters. It is early for such fierce weather and I fear, as you do, that if it continues it will make everything more difficult.

It is six months before we can hope for any rise in temperature. Forgive me if I sometimes catch myself dreaming of walking under the trees on The Mall with you in sunshine or, even more wonderful, being able to walk with you in the gardens here.

Time moves on and I have a client to see in an hour's time and papers and accounts to consult before he arrives. I see you in my mind's eye, sitting at that handsome desk that Sir George visits so reluctantly, wearing your warmest dress with even more papers stacked up in front of you than I have now.

I shall write again this evening or tomorrow, by which time I may have news of the planned expedition in December. It will be a small number of people like myself revisiting, in order to reassess the need and the possibilities for meeting it in the nine counties of Ulster.

Take care of yourself, my dear one.
I hold you always in my thoughts and prayers,
Jonathan

The letters that flowed backwards and forwards between Ardrea and White Hill House brought warmth and cheer to both Sarah and Jonathan, but there was nothing anyone could do to mitigate the severity of the weather, as gales followed storms, and snowfall was a regular hazard on Sarah's journey to work. Even without a covering of snow, the temperature stayed low as November turned to December and the *Armagh Guardian* reported the first deaths from starvation in Cork and Kerry.

It was so cold in the evenings that front doors were shut for the first time in years, not against unwelcome visitors, but to keep in what warmth a good fire could produce.

Mary-Anne got to her feet the moment she heard her door open.

'Ach, Sarah, it's great t' see you. I know we said we'd meet the nite, but it's so bitter I wasn't entirely expectin' you,' she said, as she took Sarah's sewing bag. She helped her unwind her heavy woollen shawl and hung it up near the fire so it would be warm when she had to go home again.

'I was just readin' the paper,' she said, after she'd given her friend a hug, 'but that wouldn't do you much good this weather,' she said sharply, as she sat down again.

'Anything strange or startling?' Sarah asked, suddenly thinking of John who had used the phrase, one she had never heard before, until she left Lisnagarvey and came to the forge at Drumilly.

She glanced at the abandoned newspaper dropped down beside Mary-Anne's chair and then, feeling a sudden sadness for a world that had disappeared, not only with John's death but with everything that had happened in the time since, she turned to look down at the deep red glow of the wood fire. She felt warmer already and the flickering flames and the crackle of wood brought an unexpected comfort for the sadness that had come upon her.

'Ach sure what are they reportin' on Cork and Kerry for when there's plenty o' death's roun' here to report? But the poor people here don't have the benefit of a fancy post-mortem,' she went on crossly, as she settled herself again.

'Shure yer hans are stone cold, Sarah,' she said abruptly. 'Like two bits of ice when I helped you with your shawl. Will I make us a drop o' tea now or wou'd ye rather try to get warm first?' she asked, looking concerned.

'No, don't get up,' said Sarah quickly, aware that Mary-Anne was upset by what she had just read and was ready to jump to her feet if a mug of tea would help cold hands. 'I think I'm getting used to the cold now,' she said reassuringly. 'I sometimes have to get down from the trap and walk if Daisy is uneasy. She doesn't mind snow, but if there's ice she doesn't want to move . . . so I have to lead her till she gets used to it.'

'Ach dear, I diden know that,' Mary-Anne replied, her voice softening. 'Don't tell Scottie for any sakes. He'll worry himself t' death if he thinks anythin' might happen to you.'

Sarah smiled and sniffed appreciatively at the scent of the fresh applewood log which Mary-Anne had just put on the fire. She opened her sewing bag and took out a baby's dress.

'So, are you tired of making work clothes or is this good news I haven't heard yet?' asked Mary-Anne, sounding more like her normal forthright self.

'I'm not sure to tell you the truth,' Sarah replied, with a wry smile. 'It's Annie, the housemaid at Castle Dillon. She and James, the youngest footman, have been going together for a year or more, but they were trying to keep it a secret. I'm amazed at how well they've managed it, but once Annie stopped looking half-starved I did notice she'd begun to get a little tummy. I'd nearly made up my mind to ask, when she came an' told me herself that she must be in the family way. D'you know, Mary-Anne, I don't think she knew how it had happened. She thought it could only happen if you do "what ye mustn't do that's wrong." And when I asked her what she meant by that, she said, "I must never let James come into me," and she assured me that he hadn't.'

'Dear a dear, the poor wee lass, an' no mother to help her. Whit'll she do atall?'

'Well, I'm gathering myself to ask Bridget Carey for advice. She once frightened the life out of poor Annie, told her if she didn't mind her manners she'd send her back to the workhouse. Do you remember, it was Annie called me "My lady" on her first day at work? And it was my first day as well . . .'

'Ach aye, I remember ye tellin' me that story,' Mary-Anne said laughing heartily. 'What age would she be now?' she went on more soberly.

'Sixteen and a half now. At least it sounds better than fifteen. She was a good way off sixteen when she came to Castle Dillon.'

'So what will Bridget Carey do? Throw her out or send her back to the workhouse?'

'Not if I can help it,' said Sarah briskly. 'But I certainly can't see how to go about it. I'm waiting for inspiration.'

To Sarah's surprise, she saw Mary-Anne was thinking hard. Usually with her friend there was an instant response, to see her lost in thought was most unusual. Sarah got on with her sewing and waited.

It was two nights later, Wednesday, the night before the second market stall in December, when they met again in Sarah's sitting room. The small room with its tiny fireplace and mirror over the mantelpiece had seldom been used in the two years of Sarah's marriage, the kitchen being larger and more welcoming. John insisted that his mother kept it spotless for the minister calling, or the doctor, but that no one else ever set foot in it. Now, it was in use all the time. Occasionally, as before the visit to Tartaraghan, it had held sacks of meal, but now it did have a regular weekly function.

Piles of clothes, collected by Scottie and Jamsey accumulated during the week and on Wednesday evenings Sarah and Mary-Anne priced the garments, sorted them into bundles and tied them up ready to be loaded into the trap early on Thursday morning, before Scottie and Jamsey went to their own work in the forge and on the farm.

Despite their hard work humping and tying bundles, they were both stone cold by the time they'd finished in the unheated room. Sarah had thought about lighting a fire, but she'd been anxious about the state of the unused chimney. Besides, the fireplace was so small she doubted if a fire could produce much heat even at the best of times. They'd agreed that with the likelihood of smoking out the clean clothes, it just wasn't worth the risk.

They both shivered as they came back into the warmth of the kitchen and Sarah put the kettle down to make tea.

'You look pale as a ghost, Sarah,' said Mary-Anne.

'Well, you needn't worry about me, for you look just as bad,' Sarah replied, laughing. 'We'll be fine when we've had a mug of tea and a bit of cake.'

'This cold is desperate bad news,' Mary-Anne said anxiously, as she drew up close to the fire which Sarah had just made up with small logs and some pieces of coal. 'I'm afeerd that with no good hot food the cold will do more harm to people than loosin' the potatoes. What are we goin' to do at all, Sarah? An' all those poor people around us wi' hardly the makins of a fire an' nothin' for their supper forby. Is there any hope at all?'

'A bit, but not a lot,' Sarah replied as she brought the teapot and mugs from the dresser. 'They've got some boilers going in Tartaraghan now but there's still arguing going on over relief works. "Presentments" is the big word I had to learn. It means arguing who pays for getting the work started. Then, even after months of arguing and work starts on drainage, or roads, or whatever, some of the men coming forward are so weak with hunger they can't do a full day's work, so their money gets docked and they still don't get enough to eat.'

'I heerd that the workhouse is full, an' full of fever as well. Is that right?'

'I'm afraid so,' agreed Sarah, as she made the tea and let it stand to brew by the hearth. 'They were built to hold a thousand people but it's way over that even with using the attics and some workrooms. They're trying to get the old cholera hospital going again for the worst cases and fever sheds are going up in the grounds, but it goes from bad to worse. There's more coming for help every week. Some of the doctors who attend have got fever themselves, but it's the poor children who are dying in droves. The younger they are, the less chance they have.'

'So if that wee Annie of yours were sent back to the workhouse there'd not be much chance of her, or the chile, ever comin' out of it. An' that poor man, James, did ye say his name was? What'll he do if he loses her an' maybe his job as well?'

'I hope it'll not come to that. If it looked like that I'd go to Sir George, but he's still in London and I'm not sure when he's coming back. The roads are in a bad way with the frost and ice and Lady Emma hates travelling in winter. He's not very likely to come on his own till after Christmas.'

'So did ye see yer woman, Mrs Carey? How did that go?'

'Well, a lot better than I expected and there were a couple of real surprises for me,' said Sarah directly. 'It seems that James is the son of the butler, who calls himself Smithers, though Bridget says his name is actually Smith. She says he had an affair with a kitchen maid who had a child and died a few weeks later. Smithers denied all knowledge of the girl and Sir George's grandfather had the child adopted by one of the women staff in his Dublin house. The little boy went to school with the Molyneux children until he was ten or eleven and then when they all went to public school or boarding school and finishing school, he was left behind to become a servant.'

'An' yer man Smithers was his boss, was he? An' did he still not admit who James was?'

'No, according to Bridget, who was a kitchen maid herself in those days. James looks like his mother, who was a lovely girl with dark hair and dark eyes, and Smithers never had a good word to say for him. Bridget says he was a willing enough lad and did his best to do his work, but she thinks he had no great interest in being a servant.'

'You tole me the other nite that Annie thought they'd done no wrong. Will Mrs Carey take any heed of that?'

'That was my biggest surprise,' Sarah said, pouring their tea. 'She actually told me about the village in Clare where she was brought up and told me an expression she often heard. She said: "There's some girls could pick it up off the grass." I had to ask her what she meant and she said: "Sure a bit of rough and tumble in the hay field without a full act of intercourse and they'd fall pregnant." That's what she said and I know she doesn't invent things.'

'An' she's quite right too. I've heard that same expression and I've heard of a servant girl delivering her own child in a lavatory and not even knowing she was that way in the first place.'

'I'm going to write to Sir George and suggest they are allowed to marry. I'll tell him that Mrs Carey is reluctant to lose two good workers and that a room can be found for them in the stable building. Between you and me, once Bridget told me he could read and write, I suggested to her we could find him a job keeping stocklists and filing accounts. That actually went down very well with her, there's a lot of that sort of thing she really dislikes, but it's part of her job.'

'Well now, isn't that a bit of good news to brighten us up, for we're sure to be froze the morra in Armagh,' said Mary-Anne. 'You can also drop a wee hint to Bridget Carey that ye know a wumman who has a room ready if the girl goes into labour. So she won't be put out at all in her routine. All she needs to do is sen' her up to me and sure isn't there carriages galore in them big stables ye were tellin' me about? Forby Daisy just waitin' there ready to go home.'

'But what about Billy and Jamsey, Mary-Anne, you don't expect them to give up their room, do you?'

'An' why not? Sure I said maybe one day they'd need a han' from their ma with a we'an of their own. Wou'd it not be a good idea to help her to keep her han' in, doin' a job they might need?'

Sarah laughed. There was no doubt when Mary-Anne put her mind to something she got there in the end. As she helped her friend wrap up warmly for her walk back up the hill, she remembered the one occasion when Jonathan had visited her, full of anxiety about her well-being, and left some time later saying he would hardly notice the journey back because his heart was so light.

Whatever tomorrow brought, there was joy in knowing that Annie and James now had another friend, and a more reliable one it would be hard to find.

CHAPTER TWENTY-THREE

Friday was always a busy day for Sarah at Castle Dillon whether Sir George was in residence or not. To begin with, Thursday's post sat unopened on the highly polished desk and, before noon, Friday's post would also arrive, carried on a silver salver by James.

By the time Annie had appeared with tea, neatly arranged as always on a tray, bearing a cloth with a crocheted border that was spotlessly clean and well starched before it was ironed, Sarah would have some measure of her tasks for the day. Once Friday's post arrived, she could then decide on whether it would be best to take half a day's work home to complete at her own kitchen table, or whether it would be better to come in for the whole day on Saturday.

The advantage of coming in was that she would be

undisturbed at her desk and have her lunch cooked for her, but the disadvantage was having to get up early to make sure there was a midday meal for Sam and Scottie.

As Sam regularly pointed out, he was not entitled to a midday meal – that was a requirement that only applied to apprentices. Sarah had finally stopped trying to persuade him that it was no trouble and little expense to offer him a meal given how hard he worked. She had often reminded him how often he did jobs for her which were certainly not forge work, but that hadn't reassured him either. Now she just smiled if he protested.

'Now, Sam, who would keep an eye on Scottie and make sure he ate up all his food if you weren't here?' she would say. Sam would laugh heartily, for Scottie had a good appetite and left his plate so clean he might well have been accused of licking it.

Friday 11th December 1846 on Sir George's calendar began no differently from many other Fridays. Daisy was handed over to Robert Ross who had become a favourite with her. She blew down his neck affectionately and nibbled his ear. Robert had Scottie's gift of making animals feel easy and Sarah could sense Daisy's disappointment if Robert had gone on some errand into Armagh. Tommy, his helper, was perfectly competent, but Robert had won Daisy's affection.

A fall of snow in the night was still lying on both roads and fields. On parts of the back driveway exposed to the chill wind, it had turned into a crust of ice and a narrow path had been cleared from the stables to the housekeeper's entrance. Sarah followed it gratefully, for walking on the adjacent snowy surface would have been like scrunching over a pebble beach, hard on the back and potentially dangerous.

She settled herself with Thursday's letters and felt her spirits descend as she began to read the current week's workhouse report. It was all bad news: the fever was carrying off so many, but even more poor people were queuing up to take their places so the admissions just kept on rising. Worse still, a number of staff members had fever themselves. The pharmacist had already died. One look at the guardian's expenses for the week told her that the debt was also increasing all the time; the average cost of feeding a pauper had gone up steadily since the last of the potatoes and turnips had been used.

She took a deep breath and began to make notes for an abstract to send to Sir George. He was not at all interested in the arguments over diet, but he was always concerned over the effect of costs which would have to be met from the rates and over the progress of local presentments for relief works.

He had begun drainage schemes himself on his own land and at his own expense, but he knew they were but a drop in what he called 'a bucket with a hole in it'. Only at county level could schemes large enough to be of value be funded. And even if the government did agree to match local funding, there was then the problem of finding the local funding in the first place.

She had a number of abstracts to send out to local landowners before she even began on the rest of the pile. Mostly they were regularly recurring queries that flowed in with steady repetition, but they still had to have a written answer.

The tentative knock at the study door took her by surprise. Though she'd been aware for some time that her porridge had been a long time ago and admitted she was longing for a cup of tea, she had still lost track of time. Annie, now balancing the tray one-handed, shut the door behind her with a practiced push and walked steadily over to the desk.

'Hello, Sarah, did the stall go well yesterday?' she asked, smiling.

'Yes, it did. A bit down,' she added thoughtfully, 'but I think it was only because it was so cold some women stayed at home. Do you like the snow?' she asked, half-joking, for most people, even the children, had got weary of the regular falls and it being so cold.

But Annie did not answer. Having put the tray down on the desk, she was still standing beside it, waiting to see if Sarah would ask her to sit down for a minute or two, as she often did. Suddenly, she doubled over, her arms hugging her stomach, her eyes wide as she moaned with sudden pain.

'Annie, what's wrong?' Sarah said, dropping her pieces of paper and coming from behind the desk to put an arm around her.

'Would it be "the time of the month"?' she asked, knowing that sometimes, even in pregnancy, one could have unexpected pains at that time.

'No, I've niver had a pain like that before,' Annie said, gasping and wiping sudden tears from her eyes. 'D'ye think it's the baby comin'?' she asked, her eyes wide, her voice now steadier.

Sarah's first thought was what a mercy it was that she and Mary-Anne had talked about Annie as they had on Wednesday evening, but about the pain she couldn't be sure. She had lost two children herself, but the first was very early in pregnancy and the second only a month or two further on. Annie was certainly much further on than she had been.

'Sit down, Annie, and just try to breathe normally,' she said, taking a cup from her own personal drawer in the bottom of the desk. She shared the tea between them and watched Annie carefully, noticing her hands shaking as she drank, her skin deathly pale.

When the pain came again a few minutes later, she got up and pulled the bell, praying it would not be Smithers who came to answer it.

'Sarah, I think I'm bleeding on the good chair,' Annie whispered, her voice dropping even lower in her distress.

'Don't worry your head about that; we'll get some help in a moment. Drink your tea now like a good girl,' Sarah said steadily, as she tried to keep her own anxiety firmly under control.

One of the other housemaids knocked briefly and walked across the room towards them. Sarah breathed a sigh of relief when Lizzie, only a little older than Annie herself, took one look at her friend and immediately focused on Sarah.

'Lizzie, dear, I have three messages for you and I want you to be as quick as you can. Now, can you manage to remember three things?'

Lizzie assured her that she could and listened hard.

'I want you to go to Mrs Carey and say Mrs Hamilton needs her help in Sir George's study and will she please come immediately and bring some clean napkins.' She paused and waited till Lizzie nodded. 'Then I want you to find James and tell him Mrs Hamilton needs his help in Sir George's study right away. And thirdly, I want you to go out to the stables and tell Robert or Tommy that Mrs Hamilton needs transport immediately at the front entrance to go to Drumilly Hill and back.

'Can you remember all that, Lizzie?' Sarah asked, a hint of anxiety in her voice.

'Yes, I can,' Lizzie said firmly, as she glanced sideways at Annie. 'If no one's lookin', I'll run,' she said, making for the door.

Lizzie was as good as her word. Minutes later, James arrived, got down on his knees beside Annie, held her hands and told her she'd be all right, that Mrs Hamilton would see to that. When Bridget Carey swept in, she took one look at Sarah and asked James to go and fetch Annie's shawl and an extra blanket from her storeroom.

When he came back, Annie was on her feet, a clean napkin covering the damp patch on the chair. He helped her wrap her shawl around her and then picked her up as if she were no weight at all and carried her to the front entrance where Robert himself helped Sarah up into the driving seat, wrapping the warm trap rugs he had brought with him around Annie the moment he saw her little pale face.

'Can I come with you, Mrs Hamilton, please?' said James, steadily.

Sarah paused. Leaving the house without permission was a serious matter. But it would help both Annie and him if they could meet Mary-Anne together.

'Yes, you can. We won't be long.'

She turned to Robert, now standing by Daisy's head.

'Robert, would you do me a favour? Would you go to Mrs Carey and tell her I've removed James without permission but only for a short time? And could she please tell Smithers if the question should arise?'

Robert smiled and nodded briskly. He knew well there was no love lost between Smithers and Mrs Carey but if anyone could deal with his bossiness it would be her.

'Take care now, safe journey,' he said, saluting them as they drove off.

Once Annie had been delivered into Mary-Anne's safe keeping, Sarah knew she'd have to get James back to work, but the young man, who'd made such an effort to be steady for Annie's sake, was now much easier in himself. When they arrived, Mary-Anne had assured him that they'd done the right thing to bring Annie to her till they saw what was happening. She managed to make them both smile when she reassured James that she'd never lost a father yet.

While Mary-Anne and Sarah had a quick word together, James sat with Annie. She now looked less pale and as he got up to go, she assured James firmly that he wasn't to worry. She'd be fine now with Mrs Halligan to look after her.

It was Sarah who felt completely exhausted as James

helped her back up into the trap for the return journey.

As she came back into Sir George's study, she noticed that the chair where Annie had sat had disappeared, Friday's letters had arrived and there was a note tucked into the blotter.

It was brief and to the point. Bridget Carey would be expecting her for lunch in her own room.

By the time Sarah arrived home before it was fully dark, she was longing for the quiet of her own fireside. It would be an hour or more before Scottie appeared for supper and she needed the time badly to absorb all the happenings of the day.

Among the pile of Friday's delivery, there was one from Sir George in London. He told her he was hoping to come to Castle Dillon sometime in the next few days, probably accompanied by his eldest son. Lady Emma was reluctant to travel in such bad weather and did not think it would be good for the children. Sir George wanted her to begin at once the arrangements for an earlier than usual staff Christmas party as she had done last year with the help of Mrs Carey.

Clearly he intended to be in Dublin on Christmas Day itself but did not want to disappoint his staff at Castle Dillon. At least Bridget Carey was now a friend, as well as a colleague, a practical woman with no time for making a fuss, but it was going to make a lot of extra work just when she was hoping to have a little extra time off during Jonathan's visit.

Except that the timing of Jonathan's visit was now in

some doubt. He was certainly coming to Ireland and the itinerary planned with some fellow Quakers was going ahead, but he was writing to warn her that bad weather in Donegal might affect their plans to spend some time together over the Christmas period.

Among Friday's letters, she found a short note from him, sent to Castle Dillon at the same time as a letter to Drumilly in case her postman had not been able to get up the hill. From what he said, it looked as if the weather in Yorkshire had been even worse than in Ulster. He'd ended by warning her that sailings might be cancelled if there were more gales like those in November.

She sat looking into the flames of the restored fire, grateful for the cheering warmth but feeling incredibly sad. She had been so looking forward to seeing him, sharing with him all the plans and projects they both had, the successes as well as the failures in their efforts to help people in dire straits.

Now, if there were gales, he might not get to Ireland in the first place and even if he did, the plans they had made would have to take second place to the commitment he had to his colleagues from the Quaker Central Relief Committee who were charged to provide updates on projects already in place in some of the most deprived areas.

How long she sat, she had no idea, but when she heard footsteps outside the kitchen door she assumed it was Scottie arriving for his evening meal. She realised she'd closed her eyes and must have dozed off. She had not even got as far as beginning to lay the table.

But it was not Scottie who came in: it was Jamsey, a

dusting of fresh snow on his hair and shoulders. It needed only one glance to see that he brought news, and good news at that.

'Great news, Sarah,' he said, taking off his jacket. 'That wee Annie has had her baby, a wee boy, and Ma says he may be small but he's lively. She said to tell you she thinks they'll both do.'

To her great embarrassment, and to Jamsey's surprise, he saw Sarah's eyes stream with tears.

'Oh Jamsey, what a lovely Christmas present,' she said, as she searched for her handkerchief to mop them up.

'I'm going over now to Castle Dillon to tell James,' he said happily. 'He'll maybe get let out to come an' see Annie the morra.'

Sarah nodded and said she hoped the snow was only a shower, but she knew Jamsey was a determined young man and a good driver. Clearly he had already made up his mind. He was going to Castle Dillon, snow or no snow.

'When you get there, Jamsey, ask if you can speak to Mrs Carey. Tell her, Mrs Halligan says, "she was right about the stain on the chair", and that all is well. She'll know what that means. And tell her I'm so grateful for all she's done to help. She'll probably arrange for James to come up tomorrow to see his son,' she ended quickly, as she felt tears well up again.

'Ach, isn't it great to have good news for a change?' said Jamsey, unexpectedly. 'I'll away on and leave ye to tell m' friend Scottie when he comes in for his tea.'

'I will indeed,' said Sarah happily. 'And you can tell your mother when you get back home that she has another satisfied customer to add to her score. You may not know, Jamsey, for she doesn't talk about such things, but she looked after me when I was in a bad way after John died. Without her, I might not be celebrating with Annie and James tonight.'

CHAPTER TWENTY-FOUR

There was no improvement in the weather as Christmas approached. On one or two days it was so bad that Scottie refused to harness Daisy, saying it was too dangerous for both her and Sarah to try to travel on such icy roads.

While Sarah suppressed a smile, knowing what Mary-Anne might say about Scottie's protectiveness, she did recognise the danger and accepted that it was just not worth the risk. If Daisy were to fall, she might be badly injured and the thought of her having to be despatched by a vet was far too painful to contemplate, especially after all the journeys she'd made possible since Sarah's first visit to Castle Dillon.

There was, of course, someone else who would have vigorously supported Scottie's firm approach, but of her dear Jonathan she hardly dare think. In the last week before Christmas she'd had no letter for several days, so she still didn't know if he'd been able to reach Belfast or whether perhaps he had managed that, but had then been so behind schedule he'd had to go straight on to north Donegal, the first stop on the schedule drawn up by the London Relief Committee of the Society of Friends.

He had taken great care to warn her thoroughly, knowing how she might worry, that even if all went well, she might still not receive his letters very promptly or even in the correct order. All they could do was hope that their dearest wish would be granted and he could stay a night or two in the Charlemont Arms on his return from north Donegal to make up for the visit he'd hoped to make between his arrival in Belfast and the date he was committed to travelling to the north-west with his colleagues from the Relief Committee.

Meantime, at both Castle Dillon and Drumilly Hill, everyday life seemed to get harder day by day. Even when Sarah was forced to stay at home, there were so many neglected tasks to catch up on that she worked hard all day and wondered by the evening why she had not been able to achieve more.

While she and Bridget Carey had been busy preparing for Sir George's very successful staff Christmas party, she'd barely managed to prepare food and fresh bread for Sam, Scottie and herself. Now, she found she was always searching for clean collars to freshen up her work dress and a second, even warmer dress, she'd begun in late November was still laid out in pieces in her bedroom.

But she did admit, most willingly and gratefully, that what took up a lot of her time at home was counting money. Not only did she fill more and more small brown envelopes for women who sewed for the stall, but she now had to write regular thank you letters to both Ben and John's brother, George, for their regular gifts of dollars.

George had not only returned to her the money she'd given him so he could emigrate with his family, but he had set up a Relief Committee in Quebec, where he'd found work. He sent her dollars that had been collected by both Irish emigrants now settled and in work and kindly Canadians who had known hardship in their own past lives.

Ben had drafted in his workmates in a factory turning out agricultural tools and equipment and continued to send dollars whenever he'd accumulated a significant sum.

Most generous of all was Helen, her dear friend from childhood, who had mobilised her local friends in Charleston to take it in turns to meet at each other's homes and use their skills in making patchwork quilts. From what Helen said, and knowing both her love of colour and her skill with a needle, Sarah could imagine what lovely creations the handmade quilts were. She was not at all surprised they sold for such high prices to the owners of the big houses, both in South Carolina and in Georgia where friends of Helen's husband had set up a support group. But organising it all did take time. She often laughed with Mary-Anne at how amazing it was that putting money in envelopes should be such a time consuming job, but the truth was that now the cold weather appeared to have settled in for the winter, the trade on the market stall was growing all the time. Sarah herself now had little time to sew, but she more than used that time with the amount of calculating the job required.

It was on Friday 19th December, another snow ridden day that, to her amazement, the postman had managed the hill aided by his rubber boots and now sat down willingly for the tea she offered at her kitchen table. Together they looked at the letter he took from his bag. It was postmarked Donegal and looked as if it had taken over a week to come, the address smudged as if the envelope had been caught in a shower of rain or snow.

She could hardly wait for her postman to thank her and say he must be going so that she could read it quickly to see if it held out any prospect of her and Jonathan being able to meet.

She then drew over to the fire and settled down to read it slowly, so grateful to be able to share Jonathan's immediate concerns and to have something of his which would tell her how he was faring, a small comfort when she would willingly travel with him if only circumstances were different.

Dunfanaghy,
10th December 1846

My dearest Sarah,
I am writing this by the flickering light of an ill-functioning oil lamp in a very cold bedroom in the only hotel in this small town. I cannot tell you what a joy it is after all that has happened in the past days to be sitting here writing to you, knowing that we still have hope for a meeting and for the letters we share.
I have to confess to you that I thought I would

never see you again. We set out from Liverpool in rough weather, but the rocking and pitching of the ship when we left the shelter of the Mersey was as nothing compared to the sudden gale that hit us when we were in the middle of the Irish Sea. I could not bear being thrown around in my tiny cabin facing the prospect of going down with the ship, so I went out onto the deck and clung to a coil of rope attached to the structure. I was there when part of the rigging fell down and landed only yards away from me.

I could see that even the seamen were frightened and for a time we turned back, presumably seeking quieter waters, but there were none to be had and in the end the captain must have decided our only hope was to run before the storm and end up wherever it might leave us.

Our chances of survival seemed to me to grow smaller with each passing minute, but I thought about you and prayed for strength. As you see, my prayers were answered. We found haven somewhere in Scotland and were kindly treated there, staying a day and a night, till the gale abated. The second attempt to cross to Ireland was still turbulent, but it was a shorter distance and, compared with what had gone before, I was positively confident that we would meet again.

Sarah, my dearest, can you still love a man who has to confess to being so afraid? Knowing you as I do, I think you could, but I wish I could have been stronger.

Because we arrived two days late, the coach awaited us in Belfast and so we set out directly for Donegal. That journey was made difficult by the frequent snowstorms. We arrived here in the middle of the night and I confess I was so exhausted that I could no longer put pen to paper. Foolishly, I had not brought paper with me and I could hardly ask the innkeeper to provide me when he appeared in his nightshirt with a flickering candle.

How long it may take for this letter to reach you I dare not think, but I know you will not give up hope until all hope is indeed lost.

We began our work this morning, much helped by a respectable merchant in the corn and flour trade. He confirmed in every detail the dreadful reports we had had from various sources in the area. The small farmers and cottiers have sold all their pigs and fowl and even their bedclothes and fishing nets for the one purpose of gaining the wherewithal to buy food. He said it was common enough for families of five to eight people to subsist on about two and a half pounds of oatmeal a day made into a thin gruel, about six ounces of meal for each!

This, my dearest, is heartbreaking to us, for Dunfanaghy Bay is teeming with fish, as I think I told you earlier in the year. The problem is that their fragile curraghs are only suitable for fair weather fishing. They need robust boats and people to show them how to make best use of them. But the plans we set in hand to get this going in the early summer *have not materialised. Meantime, people starve for want of help.*

To address that situation is, of course, our purpose here and we have come prepared and will do what we can as quickly as possible. I know from past visits to my cousins that this is a beautiful place: I have been here in springtime when every hedgerow is full of primroses and in summer when the mountains are ablaze with heather, the sky a blue dome with great white clouds piled up like castles. How I would love to be with you here when this great affliction has passed away. But then I would be happy to be with you anywhere. That is my most fervent prayer, that we can be truly together and share whatever time we are given.

I shall write again as soon as I can, but know that I am, for the moment at least, safe from the perils of the sea and travelling with good companions who share our hopes.

Take care of yourself, my dear one. I long to see you again.

Your sincere friend,
Jonathan

Buoyed up by relief and delight, Sarah returned to Castle Dillon on Monday after her enforced absence with a lighter heart and was greeted with more good news. Sir George had now departed for Dublin, but he had left instructions with Bridget that Annie and James were to be found lodgings somewhere in the house or stables, and that she was to make provision for a young person to look after the child so that Annie could carry on with her work.

Sir George had obviously spoken to the incumbent of St Aidan's, the parish church of Salter's Grange, for in the letters awaiting Sarah's attention she found a courteous note from him. It offered a date and a time at which the young couple could be married and then have their child baptised.

Meanwhile, Bridget had been busy. Finding that one of her ground-floor storerooms actually had a fireplace, she'd had the room emptied, thoroughly aired and then furnished from discreet subtractions from some of the smaller guest bedrooms. The happy couple now not only had a bed and a table and chairs, but the means of making a pot of tea or a bowl of porridge, a luxury they could only have dreamt of when they climbed the ladder in the barn, cautiously and separately, so that they could be together.

On her next visit to Armagh to deposit cheques for Sir George, Sarah bought them a cake tin and some china mugs, then baked them a cake to put in it. When she gave it to Annie the next day, she asked her if there was anything she still needed.

Annie shook her head. 'Sure haven't I a thousand times more than iver I had in all my life,' she replied, close to tears. 'James and little Patrick, and a home of our own, an' a girl comin' from the workhouse to look after him. Sure how could I need anythin' more an' now your lovely tin to put cake in and mugs to give out to our visitors. Sure I couldn't want more if I were the Queen herself.'

Their joy was palpable, touching all the staff. Each

one of them had made some small contribution to their single-room home and the wash room they would share with some of their colleagues.

But the most generous, and most surprising, gift of all was from Smithers. He presented the young couple with a proper cradle so they could return the drawer that Bridget had lent them to the dresser in the main kitchen.

His change of attitude towards James was now visible. Most of the staff assumed it was because James himself had 'had promotion', having now been given tasks of stocktaking and accountancy which Bridget was more than happy to shed, but Sarah suspected that Bridget had once again had a word with Smithers.

Sarah did raise the question when they had lunch together in Bridget's room, but Bridget only smiled. Whatever secret she held, she intended to keep it, but that didn't mean she wasn't prepared to use it to the advantage of Annie and James.

Drumilly Hill,
24th December 1846

My dearest Jonathan,
What joy that you have received two of my letters when I had hardly dared hope that mine might travel any faster than yours to me. How I wish I could personally thank that merchant you mentioned who, finding them at the hotel, sent them to you in Bunbeg with a carter he knew who was going there. Our Christmas angel. May he be blessed.

After your harrowing journey from Liverpool and the discomforts of winter travelling, I was so pleased to have some glad tidings to share with you. The arrival of little Patrick, now baptised, and his parents' joy, seems to have cast a glow over Castle Dillon. Despite the miserable weather, which has at least brought a welcome thaw, everyone seems to be in good spirits and determined to celebrate Christmas Day, even though the Christmas party was some two weeks ago.

I was invited to join the rest of the staff for dinner tomorrow but I had already said I would go to Mary-Anne, who kindly invited Scottie as well. It is her first Christmas without Billy and, although they could hardly be described as a loving couple, they did care for each other.

Apparently Mary-Anne received a gift of a goose last Thursday at the stall when I was busy with customers. Only later did I find that all the women who sew for us had been saving a penny a week in December, knowing that if Mary-Anne had a goose then I would be sure to share it.

I don't think Scottie has ever had goose and he does so enjoy his food.

My dear, what a homely letter, and yet I should not apologise for it being so. We speak as we see and say what is in our hearts. That is not simply a measure of honesty such as we both value, it is a measure of love. What is of importance to one, however homely, or indeed however elevated, for we do sometimes wax metaphysical, is always of importance to the other. The sharing is part of our loving.

I think often of Annie and James: their devotion, their longing to be together and their joy. We are so much older, dear Annie is only just sixteen, but I see no reason why we too might not find that same joy and a place to be together, if we are patient.

I shall be looking out for the letter that tells me you have completed your task and that we may find an opportunity to greet the new year together.

Your sincere and loving friend,
Sarah

CHAPTER TWENTY-FIVE

Arriving home on Thursday evening, Christmas Eve, laden with bags of coins and two bundles of clothes – the unsold residues from one more very busy day – Sarah's first glance was to the kitchen table. It was bare and clean, as Sam and Scottie had left it after the midday meal she had left for them to reheat. On it lay the very best Christmas present she could have wished to receive, a white envelope with her name upon it, the hand unmistakeably Jonathan's.

She dropped her heavy bags of money gratefully on the table, carried the bundles of clothes into the sitting room, unwound her damp shawl and sat down by the fire, overjoyed by the hoped-for arrival.

Though the letter was short, written hastily in an inn where they had stopped for some midday refreshment, she was not disappointed. It confirmed that Jonathan would be arriving in Armagh late on Tuesday 29th. He hoped she could join him at the Charlemont Arms on Wednesday morning and hopefully on Thursday as well, which was New Year's Eve, if she was not committed to the market stall. It was perfectly clear he was hoping she might find someone to help Mary-Anne on the stall so they could have a second meeting before he left on the afternoon coach for Belfast.

Knowing there was so little possibility of a letter reaching him before his return she began laying the table for supper, planning that afterwards, before she started counting money, she would bake a cake to take down to Mary-Anne. Her friend would be spending her evening plucking the goose and preparing to cook it, no easy task over an open fire. The goose would need basting regularly in her largest pot, but Mary-Anne would find a way. It was one of her most endearing characteristics: she would never admit defeat until she'd tried all the possibilities she could imagine.

Sarah was sure the goose would be a great success and it was. Scottie, Jamsey and Billy tucked in so vigorously that Mary-Anne raised her eyes heavenward and said, 'D'ye think maybe I shou'd 'ave asked fer two?'

'Well, I for one could certainly get used to eatin' it,' said Jamsey with exaggerated politeness.

'So, you think it's "better than a blow of a stick", as the saying is,' said Mary-Anne.

Sarah laughed and enjoyed the banter, but she knew her thoughts were with Jonathan; the only sadness in the happy day was the thought they might never eat a Christmas dinner at their own table.

She pushed the thought away and joined in as vigorously as she could, knowing she must go home before darkness fell to count money and fill envelopes so Scottie and Jamsey could start delivering tomorrow. She was only too aware that they would be bringing money for food to women who may have dined on Christmas Day only on the customary bowl of porridge.

When all the morning tasks were done on Wednesday 30th December, Sarah went upstairs to wash and change her kitchen clothes. With some help from Mary-Anne, she had at last managed to finish the new winter dress. The same pattern as the favourite blue dress in which she had driven for the first time to Castle Dillon, this one was a much darker blue in a heavier fabric, but Sarah was pleased when she tried to see herself in the starred and crazed glass of the mirror in the old wardrobe that stood in the bedroom.

The day was cold and damp but there had been no more snow. The remnants of the last fall lay like white shadows below the hawthorn hedges, shrivelling as the morning moved on, when the roadside verges then began to reappear, damp and squashed but still a vivid green.

Now that the long-awaited meeting was to happen, Sarah found herself anxious. Perhaps Jonathan would be delayed like last time when he'd encountered a gang of hungry men in the bread shop. Or perhaps the coach had been delayed by snowdrifts on one of the mountain passes. She checked herself. *Oh ye of little faith*, she said to herself. You must travel in hope.

Their meeting was to be at noon and although she

herself was ten minutes early, Jonathan was already there in the stable yard of the Charlemont Arms waiting patiently. He looked as if he might have been there for a long time, probably as anxious as she was not to be late.

He came towards her the moment he caught sight of them, helped her down and took her in his arms, kissing her on both cheeks and holding her for a few moments. To Davy, the stable boy, who had his back towards them, he gave a coin and watched as he walked away with Daisy and the trap.

'You look wonderful, Sarah,' he said sheepishly, as he released her and they walked towards the entrance. 'But I'm sure I'd still think that if you'd been doing your housework in your oldest clothes. I think I'm prejudiced.'

'Then we both are,' she said beaming. 'Perhaps we must just confess all our weaknesses and hope we'll grow out of them.'

The dining room was already busy, noisy with men's voices and steamy from damp clothing and the huge log fire. Sarah's heart sank as she remembered the voices of some very loud men on their last visit. To her great surprise, Jonathan seemed just as distressed.

'Would you mind waiting a few minutes? I really think we need somewhere quieter,' he said, leading her to a reserved table.

And that was how they came to have their meal in a Committee Room, as the head waiter called it, one of the many rooms they hired out for functions.

The food was good and the quiet was blissful. They

laughed at themselves and their reluctance to share their space with anyone else as they began to talk about Jonathan's expedition and the news from Castle Dillon.

There was sadness to be shared as Jonathan confessed how much worse things had become in Donegal since the last visit he had made. He was uneasy with the new government's pronouncements about self-help and laziness, and the number of evictions taking place. Absentee landlords were using unpaid rent as an opportunity to evict tenants, taking away the possibility of cooking even the meagre rations handed out by various charitable bodies, as well as leaving them totally exposed to the weather.

For her part, Sarah had to share the very sad news, just arrived from London, of the death of Sir George's youngest son, his namesake, from scarlet fever at only two years and eight months old.

They both wondered why Lady Emma had remained in London when Sir George had come to both Castle Dillon and Dublin, but the only reason that seemed to make sense was her concern for the children. Perhaps she feared the rampant fever which was not in any way confined to the workhouse or to people underfed and cold, but was also affecting doctors, schoolteachers, and other professional people who were not deprived of either food or shelter.

A fire had been lit for them in the Committee Room and after their meal they sat in armchairs on either side of it. Sarah found herself thinking of Annie and James and their one-room home. This room was far bigger, warm and heavily curtained, but it was only a temporary shelter from the lives they were forced to lead, quite separately, with the width of long coach journeys and the dangers of the Irish Sea coming between them.

'Did you bump your head?' she said lightly, when she realised she had fallen silent.

'Oh this,' he said, touching his forehead and looking startled. 'Does it spoil my beauty?' he asked, trying to make her laugh.

There was something in his tone that troubled her. He had suddenly become uneasy and his attempt to deflect her attention had reinforced her sense that the scratch – now showing up more clearly as a bruise – was not just a trivial accident.

'What happened, Jonathan?' she asked steadily. 'Tell me what happened.'

She knew he would have to tell her, but as the pause between them lengthened she became more anxious herself. What could possibly have happened that would have exposed him to even minor physical damage?

He sighed and turned his face away from her, his shoulders drooping momentarily as he took a deep breath.

'I had to go to visit The Retreat this morning,' he said slowly. 'I didn't want to go but I consider it my duty and I know you'll understand why I don't speak of it. It is a duty I owe to my wife's family even if the person who once held that position is no longer the woman I once knew.'

He paused, unable to go on, until she leant forward, took his hand and said, 'Just tell me, Jonathan. It can't hurt you now. Or if it does, I'll share that hurt with you.'

He looked up at her, his eyes moist and said, his tone flat and featureless: 'When she saw me, she flew into a rage, picked up a heavy vase and threw it at me. When I managed to avoid it, she then threw herself upon me, trying to scratch my face or my eyes, I don't know which,' he said, shaking his head. 'I must have lost my balance or caught my foot on the carpet and to fell to the ground. By that time, one of the attendants had seen my plight and came to my rescue. They told me afterwards they're familiar with such outbursts and the attendant overcame her quite quickly, though he had to call for help to lead her away because she struggled and kept on shouting at me and clawing the air.'

Sarah got up, knelt by his chair and put her arm round him. 'Poor Jonathan,' she said quietly. 'I'll kiss it better,' she said, bending towards him and placing a kiss firmly in the middle of the swelling bruise on his forehead. 'You should have told me right away and we could have got a cold napkin for your forehead. There's still a lot of snow in the stable yard if the hotel hasn't got ice for its white wine,' she said lightly.

He smiled weakly. 'I'm the man who wants to protect you from all harm and I have to be kissed better like a child,' he said ruefully.

'Jonathan, we're all children when we're hurt or anxious, but don't you think two children might be able to make one grown-up?'

'You have a point, my love. I often think if I could have you by my side what wonders I could accomplish,' he said, clasping his hand over hers.

They shared the hours of the afternoon. Darkness fell so early that Sarah, now more at ease travelling in the dark, said she could stay for a light supper, but must not delay beyond that in case the temperature went down and the roads, so cold already, began to ice over before she reached Drumilly Hill.

Jonathan agreed and said that however much he wanted to be with her, she was not to take any risks for his sake.

'Not when we have tomorrow, my love, thanks to that kind woman, Sophie Lawson, taking your place on the stall.'

'I'm very fortunate, Jonathan, I have good friends, but sometimes I long for my best friend of all,' she said, as he walked with her to retrieve her shawl and rug in the cloakroom and collect Daisy from the stable yard.

Their goodnight was brief in the cold air with people and traps coming and going around them in the stable yard, but he walked ahead of her up the cobbled entry leading to English Street so he could wave to her, as she turned right and moved slowly down the empty street on her solitary journey home.

The night was cold and damp but there was no ice at this early hour – overnight might be a different matter. She arrived home safely and found Scottie waiting for her though it was nearly eight o'clock.

'Oh Scottie, you should be away home long ago,' she chided him gently.

'An' leave you yer lone to unharness Daisy and get her into her stable? Sure it's been a long day for you and you up cookin' since before breakfast,' he said, as he helped her down, spoke to Daisy and began to unharness her in his usual expert manner.

'Would you drink a mug of tea, Scottie?' Sarah asked, wondering if he was feeling lonely.

However well he was managing – living by himself and making some friends of his own – she had not forgotten how lonely she had been, night after night, when there was no John, neither a weary presence sitting exhausted by the fire, nor a tender companion often too tired to make love when he took her in his arms.

It was those sheltering arms that seemed to make the hard work of every day entirely worthwhile, something to look forward to when the fire was smoored, the lights out and the house silent. However feeble Scottie's old granny and how unable she was to shelter him, there was no doubt she loved him and was a presence in his life.

Tired as she was and longing to sit quietly by the fire he'd looked after for her, Sarah was not surprised when he said, 'Thank you. That would be very nice.'

The kitchen was warm as he'd kept both inner and front doors tightly shut to await her coming. He put the kettle down, brought out mugs and the cake tin before she'd even unwound her shawl, beads of moisture on it glinting in the lamplight. He had trimmed and filled the lamp, topped up the coal bucket and the log basket and laid the table for breakfast, to save her one more small task before bed.

She sat down gratefully, wondered what she might say that would be of interest to him, apart from asking about his work in the forge. He was easy with her, but was still not yet used to having someone to talk to, apart from Sam Keenan, the Halligan boys and Mr McMahon. That, perhaps, was the problem she reflected, as she made the tea. There were no women in his life: no mother, no sister, no aunt, not even some elderly female friend of his mother or father.

But before she had settled herself in her chair and saw him take a bite of the cake she'd cut for him, he looked up at her and said, 'D'ye think Annie and James have done the right thing, marryin' other when they're only servants?'

'Why d'you ask, Scottie?'

He was looking awkward and she realised that he probably didn't know why he was asking. It was just something that had come into his world and he didn't know what to make of it.

'It's hard to work out what the right thing is for other people. I think it's right for them, they were both lonely and they obviously love each other. It might have been better to have waited a bit longer, but things sometimes happen that one isn't expecting. The main thing is they really care about each other.'

'Like you and Mr Hamilton?' he said quickly.

'Yes, indeed. We hadn't known each other long, but we knew we loved each other, so we married,' she said quietly, a little taken aback by the question.

'And if there were someone you loved now, you'd marry them?'

'Yes, I would, Scottie. Life is short at the best of times, if one is fortunate to find someone to love, who loves you, then you marry them.'

'An' you'll marry the English man who comes to see you?' he said, looking down into his mug of tea.

Sarah paused. There was no point in asking how he

knew about Jonathan, not in a small community like this. A chance remark, an easy exchange with the postman, a stable boy from the Charlemont Arms who came to the forge with a horse because he knew Sam, or Scottie, or had a difficult horse.

'I can't marry the man you speak of even if I do love him. He has a wife who is ill and won't get better, but that means he isn't free to marry.'

'But you'd marry him if you could?'

'Yes, I would,' she said gently. 'Would you mind if I did?'

'I thought I would,' he said promptly, 'for I've no one belongin' to me, but that's not fair,' he went on. 'Why should you be on yer own if there's someone you'd like to be with. An' maybe one day I might meet a girl that liked me.'

'I'm sure you will, Scottie. She'd be a lucky girl.'

'Why would she?' he asked baldly.

'Because you are kind and thoughtful and don't think you're the only person in the world that matters. Some men see women as housekeepers or mothers, not as women with thoughts and feelings and loneliness. But you'd understand about that and not think it was all about you.'

'Aye, I know about being all on yer own. But it's better than it was. When Mr Hamilton died, I thought I'd got no one left but Granny, and then I found there was you, and Ben, and Sam Keenan. An' now there's Jamsey and Billy, an' all those women we deliver money to. They always have a good word for me, an' ask me how I'm doin'. It would put heart in you,' he said, finishing his tea. 'An' I didn't understand about that till now.'

He stood up and she realised yet again how much he had grown. It looked as if he'd grown in other ways as well. She smiled at him as he stood looking down at her.

'Jamsey says Sophie Lawson is helping his ma on the stall the morrow. Will ye be going to see yer friend?'

'All being well, yes. He's going back to England and won't be back till April,' she explained. 'I'll go mid-morning in the trap, have lunch with him and stay to see him off on the Belfast coach for the evening boat to Liverpool.'

'Ach dear, that'll be hard, him goin' back an' you fond of him,' he said quietly. 'I think Annie and James were quite right,' he added firmly, as he stood up, pulled on his jacket and wished her goodnight.

CHAPTER TWENTY-SIX

Sarah sat down quickly after she'd seen Scottie to the door then shut it behind him for the night. Suddenly she felt quite exhausted; the headache that had come on as she'd sat talking to him was rapidly becoming a pulsing throb. All she could think of was getting to bed and lying in the darkness with her eyes closed.

She hung her dress over the bedroom chair to avoid the effort of putting it on a hanger, shivered violently as she got into the cold bed and then fell asleep in minutes. Her sleep, however, was troubled and full of strange repeating images, particularly one of a woman who kept pursuing her and trying to scratch her eyes out. She awoke coughing before her usual early hour but couldn't get back to sleep again, though she felt exhausted and knew she didn't have to dress and get ready to go into Armagh until mid-morning.

Despite the chill of the grey day, she felt hot and uncomfortable when she eventually got up and started the morning chores. She was so grateful that she didn't have to spend the day with Mary-Anne on the market stall being helpful to women who counted out pennies and looked at garments they knew they couldn't afford. It was the only time she'd had a day off from the market stall since they'd first laid out their products, mostly their own work, well over a year ago, not knowing how their plans might succeed or fail.

Despite a spoonful of the medicinal mixture that John always swore by, her cough was uncomfortable, her mouth dry and her throat rough. She couldn't face breakfast but drank her mug of tea gratefully.

'Come on, Sarah, this won't do,' she said aloud. 'You'll have to gather yourself for going to Armagh. You don't want Jonathan to worry that you might not be feeling well,' she said to herself. But the thought of getting to her feet, seeing to the fire and preparing the midday meal for Sam and Scottie was intimidating.

Sometimes you just have to pretend you're fine when you're not. It's a wee bit like a white lie. There's no badness in it, no intention of deceit, just a kind thought for the other people who might be anxious.

She smiled to herself. How often her grandmother's words brought comfort as well as wisdom. She would never deceive Jonathan willingly but with a long journey before him, perhaps another rough crossing, or another night to be spent waiting for a storm to die down before he could even begin his homeward trip, today was not a day for him to be made anxious.

She gathered herself and struggled through the morning chores. It was just as she was about to go upstairs to wash and change her clothes that she heard a knock at the front door which she had not yet opened.

As the hammers were ringing out from the forge as usual and it was too early for the postman, she wondered who it could possibly be, but the man who stood there when she opened the door was clearly a messenger. He held in his hand a white envelope, one so familiar that her heart leapt to her mouth. What could possibly be wrong that Jonathan was writing to her when they were due to meet in an hour's time?

'Is there any reply?' the man asked brusquely, before she had even opened it.

'Yes, I should think so. Do come in. Would you like a cup of tea?' she asked, hoping he would say no and she could tear open the envelope and see what the single sheet had to say.

'Aye, well . . .' he said, in a tone she had come to understand. It meant yes.

'Do sit down while the kettle boils. I'm afraid it might be a couple of minutes as I've just made up the fire.'

Unable to wait a second longer, she unfolded the sheet and saw the familiar hand, a message clearly written at speed.

Sarah, my dearest,
I have just had a messenger from The Retreat telling
me that it became clear last night that my wife now
has a fever. Their medical man insists I contact

anyone I've been in touch with. A mere handshake
can be enough, he says, with some of the virulent
fevers that are spreading apace.

I kissed you yesterday in ignorance, and you kissed
my forehead when I confessed about how I'd got the
scratch. Oh, my darling, if I could have infected you
unknowingly, my heart shall break. He has suggested
that I go home immediately, well-wrapped to avoid
any contact with other passengers in a coach, or boat.

Clearly, we cannot meet. I shall await a note from
you impatiently from the present messenger.

Your distraught friend,
Jonathan

'You came on the right morning,' said Sarah, amazed at how cheerful she could sound. 'There's still cake in the tin,' she added encouragingly as she made tea, all the while thinking what she could possibly do to reassure Jonathan.

The messenger, who had been sitting by the fire, looking round him and whistling soundlessly, perked up and said, 'Aye, a piece of cake would be very nice.'

She cut a generous slice, poured his tea and said easily, 'I'll just be a minute or two. I need to send a word in reply.'

'Take yer time, there's no hurry,' he said, eyeing his plate of cake as she took out her writing materials from the dresser.

My dearest Jonathan,
I am so very sorry not to see you this morning, but
I'm sure the doctor who visited The Retreat has said

the correct thing in urging caution, even if it turns out to be quite unnecessary. I am feeling perfectly well, just so sad we have been deprived of our meeting.

All I ask is that you take great care of yourself and watch out for any early sign of illness. I shall do the same and we both have good people to look after us should we be unlucky. Never forget what we both agreed once, that strength of spirit can overcome many misfortunes.

My loving thoughts are with you,
Sarah

'Here you are,' Sarah said, trying hard not to cough. 'I'm sorry to have delayed you, but my friend was worried I might not be well.'

'Sure I'll tell him you're the picture of health and gave me cake to my tea,' he said grinning, as he put the envelope in his pocket.

'What a good idea,' she said, beaming at him and hoping he would go quickly.

Moments after she shut the door behind him, the cough that had been threatening for minutes broke surface. She coughed till she was exhausted, and then sank down on the chair by the fire, sweat breaking on her face, her forehead throbbing with pain from the headache that had suddenly recurred. She admitted that she was not well, but at least she could say honestly that it didn't look to her like fever.

At mid-morning, when Scottie went to harness Daisy, he came to the door to see if there was anything to go with her, so he could take whatever it might be and find a suitable place to store it under one of the seats in the trap. As he came into the kitchen, he took one look at her, sitting by the fire with her hand to her head, still wearing her morning clothes. He could see she was not well. When she tried to speak to him and was interrupted by a bad bout of coughing, he turned on his heel and went back to the forge.

'Sam,' he said, as calmly as he could manage. 'Mrs Hamilton isn't well and Mrs Halligan is in Armagh. What are we going to do?'

Sam dropped his hammer promptly and came to the door of the forge where Scottie stood. 'Is she on her feet?' he asked.

'She's sitting by the fire, but she should be in her bed. I've never seen her look so bad, an' she has a cough would deafen you,' he added, as they walked the short distance across the front of the house to the open front door. They went in to the kitchen together and found she was nowhere to be seen.

'Maybe she went out to the privy?' said Sam steadily, having looked around and listened.

They waited a few minutes, hoping to hear the distinctive click of the latch on the back door. When another few minutes had passed, they went out through the back door themselves. They found her lying face downwards on the ground.

It was when Sarah suddenly felt sick that she decided to go out to the privy, but she didn't actually get there. Every step felt like a major effort, her head throbbing and her cough threatening to erupt at any moment. It was a bout of coughing that confused her. Suddenly, she slipped on a patch of melting ice and felt herself fall helplessly forward. She hit the ground head first, felt the damp, stony surface rough under her cheek and the warmth of blood trickling across her forehead before she passed out.

'She's hurt herself,' said Scottie, seeing the blood as Sam dropped to his knees and turned her over. 'Will I away for the doctor?'

'It might come to that,' said Sam, as he eyed the gash on her forehead. 'But we need to get that blood stopped now,' he went on. 'Away in and get one of them clean puddin' cloths from the dresser and soak it in the bucket in the wash house. The colder the water, the better. Use today's bucket. Wring out the cloth and bring it here, as quick as you can. Have you a clean handkerchief?'

To Sam's amazement, Scottie handed him a crumpled but unmarked handkerchief before he ran off into the house. He used it to wipe away the trickles of blood and then pressed it firmly against the gash itself.

Sarah couldn't understand why there was no window at the foot of her bed. There had always been a window there. Then she saw a woman sitting beside her. It was not the woman who had tried to scratch her eyes out. The woman had her head down and was holding her wrist. She was counting quietly to herself as Sarah fell asleep again.

It was a man's voice that woke her up. He was standing in front of a window to the side of the bed where she lay, with his back to her talking to someone. She couldn't make out what he was saying but the woman's voice was familiar. She just couldn't put a name to it because her head hurt so much.

'Yes, I think there is concussion,' he began, 'but the wound is not *very* deep. She'll probably have a headache for a while and may feel sick. Don't force her to eat but give her plenty to drink and I'll send you a bottle for the chest: there's certainly an infection there, but she is well nourished. Unlike most of my patients, she should recover, given time. Now, I must be on my way, I am required at both the workhouse and The Retreat.'

There were footsteps and other voices and then silence. She found tears streaming down her face. She would never see either of them again. Neither John, nor Jonathan. She would die and leave them both lonely and the woman with the long fingernails would run after her every time she shut her eyes.

Then, she heard a voice she knew. 'Come on, Sarah, open yer eyes an' take a drink of tea.' She knew then that the woman with the fingernails had run away because she was afraid of Mary-Anne.

It was three days before Sarah was able to sit up and drink a cup of soup.

She felt as if she'd been on a long journey and it was only today that she fully recognised Mary-Anne's room, the one where Jamsey and Billy used to sleep before Annie came here and had her baby.

Her head still hurt if she thought about anything, but the coughing had eased. She could still taste the medicine in her mouth, though she didn't remember taking it. It was the same taste as the one John had always sworn by. Looking around her for the first time, she saw the large bottle, half-empty on the windowsill to her right.

'Oh, so you've got yer eyes open again, have you? How are you feelin' the day?'

'What day is it, Mary-Anne?' she asked, surprised that her voice came out so weakly. It didn't sound like her at all.

'It's Monday. Wash day if ye were at home, but it'll be a day or two yet before you're going anywhere,' she added briskly.

'Monday?' she repeated incredulously. 'What happened? Have I been here since Thursday?'

'Well, unless you've been slipping out when I haven't been looking, ye've been here since Sam and Scottie brought you down with a bump on yer head an' a cough you cou'd hear in Armagh,' said Mary-Anne crisply.

'Oh Mary-Anne,' Sarah gasped, 'what about the money? All those poor women waiting for money from the stall and me lying here.'

'Aye, ye were talkin' about them one night and about yer man Jonathan anither. Then I heerd you talkin' to yer grandmother an' someone called Helen. Wou'd that be yer friend in America?'

Sarah realised that Mary-Anne was smiling. She couldn't think what might have amused her.

'Why are you smiling?' she asked, a hint of anxiety in her voice.

'I'm smilin' because there's not a lot wrong wi' yer brains if ye can mind about the muney. The next thing you'll be sayin' is that yer hungry and cou'd do with a mug of tea,' she said, leaning forward and giving her a hug. 'Scottie did the money and he an' Jamsey got it all out on Saturday, so it was only a day late. It's only you that's behind yerself,' said Mary-Anne, breathing a great sigh of relief.

If Sarah had a rather vague impression of the first days of New Year 1847, she soon caught up with events in both the local community of Drumilly, as well as events at both Castle Dillon and Armagh as soon as she got back to work. Gales and snow and low temperatures continued through the whole month, there was a backlog of paperwork to be done and although she still got tired very easily and had the remains of a cough, she tackled it as best she could.

She was so grateful to her friends, not just Mary-Anne who had yet once again sat with her, nursed her and brought her back to herself, but Scottie and Sam who'd taken care of themselves, kept her fire going, made food and even baked bread to await her return home. Going back to work on Wednesday 6th January, she was grateful when her friends at Castle Dillon were glad to see her and simply assumed the snow on Drumilly Hill had made it impossible for her to come sooner.

But however thankful she was for her own well-being, she saw with increasing sadness the enormity of need in the wider world. Fever was now rampant, not only in the overcrowded workhouses, but in the countryside as well, cutting through swathes of poor, half-starved people, their numbers increased yet further by absentee landlords who used their unpaid rents as an opportunity to secure their eviction.

She asked herself what possible hope there was for families with no income, without either food or shelter, in areas where remoteness or indifference meant there was no help to be had readily at hand.

As she opened letters and forwarded abstracts to Sir George who was still in Dublin, she searched in vain for some better news, but there was none to be found: neither in rural districts like Tartaraghan, a mere few miles away, nor in the southern and western counties of Ireland, where, unlike in Ulster, there were few landlords on the ground. There, only the local clergy, with limited means themselves, tried to help the suffering population by writing letters asking for help, many of which were ignored.

The only piece of good fortune that came to help her was when she found that Jonathan had indeed crossed the Irish Sea on New Year's Eve, but that was the last sailing for almost a week due to sustained westerly gales, probably blowing as vigorously across Yorkshire as on the Irish Sea itself.

After the memorable crossing in December, which Sarah was sure he would never forget, he would be only too well aware of the effect of bad weather on the post. In fact, when a cluster of letters arrived in the middle of January, she discovered that a lack of letters from her had only just begun to trouble him when the first one she had written arrived some ten days after he'd sent his messenger to her.

With the roads so very bad, Sarah solved the problem of going to work by travelling in the middle of the day, if there'd been another fall of snow overnight. With the morning's partial melting the road was passable with care,

Daisy now adept at 'picking her steps', as Scottie called it. Sarah then took up Bridget Carey's suggestion that she stay at Castle Dillon one or two nights at a time, depending on the weather and making use of one of the small guest rooms which Bridget had prepared for her.

However much she would have preferred to sit by her own fireside, she was able to use the overnight stays to catch up on the piles of letters that had accumulated in her absence and to write letters of her own, not only to Jonathan but to her other friends as well.

Annie and James were so delighted to see her back. She made time to visit them in their room in the early evening after supper in the servants' hall, before she went back to work in the study. She got to know Beth, the good-hearted girl from the workhouse, whose task it was to care for little Patrick during the day when Annie and James were both at work.

She was pleased to find that James was coping well with his new household duties which involved stocktaking and accounts for Bridget. When he asked her for help with account keeping, she was delighted by his new-found confidence and more than willing to spend a part of each evening teaching him. He was an able pupil.

Mary-Anne and Sarah agreed that if she wanted nothing said about either her accident or the chest infection, it was a simple matter to ask Scottie and Sam, Billy and Jamsey to say nothing.

Sarah was relieved. If Jonathan need not be told, then it was one less anxiety for him to carry. He already carried so much without complaint, from the challenges of his work as a manufacturer, albeit shared with his brothers, to the research he had committed himself to on behalf of the Quaker Central Relief Committee.

Their letters were open and honest about all that happened to them, but Sarah was sure her grandmother would approve of this single omission. Let Jonathan have the comfort of knowing she was well without reminding him of that unhappy day when he'd had to send her a messenger and depart without a proper goodbye.

CHAPTER TWENTY-SEVEN

Sarah opened her eyes suddenly and saw a bright line of light where the curtains on the south-facing window had not been closed carefully enough the previous evening. She smiled. It often happened when she was tired out, the candle flickering in her other hand, the window completely black unless there was a moon reflecting off the snow.

What a difference it made to getting up in the morning when there was sunlight. She got out of bed, wrapped the extra rug from the foot of the bed round her shoulders and tramped across the wooden floor to stand on the rag rug she'd made in her first year as a bride in her new home.

She drew the curtains back, looked in amazement at green fields and trees dripping in the sunlight. The last day of January and there was no new snow in the night. Clearly it was not so cold, for only in a thaw would there be jewels on the trees.

She felt her spirits rise as she pulled on her morning clothes: a heavy skirt and a very old silk blouse, many years ago a Sunday best, now worn and much-mended but treasured for its continuing warmth under a knitted woollen top.

Saturday and no Castle Dillon today, her work all up-to-date, she could do some of the things she only thought about when what had to be done was only too obvious. And then, of course, it would be light much longer than last Saturday. She'd not have to remember to get in the wood or the water, before the day ended in darkness as early as four o'clock.

She'd had some strange dreams last night and now images began to float back to her. She imagined she could smell hawthorn, the May blossom, and the touch of the rug on her shoulders felt like the delicious warmth when one could stand in the doorway, back to the sun and feel the kindly heat taking away the ache produced by heavy buckets and tending to the fire on the hearth.

She laughed at herself as her bare feet got cold, pulled on her clothes and ran downstairs to stir the fire and make porridge.

She worked all morning and marvelled that the sense of pleasure simply did not fade with the passing hours. When the postman came into the kitchen and placed a fat letter on the table, she simply assumed that Jonathan had been able to spend a whole evening by his own fireside.

This was how he always tried to share it with her.

After the postman left she went upstairs, washed and changed, the letter sitting on the table like a child's promised treat, only to be savoured when the appropriate things had been done. Laughing at herself for her imaginings, she made up the fire, peeled vegetables for the midday meal and finally sat down at the table to open the envelope and smooth out the multiple sheets.

My dearest Sarah,

How I wish I could take you in my arms and whisper in your ear, for what I have to tell you makes me so hesitant and so anxious, lest you should think me in any way unfeeling. I know not where to begin, alternately overcome by joy, and then by the frustration of not being able to speak directly to you.

My dear one, I have just received two letters both of which I should have received several weeks ago. One of them contained a death certificate for my wife issued by Dr Leslie, the medical attendant at both the workhouse and The Retreat, plus an account for funeral expenses. It also enclosed a letter in which I was informed officially by the director of The Retreat that my wife died only three days after I left you.

You will indeed remember only too well that she had fever. It seems the advice I was given when it was diagnosed was not alarmist, as we might have thought. Burial was required immediately because of the nature of the fever she had. There was simply no question of informing me, so that I could make appropriate arrangements or return to attend the funeral.

The second letter, which I received at the same time, was a note from my brother-in-law written some days after the funeral itself. A man considerably older than myself, he is somewhat reserved, so what he said took me aback completely. I shall copy it for you just as he wrote it:

'Jonathan,' he began, 'you have done your part. You said you could provide well for my sister when you married her and you have done that. You have ensured that she wanted for nothing, "in sickness and in health" as we Anglicans avow. Now, she has no more earthly needs once the funeral expenses are settled.

If I may be so bold, I would like to tell you that if you were to engage with some other woman and want to make her your wife, then none of us would wish to see you delay making a new life for yourself. It may well be a custom in your faith group to show respect for the lost one by delaying any other potential marriage, but I hope you will not feel bound by this tradition at the expense of your own happiness.'

My own happiness, my love, my Sarah. He may or may not have found out that we are friends, but his words are sincerely meant and they contain a gift I could not have dared hope for.

You gave me your promise last year, beneath the summer-leafed trees on The Mall, may I now ask you, in all humility, to make me the happiest man alive and name a day, as soon as maybe, when we can become man and wife?

Please write as soon as you can. I am not sure I can contain my excitement or my joy till I have your letter in my hand.

My love and thoughts are ever with you,
Jonathan

POSTSCRIPT

The Irish Famine was not said to be over for several more years and the huge number of casualties is still being argued over in the twenty-first century.

It is certainly true that a million or more died, though probably more from illness than from starvation. A million or more emigrated, a process that has continued ever since.

Some of the characters in this novel are historical persons. Sir George Molyneux mourned his ten-year-old son in March 1847 when this little boy, his eldest son and heir, died of scarlet fever. Sir George himself died a year later, aged thirty-five, his wife, Lady Emma, marrying in England a year after that.

But five million people survived, including many of those recreated in this novel, a fiction that tries to be true to the facts and to the courage of those like Sarah and Jonathan who 'did what they could, did it in love and saw that often it was even more than they could have hoped'.

Their descendants are still doing just that in 2016.

Anne Doughty,
Belfast